New-Slain Knight

Also by Deborah Grabien

Cruel Sister
Matty Groves
The Famous Flower of Serving Men
The Weaver and the Factory Maid
Plainsong
Eyes in the Fire

New-Slain Knight

The Haunted Ballad Series

Deborah Grabien

THOMAS DUNNE BOOKS / ST. MARTIN'S MINOTAUR ≈ NEW YORK

This is a work of fiction. All of the characters, organizations, and events portrayed in this novel are either products of the author's imagination or are used fictitiously.

THOMAS DUNNE BOOKS.
An imprint of St. Martin's Press.

NEW-SLAIN KNIGHT. Copyright © 2007 by Deborah Grabien. All rights reserved. Printed in the United States of America. No part of this book may be used or reproduced in any manner whatsoever without written permission except in the case of brief quotations embodied in critical articles or reviews. For information, address St. Martin's Press, 175 Fifth Avenue, New York, N.Y. 10010.

www.thomasdunnebooks.com
www.minotaurbooks.com

Library of Congress Cataloging-in-Publication Data

Grabien, Deborah.
    New-slain knight : a haunted ballad mystery / Deborah Grabien.—1st ed.
        p. cm.
    ISBN-13: 978-0-312-37400-6
    ISBN-10: 0-312-37400-3
    1. Musicians—Fiction. 2. Cornwall (England : County)—Fiction. I. Title.

PS3557.R1145 N49 2007
813'.54—dc22

                                                                2007024851

First Edition: November 2007

10 9 8 7 6 5 4 3 2 1

For my daughter Joanna, my niece Marisa,
And for the good friends who cover my back.

Acknowledgments

Thanks to my WIP readers: Anne Weber, Hillevi Wyman, Richard Furman, Beverly Leoczko, Marty Grabien, Rebekkah Martin, and everyone else who regularly called me on the twists and turns of this one.

I also need to thank my husband again. Nic, dear, thanks.

A quick note: Since many of my readers may raise an eyebrow at my choice of locale, let me offer reassurance. While I've set this story in Cornwall, I am in no way trying to poach on the superb Daphne du Maurier's preserves. I've been a fan of hers all my life.

So, while this particular novel, in its dealing with the Cornwall of centuries past, may evoke in people lucky enough to have read it some faint echoes of du Maurier's *The House on the Strand*, any reminder is pure luck on my part. If it does remind you, consider me honoured.

New-Slain Knight

Prologue
St. Ives, Cornwall,
June 1986

In the large upstairs room at the pub called the Duke of Cornwall's Own, a local band, the Tin Miners, were playing to an enthusiastic audience.

The place was full. The printed notice posted up beside the door stated that the room's official capacity was seventy-three people. On this hot summer evening, that number had been exceeded. It was a mixed crowd; some, bantering with the band and calling out requests, were clearly local to Penzance and the surrounding towns. Others were tourists, from places in the United Kingdom outside the Duchy of Cornwall. Some, obviously foreigners, had come along hoping to get a taste of genuine Cornwall. They'd likely been steered here by local friends, or their innkeepers.

The Miners were wailing away, doing an instrumental break in a song written by the band's fiddler, Kenwyn Maddox. The break was long and complex, but the band had it down and kept it going with no trouble at all. The audience, most of them well lubricated with beer or cider efficiently dispensed from behind the upstairs bar, were enthusiastic. A few people even braved a glass or two of the local mead.

From behind his seat at the upright piano, Gowan Camborne scanned the crowd and did a mental head count. He'd been doing these counts for a good long time, now; his first public performance, a piano solo at the local Institute, had been at age twelve. Now, just turned thirty, he could average out the front of house attendance without missing a single downstroke on the keys. He invariably came within five people in either direction of the actual crowd number.

There were some lovely women out there tonight, Gowan thought. That blonde, for instance, standing alone off to the side, with a pint glass in her hand—he'd not seen her before. Chances were she was a tourist; with that gilt hair and those cheekbones, she might well be Scandinavian. A pretty thing she was, and unattached, it seemed.

Closer to the stage, by a small table right up at the front, was a dark-haired girl, as lovely as anything Gowan had ever seen. Young, though—far too young to be any meat of his. She looked no older than fifteen, ripe and ready, but he stayed away from girls that young. Besides, she was with her family, or at least what looked to be part of a family: an older woman, already fading in her thirties and not near as pretty as her daughter, and a boy a bit older than the girl. He had a sulky look, the brother did . . .

The rhythm of the song shifted, and the band shifted expertly along with it. The Miners' bodhrán player, Lowenna Maddox, was handling her drum with a verve and intensity that, considering she was actually a pianist herself and merely played the drum as a hobby, said something about the level of musical ability in the Maddox family. Kenwyn's sister was a recent addition to the band, but the Miners were like that, fluid in terms of the personnel; musicians joined the band, played for a while, and then moved on.

Lowenna, Gowan thought, was a pretty thing, very pretty indeed in that soft flowery skirt she was wearing, and with that rippling mass of superb chestnut hair. He'd brushed against her as they'd come onstage, letting one finger trail lightly across the gleaming cascade of curls that came nearly to her waist.

He'd startled her, that was sure—she'd jerked and looked over her shoulder at him. She hadn't smiled, but then she rarely did.

With her attention caught and her eyes focused on him, he'd smiled himself, and kissed the tip of his finger, as if he'd found nectar there.

"You've got beautiful hair, you know that? It tastes like the summer," he'd told her, and got what he wanted: an indrawn breath and a fast hard blush, the colour of berries, staining her cheeks.

Now, with the song and the show nearly ended, he caught her glance once more. The look she gave him—a smoulder, embers deep in the enormous eyes, the sudden flutter of her lashes, the curving up of a pair of full lips—told him what he wanted to know. His fingers ran up the keyboard suddenly, a rippling triumphant little dance of sound.

He didn't stop to wonder whether Kenwyn would mind when his sister ended up in the bandleader's bed; the thought never came into his head. Nor did he consider whether the timeworn chestnut about not making a mess where you eat ought to get in his way. Gowan rarely thought about externals when sex was the goal. Besides, where was the harm? Lowenna would enjoy herself thoroughly, and they would both move on. Gowan was no predator, and no heartbreaker, either. He'd never hurt anyone, not knowingly, and he'd no plan to start now.

The song was in its final four bars when a sudden outbreak of noise that wasn't music cut through the piano, the bodhrán, the fiddle. Startled, Gowan jerked his mind away from picturing how Lowenna would look stepping out of that soft delicate skirt and gave his attention to the commotion.

It was the not-quite-family at the table in the front row. Brother and sister were scuffling, slapping their hands at each other, while the older woman, presumably their mother, tried desperately to hush them.

". . . Jenny, Mitch, you both stop this right now or I swear I'll let your father deal with you both when we get back to the hotel, what in the world is wrong with you, you know better than that, Jenny stop that . . . !"

The Miners, as if on cue, suddenly punched up the volume and the tempo. They were drowning out the noise, giving the red-faced mortified mother time to cope with her unruly teenagers, giving her the space to get one hand on the hulking boy and the other on the exquisite girl, giving the regulars the nod to make way for her as she pulled them out of the room, presumably back to an irate father who hadn't wanted to waste an evening of his European vacation listening to music he knew nothing about. And really, they were too young to be here, anyway.

At the door, the girl wrenched her arm free for a moment. She turned back, staring for a second at her brother, then at the stage. Her eye went first to Gowan himself, and then to Lowenna. Then her mother got her back in a good solid grip, and they went out, the door closing behind them.

With the disruptive teens gone, Lowenna turned her gaze toward the piano, as if hoping to share a raised eyebrow. But there was no response from Gowan; it was as if she had suddenly gone invisible. And there was a very odd look on his face.

Gowan would have no memory of playing the rest of the piece, although he did it perfectly. He was far too shocked by what he had seen in the girl's face, first when she'd looked at her brother, and then at Lowenna.

Gowan Camborne was a pleasant, cheerful man, a consummate musician, easy-going by nature. This was the first time in his life he had ever seen raw hate on a human face, or murder looking out of a child's eyes.

One

My heart is lighter than the poll;
My folly made me glad,
As on my rambles I went out,
Near by a garden-side.

On a glorious July day, Ringan Laine checked his cell phone for messages, found none, and headed out into his garden for a nice long nap under the late afternoon sun.

Part of him—admittedly a very small part, easily identified as what he usually referred to as his damned Scots Protestant work ethic—was doing its level best to make him feel guilty. The work ethic, or whatever it was, had chosen to take the form of an infuriating little voice at the back of his head. He'd rolled out of bed after lying in until nearly ten in the morning, and the little voice had been poking away at him steadily ever since.

It had begun by suggesting that there were several things around Lumbe's Cottage that needed doing. There was the toilet, for instance; that was badly in need of a good hard scrub. The voice pointed out that doing something about the sheet of ice presently keeping his freezer door from closing properly might be a wise idea. It raised the question of washing nearly two months' accumulation of pollen and dirt and stray bits of roofing thatch from the cottage's windows. It pointed out that all these things really ought to get done before Penny, Ringan's longtime girlfriend, arrived from London tomorrow. It had finished up with the observation that after ten hours of sleep the previous night, Ringan's desire to nap in the sun was unjustified, not to mention indecently hedonistic. As a kind of coda, the irritating little voice reminded him that the strings on Lord Randall, his Martin guitar, had been in constant use on the tour he'd just finished and wanted changing.

Ringan had initially coped with the voice by doing his best to ignore it. When that tactic failed, he took a tried-and-true road: mentally telling it to sod off, ticking off the various items that wanted doing first to forestall any reoccurrence.

Fortunately, he had common sense on his side. In the first place, Penny wasn't coming down until tomorrow, so the loo could stay dirty until this evening, by which time the temperatures would have gone down to below subtropical, and he'd probably have a bit of energy to spare. He already knew what was causing the creeping glacier in his fridge, ta ever so: the ice-making device had apparently nursed thoughts of world domination while he was off on the road for five weeks with his band, Broomfield Hill. He'd left a message with the local appliance repair people and, anyway, he'd already disconnected the icemaker. Cleaning the windows was about as stupid an idea as anyone could get in this heat—besides, the BBC weather service had said there were storms offshore, so rain was coming during the night, most likely. Obviously, the intelligent thing to do was to let the rain do the windows for him, instead of he himself getting up on a ladder and probably keeling over and crashing to the ground from sunstroke. As for Lord Randall's tired strings, those could damned well wait. Penny was coming down tomorrow for three weeks and what he had in mind for a high percentage of those three weeks had nothing at all to do with guitars.

With the voice at least temporarily silenced, Ringan let himself into the miniature tithe barn that, these days, he used partly as a rehearsal space and partly for storing things that were only ever used out of doors. Even on the hottest days, the barn was cool; the foundations, nearly six feet in height and made of the petrified earth and dung that the locals had been calling "cob" for a thousand years at least, took no warmth from the sun or the air and gave none back. The crucked oak beams that made the roof look like a small-scale model of the Abbey Barn, that world-famous tourist attraction a few miles away in Glastonbury, seemed high and remote.

The interior was always mostly in shadow, the sun's rays never reaching fully in. Ringan, stepping carefully around the heavy wrought-iron chairs and table he'd put away for safety while he toured with his band, moved gardening tools and disintegrating lawn umbrellas to one side, and glanced up and around. The instinct to see if he could catch any sign of movement was now as ingrained as any habit could be. Once, there had been other shadows in here, two people caught between death and eternity. They were gone now, those two, gone to whatever corner of time and space offered sanctuary to such as them. . . .

But there was nothing, and Ringan dropped his eyes. He hunted through a small pile of seemingly random objects just inside the door, telling himself, as he always did, that he really ought to put a few hours aside and organise his bits and pieces. Pulling the low-slung canvas chair he wanted free of the rest, he straightened his back and, once again, found his gaze moving from one end of the barn to the other, sweeping from the near-darkness of the building's distant corners and ancient foundations to the faint dance of dust motes just inside the slitted windows. Someday, he thought, he might be able to walk into the barn—for that was all it was, now, a useful outbuilding—without remembering the lovers who had once been caught within these walls like extinct insects in amber.

Ringan got the lawn chair out under one of the apple trees and began the process of setting it up to his liking. It took some doing; the chair, with its built-in canopy and seat of faded green canvas and its squeaky brass-plated hardware, had been sitting in the barn for the better part of a year. Not only were the various bits of hardware rusty and uncooperative, the wood that formed the frame was dry and shrinking. He made a mental note: next trip into Glastonbury for supplies, add a bit of wood oil to the shopping list. . . .

"Want a hand with that?"

The voice, cheerful and a bit amused, came from just behind him. Ringan turned and found himself confronting his landlord.

"Albert! Christ, you startled me. I could use a bit of help, yes—this thing's gone as dry as a bone and the hinges are useless, pretty much. I've got to get some lubricant or something at the home centre, next time I'm there. Here, could you put some weight on the foot? I'll pry the other end open—right, that's done it."

"Those hinges sound like a soul in torment. But there's no need to buy lubricant. I've got gallons of it, that spray-on stuff, up at the House. I'll send someone down with it for you." Albert Wychsale, Baron Boult, glanced around, in hopes of finding a second chair. In his sixties and on the round side, he wasn't coping well with the heat; his face was pink, his thinning pale hair was sweaty, and he was damp and a bit wilted around the edges. Lacking a second seat, he settled himself gingerly on the grass; while the dry grass of high summer in Somerset wasn't likely to stain his trousers, the dead spikes, their springy softness leeched out by weeks of direct sunlight and unrelenting temperatures, were sharp and prickly. "I just came by to drop off your post. I got lucky about the day, because I honestly couldn't remember which day you were coming down. I've left everything on your kitchen table—the door was open and I saw your car. How did your tour go? Are you home for a while now?"

"The tour went fine, thanks. Five weeks, two dozen shows, Scotland to Cornwall. Literally, John o' Groats to Land's End. The new CD's selling very well—our fastest seller to date, in fact." Ringan, who'd been about to flop into the chair, suddenly remembered his manners. "I think I need a good cold beer. Do you fancy one? And maybe a chair? You don't look very comfortable, squatting like that."

In the end, Ringan's plan for an immediate nap was shelved in favour of getting the rest of the lawn furniture out of the barn and set up on the grass. As they edged the heavy table out into the sun, it occurred to Ringan, sweat trickling down his chest and through the front of his shirt as he swore under his breath, that the little voice in his head was getting some of its own back.

"Is something funny?" Albert finished dusting off the seat of one of the chairs and sank into it with a grateful exhale. "Because you're grinning and, honestly, I wouldn't have thought you felt much like grinning, at least not going by what you were muttering while we were moving that table. Or is that just a feral grimace?"

"Just thinking that my inner Protestant is getting its wish, that's all, what with me slogging in the heat instead of sleeping in the sun. I've got three weeks of doing sod all coming to me, and my damned work ethic kept jogging me in the mental ribs to do chores instead of take a nice kip out of doors. Where in hell did I put my beer?"

"Next to that green canvas thing, right on the grass—Butterball, get away from that and let Ringan have his pint in peace, you idiot beast." Wychsale, one hand firmly around his own bottle, shook his head as the Wychsale estate's enormous orange Persian cat emerged from behind the apple tree and began a ritual sniffing. "At least it's cooling down a bit. So, three weeks of perfect summer weather and nothing on your dance card except relaxing? Sounds like a bit of heaven—I can't imagine the sort of tour you people just did without wanting to sleep. Is Penny coming down?"

"Tomorrow, for three full weeks." Ringan felt his lips wanting to curve up into a smile. He couldn't help it. The smile was tender, edging on sensual; he hadn't seen Penny Wintercraft-Hawkes since his band had begun touring. "We've finally managed to beat the odds and have the same amount of time off at exactly the same time. And before you can ask me, I'll tell you. No, we've got nothing planned, at least beyond setting the telephones to voicemail and ignoring everything else. We plan to continue having nothing planned. And if anyone tries to get us to make plans beyond having nothing planned, I'll thump them repeatedly over the head with my guitar while Penny quotes Shakespearean insults at them."

Albert grinned but said nothing. Ringan polished off the rest of his beer, settled back in his chair, and closed his eyes. "And what's more," he announced, "any plans that we do make will not, repeat not, be shared with the rest of the world, and aren't likely to be suitable for children under the age of consent anyway. Oh, damn! Please tell me that's your phone buzzing, and not mine?"

"Sorry, no. Don't have one with me. It's yours." Albert nudged it toward Ringan with one foot. "Hadn't you better see who it is? What did you say?"

"I swore," Ringan said grimly, and flipped open the phone. "Hello? Ringan Laine here."

"Ringan? Oh, thank goodness." The voice at the other end was female, firm, slightly musical. "This is Roberta. Look, do you have a moment? I hate to bother you, but I need help."

"Robbie!" Ringan sat up fast, knocking the dregs of his beer into the grass. His older sister, a no-nonsense doctor in Edinburgh and married to a Viennese businessman, was legendary in her own family circle for a near-pathological unwillingness to ask for help. "What's wrong? Is everyone all right?"

"We're fine." Roberta Laine Eisler sounded crisp but harried. "Unfortunately, Helmut's mother isn't. We've just had word that she's in hospital in Austria—she fell down her stairs, arse over teapot. Bruises, of course, and a broken rib, but the real problem is a compound fracture of the tibia, and they suspect a damaged hip. At Renate's age, it's tricky; she's in her eighties. We need to go as soon as we can. It's an absolute mess."

"Damn. I'm sorry." Ringan shifted the cell phone from one hand to the other. He had a sinking feeling in the pit of his stomach that he was going to be sorry beyond the mere formality of the spoken word. "I probably don't want to know the answer to this, but—what do you mean, you need help?"

"Well—it's about Becca."

For a moment, Ringan's urge to groan aloud was so strong, he wondered if he'd actually done it. He could see what was coming—parents of an only child, elderly grandmother in a foreign capitol, long afternoons at said elderly grandmother's bedside, thirteen-year-old girl with nothing to keep her amused, or occupied, or out of trouble . . . "What about Becca?"

"She's at home at the moment—it's summer hols for her school. We're going to be tied up in Vienna for two weeks or so, according to Renate's surgeon. Becca'd be bored out of her mind if we took her along. Besides, she's got to practice. She's got an entrance audition for the Hambleigh Academy in August, and you can't practice violin in a hotel room, or in a hospital room, either." She had the grace to sound apologetic. "I know it's an imposition, Ringan, but, honestly, we've got no one else we can ask."

Ringan was silent. Roberta was right; there was, literally, no one else she could ask. Their brother, Duncan, was at the moment living and working in Dubai. As for their mother . . .

"We can't leave her with Mother." Roberta's voice was a bit more urgent; apparently, Ringan's silence had stretched long enough to make her uneasy. "She'd drive Becca half out of her mind."

"I know. I wouldn't suggest that, not in a million years."

He hadn't seen his niece, Rebecca, for over two years. That last time had been at a quick Christmas gathering in Edinburgh. At that point, she'd been a quiet child of eleven, a bit fine-boned and small. He and Penny had given her a biography of her favourite composer; she'd looked up at them from under long black lashes and thanked them quietly, and then disappeared upstairs with her book. She'd come down later in the evening, watching and listening as her uncle played a few Christmas-themed traditionals.

He couldn't remember a single thing about her, other than a pair of remarkable dark grey eyes, a swirl of long black hair, and her undoubted devotion to her violin. If she'd managed to get far enough to have secured an audition to the Hambleigh Academy, he thought, she must have become one hell of a fiddler. The school was posh, self-important, and elitist enough to set Ringan's teeth on edge. But it had spent two centuries earning its reputation; as a music school, it was the best Scotland had to offer.

"Ringan?"

"All right." So much for three weeks of pubbing and leisurely sex. "As it happens, I'm at home right now—I have the next three weeks free. So does Penny. She's coming down tomorrow. But I have a restoration project in Leeds beginning the second week in August, so if it goes longer than that, we've got a problem."

"Oh, we won't be gone longer than two weeks." If she was re-lieved, there was no way to tell from her voice. "We can't be. Re-becca's Hambleigh audition is on the tenth, and she'll need two days of working with her violin teacher beforehand. If Renate needs Helmut to be there longer than that, he's on his own. Be-sides, I really can't desert my practice for longer than that; it's sim-ply not fair to the covering doctors. I'll let Becca know. She really won't be a problem, and you won't really have to keep her amused, because she'll have her violin with her. And Ringan?"

"What?" Butterball had found an insect in the grass and was bat-ting it sideways with one paw. The apple trees were heavy with early fruit and echoed to the sound of birds singing, and Albert was dozing in his chair. Penny was the only thing missing. As soon as Roberta let him know how she was planning on getting Rebecca, with all her gear, from Edinburgh to Glastonbury, he was going to have to get hold of Penny in London, and let her know. And she wasn't going to be pleased.

"You're a very good brother," she told him, and rang off.

A little more than twenty-four hours later, Penny's recently ac-quired Jaguar S-type pulled up on the gravel drive that curved out in front of Lumbe's Cottage, with Penny behind the wheel. She wasn't alone in the car.

Ringan, who'd been watching for them, came out to help. The conversation with Penny the night before had not gone quite the way he'd expected. He'd given himself a few minutes to get over his disappointment over having done his family duty and wrecked his own holiday in the process. That strategy, unfortunately, had failed miserably, and had in fact done nothing other strengthen his sense of grievance.

The upshot was, he'd rung up Penny in something perilously close to a sulk. Holding the phone, he took a deep breath before punching her number; Penny's likely reaction was likely to be part reluctance to play nursemaid for an adolescent she didn't know, part disappointment at being done out of three weeks of having Ringan to herself, and part congratulation at him doing the right thing. However those proportions broke down, he wasn't looking forward to it.

"Hello? Is that you, Ringan?"

"Hello, Pen." He took a quick breath; she sounded pleased and anticipatory, and it was a damned shame that mood was going straight out the window as soon as he filled her in. "Listen, lamb, something's come up. I've got a situation, and you aren't going to like it, I'm afraid."

He told her about Roberta's call. She heard him out without interruption. Her silence was so complete, he began to get nervous; silence was not Penny's forte. ". . . So she really can't leave Becca with my mother," he finished, and heard what might have been desperation creeping into his voice. "Can she? I mean, you know my mother, Pen. She's enough to drive anyone out of their mind. Two hours with Becca stuck listening to my mother going on at her, and there'd be murder done."

Silence. Damn. He cleared his throat. "Penny?"

"Still here." She didn't sound angry or disappointed. She sounded businesslike. "Just wondering about logistics. How is she going to get to Glastonbury? Surely they aren't putting a thirteen-year-old girl on a train from Scotland? She'd need to change at least once and probably twice—considering the mess the trains are these days, she'd probably have to change once up north, and again in London. I'm thinking that if they can stop in town or at least let me know when her train is due to get here, I can meet her. That way, she can come down in the car, with me. Much less potential for disaster that way."

Ringan opened his mouth, and closed it again.

"Ringan?"

"Right here. You know, you floor me sometimes? I thought you'd be cranky as hell about this. I certainly am."

"Really? Why?" She sounded honestly surprised. "It's not as if you had any other choice, not from what you've told me. I mean, you could hardly leave Roberta in that sort of mess, and anyway, you said it yourself, inflicting your mother on that child is simply not on. That would come pretty damned close to qualifying as child abuse. Your mother is not the ideal woman to deal with a teenaged girl. So what earthly use is there in being cross about it?"

"True." It was amazing, he thought, how fast he'd relaxed. The loss of the time alone was still disappointing, but he no longer wanted to break something because of it. It occurred to him that she'd always had the ability to take the edge off his bad moods. "So, you're thinking I should ring Robbie back and arrange her delivering Becca to your place?"

"Why not just give me your sister's number?" There was amusement in Penny's voice. "I'm sure I can make her understand, if I try really really hard—I'm a big girl, I can buckle my own shoes and do up my own buttons, and everything. I even know a few words of Lallans Scots, if she's forgot how to speak English. And if there's a problem, I can talk really loudly. That usually works."

"Don't be snotty, wench," he told her affectionately, and she laughed back at him.

"You know, Ringan, I've just had a thought. Even if she's planning on practicing her fiddle until her fingers bleed, she's going to get bored. What would you say to a genuine trip to the seaside, the three of us, I mean? We could kill a handful of birds with one stone, that way."

"What, like a day trip to Brighton or something?"

"Not Brighton, and not a day trip." She'd gone from sounding practical to sounding animated. "More along the lines of tossing the girl and her fiddle in the Jag, throwing some swimsuits in the boot, and heading down to Cornwall until her parents finish coping in Vienna. Opinion, please?"

"I'd say you're brilliant, is what I'd say." He hadn't stopped to think about it, but of course she was right. Becca was going to be just as bored stuck out in the wilds of Somerset as she would have been trailing after her parents from hotel to hospital ward in Vienna. Not only that, with high summer hitting early, things were going to get hot and uncomfortable. "Do you know, if I'd been left to think of that on my own, that girl would get here and we'd have spent it sweltering and bored in the garden? I don't seem to have the parenting chromosome anywhere in me."

"True. Actually, neither do I—this was more about me remembering how impossible it was to keep Candy amused during the summer hols down at Whistler's Croft. So it's just as well neither of us is a parent."

Penny's suggestion was as close to perfect as he could imagine. Cornwall had beaches, and shops, and stone circles. It had clubs and music shops and cafés. It had castles and it had pubs. As a way of keeping Becca amused, it was nearly perfect.

The only drawback was that Cornwall also had tourists, quite a lot of them this time of year. Luckily, considering how impossible finding hotels or even bed and breakfasts for three people on this short notice was likely to prove, it had a small group of musicians Ringan had known since his earliest days of playing the traditional music circuit. Most of those friends had been providing each other with last-resort places to sleep for two decades or more.

And best of all, they were spread out all over Cornwall, from Padstow to Tintagel to Penzance to St. Ives. There wasn't a corner of the Duchy in which Ringan couldn't find a place to bed down if the hordes of tourists had snapped up the available paying hostelries.

Ten minutes later, Penny had rung him back to say that everything was settled. The Eisler family would fly into London from Edinburgh in the morning, and Penny would meet them at the airport. Becca would wave a fond *auf wiedersehn* to her parents. They would continue on to Vienna while Becca, her violin case in hand, climbed into Penny's car and headed southwest, to Glastonbury and then to Cornwall. She would be travelling light; the rest of her luggage consisted of one suitcase, and a wad of money that would ensure she didn't bankrupt her fond uncle with the various things a thirteen-year-old girl on holiday might decide she needed.

In the end, Ringan's whispering work ethic had got the last laugh. He'd spent the entire evening cleaning out the loo and the bath, making sure there was fresh bedding in Lumbe's rarely used guest bedroom, and arranging with Albert Wychsale to have someone at Lumbe's when the handyman came to repair the icemaker in the fridge. He left the windows for the promised rain to cope with. He'd even, after a bit of thought, made a phone call to one of the first musicians he'd ever played with professionally, down in Cornwall. The friend in question, who lived in a nice old cottage just outside the main drag of the town of St. Ives, was delighted to offer Ringan beds.

As an afterthought, Ringan decided to put fresh strings on Lord Randall. It was beginning to look as though he might be playing some music during the next three weeks, after all.

So, when the women arrived the next afternoon, the house was clean, there were fresh linens on both beds, and Lord Randall was ready to be played. Ringan was admiring Penny's car—she'd recently traded in her elderly Jaguar sedan for a much newer, racier model, in a silvery blue—when the passenger door swung open and his niece stepped out.

"Uncle Ringan." She came round the car and held out a hand. "Thank you for inviting me, and thanks to both of you, for letting me come down in Penny's car. I hope I didn't mess up your holiday too badly. Is something wrong?"

"No, nothing. It's just—you've grown up since the last time I saw you. I was remembering you from Christmas at my mother's house. What was it, two years ago?" She had callouses on the fingers of her left hand. "You look—different."

It was staggering. The skinny child, coltish and leggy but looking fine-drawn and a bit fragile, was now close to fourteen. She was as tall as her uncle, and what was more, she was completely self-assured. It was the self-assurance that most beautiful women have, coming from the starting point of knowing that heads would always turn for them. It was also unusual in a girl so young; that level of assurance, in Ringan's experience, came with age, and experience.

Rebecca Laine Eisler, with legs that seemed to go on for miles and a lustrous black waterfall of hair and the magnificent grey eyes he remembered holding a weight of lashes almost too long and heavy for her lids to carry, was exquisite. It was an elite class of beauty, the kind that usually finds its way into poetry or sonnets. No matter where she went, she was going to leave a wake. She was so beautiful, she was disturbing.

She grinned at him suddenly. It transformed her face, and suddenly, she was a gamine, still beautiful, but wearing her youth like a tattoo.

"I wish you could convince Mum that I was all grown up," she told her uncle. "She wants me to stay about eight years old. She says she doesn't, but she does, I can tell. And Daddy's even worse. I'm just amazed they let me come down to stay with you. They're so protective, usually."

"Becca, sweetie, of course they are." Penny had strolled over. "Do you brush your teeth every morning? Yes? Well, then, that involves a mirror, and that means you must know what you look like. They're afraid you're going to leave car crashes behind you, and grown men weeping like small boys."

Becca stuck her tongue out. The gesture produced a pair of long curving dimples. "You sound like my mother," she told Penny. "Okay, maybe not exactly like my mother. But really, who cares about boys? I'd rather play my violin."

Ringan stared at her. They were eye level, uncle and niece. And out of nowhere, with that statement, Becca ceased being a disturbing amalgam of beauty, potential, and youth, and became something and someone he recognised at a bone-deep level: the girl was a musician.

"Let me ask you something." An idea had come into his head, full-blown; it was as if it had been sitting there, waiting for confirmation that the girl was a player. "Robbie told me you've got an audition at Hambleigh coming up. Have you ever played in front of a live audience? Beyond family and friends, I mean?"

"No. Well, a few school recitals, but that was all parents and things." She tilted her head. "Why?"

"Playing in front of a crowd is a huge confidence builder." He caught Penny's eye, and saw her comprehension; she knew just where he was going, and what he was going to suggest. "And even though the admissions panel at Hambleigh probably won't be more than half a dozen people, they'll be intimidating. So getting a bit of live performance experience under your belt before the tenth of August, you'll have a weapon in your audition arsenal. How quickly are you usually able to learn new pieces?"

"Live performance?" The grey eyes were wide. "New pieces? Do you mean—what *do* you mean?"

"I think Ringan's talking about you playing some live shows in Cornwall with him." Penny had opened the boot of the Jag. She was busy wrestling her own well-travelled suitcase free. "Is that it, Ringan? You'd have to learn the songs first, of course, Becca. But what fun!"

"Yes, that's it." He saw the pleasure and anticipation lighting Becca's face and grinned. "And since the first place we're going is an old friend's house down in St. Ives, we've got just the place to get started."

Two

I walked on, and farther on,
Love did my heart engage;
There I spied a well-faird maid,
Lay sleeping near a hedge.

Two days later, Ringan woke from a light doze, took stock of his surroundings, and fixed Penny with a lazy look.

"I'll tell you what, lamb," he told her. "This is one of the best ideas you've ever had. It's seriously brilliant. If they gave out prizes for this particular sort of idea, you'd be up there accepting the Nobel."

They were lying side by side under a borrowed sunshade on the beach at Penzance, surrounded by happy holiday-makers. Offshore, under a hard bright sky, St. Michaels Mount shimmered in the heat, its irregular roof giving it the look of a castle in a fairy story. With the tide coming slowly in, the enormous stone causeway that led from the shore to the island was beginning to submerge. Along the shore, children kicked soccer balls and built castles of their own, fancy little pail-shaped constructions doomed to be reclaimed by the sea. Out along the far horizon, small shapes that might have been fishing boats disappeared and reappeared as the afternoon shadows lengthened on the water.

"Wasn't it, though?" Penny lifted her sunglasses and yawned. Her skin was already turning a tawny gold. "Hurrah for Team Me and my brilliant ideas."

"Not to mention hurrah for Team You and your shiny new

swimsuit." Ringan was grinning. "At least—it *is* new, isn't it? Because I'm pretty sure I'd remember having seen it before, or seeing what there is of it, anyway."

"Brand new, just for this. You're off the hook for not remembering it." She'd been lying facedown, with her cloud of dark hair piled up in a clip at the nape of her neck, and an oversized towel draped over the exposed bits of her that were likely to burn. The suit in question was a sleek high-cut one-piece in a deep copper colour, with nothing to speak of in the way of a back.

"I literally hit the swim shop at Harrods on my way to Heathrow to collect Becca—my old one was falling to bits." She rolled over onto her side, and propped herself up on one elbow. "You approve of it, do you?"

"Not being blind, that would be yes." He rubbed his beard, and a fine sprinkling of sand drifted free. "I think it's finally beginning to cool off a bit. Good—I really can't do this much heat at one go, and anyway we're supposed to be having dinner with Gowan, and maybe a couple of people he and I used to gig with. I don't want to be late getting back. After all, we've got his keys—since he was kind enough to let us doss down at his place while he was off on the road, leaving him locked out on his own doorstep would be a bad way of saying thanks. Any idea of the time? And where's Becca, by the way?"

"It's just gone five, and I'm right here." Becca, who'd been splashing in the sea, slid down on the oversized towel next to Penny and began running her fingers through her wet hair, trying to untangle it. Ringan, watching his niece, thought that she managed to be as graceful in this as she seemed to be in everything else she did. The movement was fluid and elegant; one moment she was standing, and the next she was tucked into a lotus of which any yoga instructor would have approved.

She was also attracting a good deal of overt attention. Unlike Penny, she was wearing the barest of bikinis, and most of the male heads in their general vicinity were turned her way.

"You know, Becca, you seem to have most of the men on the

beach panting after you." Penny had noticed, as well. "Of course, with those legs, it doesn't exactly come as a shock. Just something to be aware of."

"Well, I can't stop them looking, can I?" Becca had found a comb and was working it through her hair; the shrug was there in her voice, as well as in her shoulders. She sounded completely bored, and unconcerned. "But I don't have to care about it, do I? I mean, if some boy wants to stare at me, that's his problem, not mine. Why should I mind what they do?"

Ringan opened his mouth, and closed it again. There were, he thought, any number of things he could say: warnings about men who were predators, about women who would resent her youth and beauty and talent, about not accepting rides from strangers. The problem was, he had no idea how to say any of it.

And he couldn't help but wonder if saying any of it was actually necessary. After all, Roberta wasn't an idiot. His sister was a very smart woman, and Helmut was a very smart man. The beautiful Becca was their only child, as adored and cosseted and looked after as any child had ever been. Surely, she'd have heard all the warnings by now. In fact, considering it, that was probably why she was so blasé about it.

"Are you joking?" Penny had taken her sunglasses off and fixed Becca with a good hard stare. Ringan felt the pit of his stomach tighten up; that voice, from Penny, was not something to be ignored or taken lightly. "Of course it's your problem, or it could be. You aren't eight years old, so for heaven's sake, Becca, don't be childish. You know perfectly well what you look like. Suppose one of these blokes turned out to be a nutter, or a child molester, or someone who fancies a slap and tickle with a ripe young thing? You could shrug and say it wasn't your problem and you know, that wouldn't do you the slightest bit of good. It could be your problem, and maybe even your death."

Becca flushed scarlet. The tide of colour washed into her face, pointing her cheekbones with dull red, and then ebbed, leaving her chalky. Penny's voice was sharp, and serious, and as authoritative as

Ringan had ever heard it. There was also an urgency to it that forced his hand. If Penny was this concerned with a child to whom she had no blood connection, he had to speak. The girl was his blood, after all.

"She's right, Becca. Do me a favour and don't be naïve, all right?" He patted her hand. "For the next couple of weeks, I'm responsible for your safety and continued health, and my job isn't going to get any easier if you aren't paying attention. Right now, I'm counting easily fifty men of different ages on this damned beach who are looking at you and licking their lips. I'm not saying you can or should do anything about it, but you do need to pay attention. Can you do that, please?"

"I'm sorry." The transformation, from bored self-assured young beauty to chastised defensive child, was astonishing. Ringan, with no experience of girls this age as a reference point, found himself wondering if anything so fast and so unexpected could be normal, or genuine. Her eyes were suddenly brimming with tears, and her mouth was trembling. Even her body language seemed to have undergone a radical shift: the easy lotus tuck was suddenly taut and withdrawn, a knot of tightened muscles, as if she were somehow expecting the sky to open above her, and rain down unpleasantness. "I didn't mean—I just—it's only—"

"Not to worry—no one's narked at you." Penny smiled at her, a genuine smile. Ringan saw his niece relax, the tension going out of her posture, and found himself relaxing as well. He'd suddenly remembered that Penny had not only once been a beautiful adolescent herself, she'd been a fierce and careful older sister to the flighty and mercurial Wintercraft-Hawkes family baby, Candida.

"Just—don't ever dismiss what you're capable of provoking in people." Penny sounded serious, but no longer sharp. "All right? Because you're something special in the way of beautiful, and there are people in this world that can't see something beautiful without wanting to smash it, or make use of it."

Becca was quiet; she seemed, Ringan thought, to be considering what she'd just been told, and taking it seriously. He found himself wondering if his crisp, no-nonsense sister had ever put the subject to her daughter in the kind of language that would make her think twice.

"Well." Penny got to her feet and stretched. "We should probably start back, if we're meeting up at six. Anyway, too long in the sun the first day, and we'll be burned to cinders and there goes the rest of the holiday. I have every intention of spending all day swimming when we get to Tintagel. Why are you both looking at me like that?"

"Pot, allow me to introduce you to kettle." Ringan's voice was wry and amused. Penny, pausing with one long leg bent and her hair coming loose of its confining clip, gave him a quizzical look. She was clearly puzzled, and he shook his head at her. "That whole lecture you just gave Becca, about paying attention? Very good advice. You should follow it."

"What on earth are you on about, Ringan?"

"I think he's on about the ten or so blokes who just got whiplash when you stood up, Aunt Penny." Becca exchanged a look with her uncle; Penny, who had turned bright pink, glanced from one to the other and thought that the family connection was very clearly marked, if one knew what to look for. "I think next time I buy a new swimsuit, I'm going to try one like yours," Becca went on. "It's actually much sexier than a bikini, isn't it?"

"That's because things you imagine might be there are always more interesting than things you can actually see. And if you tell your mother I told you that, I'll thump you." Ringan tossed Penny a towel. "Here you go, lamb. Let's head back—we don't want to be late and the traffic's going to be miserable."

They gathered their belongings and headed back to Penny's Jaguar. She'd driven Jags her entire adult life. She'd had the last one the entire time she and Ringan had been together, but it had finally given up the ghost, and she'd replaced it with a sleek, sporty S-type that was every bit as luxurious as the old one had been but got better mileage on the petrol and was easier to park. Ringan had taken one look at the S-type and named it Pandora because, as he'd told

Penny, this one had the look of a vehicle where you opened the bonnet and hoped nothing flew out. She'd pointed out in return that when it came to owning and properly maintaining a Jaguar, there was a lot of hope involved. The car had officially been christened Pandora.

Ringan ended up being glad they'd left plenty of time to get back. His prediction about the traffic had been spot-on: while the drive from Penzance to St. Ives was a short distance north, the traffic on a hot summer day was brutal.

"I'm looking forward to introducing you to Gowan," Ringan told Penny. He knew better than to expect a response; she was still learning Pandora's limits and personality quirks, and tourists driving on what they no doubt considered the wrong side of the road would be tricky no matter what she was driving. "I don't think you've met him before, have you?"

"No clue." Penny's attention was firmly where it needed to be. "The name's not really familiar to me. I'll expect I'll know when I see him."

"True. Actually, thinking about it, I'm betting you haven't met him, because I don't think you'd have forgotten. Gowan is—well. Let's just say he's memorable."

That was an understatement, and he knew it, but he'd just realised that pointing out to Penny why she'd have remembered Gowan—that he'd have done his level best to charm her out of her knickers, metaphorically speaking—wasn't really suitable, not with Becca in the car.

He spared a moment to silently congratulate himself on sticking to his own long-ago decision to not reproduce; having to watch and consider every word he said was difficult and infuriating. How in hell grown men and women could be willing to rewrite their lifelong habits of free speech, simply because there was a child within carshot, was beyond him.

"Why is he memorable?" Becca, leaning forward against the rear seat restraint, sounded genuinely interested. "Has he got one of those big personalities? Or what?"

Right, Ringan thought bitterly. Sod's Law being what it was, of course Becca would be the one asking that question. He shot a quick look at Penny, but she was apparently absorbed in keeping a safe distance between the front of the Jag and the rear of the decrepit oversized truck with German tags ahead of her. There was no help forthcoming; this one was on him.

"Well . . ." *Oh, sod it,* he thought. He might as well let Becca know; after all, while he couldn't remember Gowan being remotely interested in schoolgirls, Becca was beautiful enough to make him sit up and take notice. In any case, he couldn't help being gallant. And not only were they staying under his roof, the stay was going to involve the three of them making music together, something which, in Ringan's view, was damned near as intimate as sex.

"Uncle Ringan?"

"Sorry. Just thinking. Yes, he's got a big personality, but really, it's more than that. He's got a lot of charm, the genuine article—it's not the sort he can turn on and off like a light switch; it's the real thing, bred in the bone. And he likes to flirt." He thought about it for a moment longer. "He's damned good at it, too."

Becca grinned. He caught it in the rearview mirror and once again found himself biting back on words; there it was again, that odd, fast transformation between curious child and precocious teenager. The grin was amused and uncomfortably close to sophistication. This parenting business, he thought, was trickier than it looked. Either that, or Becca was unusual in more ways than merely looks or talent.

It took the better part of an hour, inching along behind a stream of traffic, to get to Gowan Camborne's house in the Carthew neighbourhood of St. Ives. The rambling stone building was down the end of a cul de sac, within a few minutes' walking distance to Porthmeor Beach; it was set on a sandy hill, just high enough to provide a stunning view of the sea.

They'd had the place to themselves their first night in Cornwall. Gowan, on the other side of the River Tamar in Devon to play a show with some friends in Exeter, had written a note recommending a small seafood restaurant five minutes' walk toward Porthmeor Beach, wrapped the key in the note, and shoved the note under the mat. Although it had been fifteen years at least since Ringan had actually set eyes on Gowan, this informality was very much what Ringan remembered, and he was oddly reassured. Gowan didn't seem to have changed much.

They'd found the restaurant, an old reliable standby, and stuffed themselves on pilchards so fresh they'd probably been caught that afternoon. Becca, as slender as a lily stem, had surprised them both with what Ringan later told Penny must have been a hollow leg; she'd eaten enough to leave both of them in the dust. She'd gone through three courses and followed up the lot with a slice of chocolate cake large enough to feed all three of them.

Dinner had been followed by a brief local wander. The night air was soft and easy, scented with the sea and night-blooming flowers. Walking along Porthmeor, they'd stood a few moments, listening to the sough of the tide hushing against clean pale sand. Becca, clearly enchanted and with the breeze off the water lifting her hair, had kicked her shoes off and splashed calf-deep into the warm surf, laughing, jumping over the small regular wavelets breaking around her feet. This was a very different sort of coastline from the north of Scotland.

Penny, laughing, had taken off her own shoes, rolled up her trousers, and joined Becca as she stood in the surf. She'd been to Cornwall once or twice before but, as she'd pointed out, she'd been not much older than Becca was now, and that had been when Margaret Thatcher was in charge and dinosaurs roamed the earth. The warmth of the sea was glorious, impossible to resist.

Ringan's reactions were different. He'd spent time in Cornwall, and even the brief after-dinner walk had unnerved him. The place had changed. St. Ives in particular seemed to be fuller, noisier, more populated; it felt very different from the quiet, quirky artist's haven he remembered from his time there, twenty years earlier. The sight of the Island, that tongue of land jutting out into the Celtic Sea, was familiar and soothing; that it still seemed empty of anything other than the ancient chapel of St. Nicholas was marginally reassuring.

Between the food and the heat, the day had caught up with them, and they'd cut the exploration short. Even Becca had been yawning and was ready for sleep. But now, with a morning of wandering and an afternoon in the sun behind them, it was time to meet their host.

"Is that Gowan on the doorstep?" Penny sounded distracted; she was easing Pandora into a tight parking spot. "Because there's someone sitting there, and I can't think who it might be, else."

Ringan, whose mind had been wandering, jerked his attention back to the moment. Penny was right; someone was sitting on the top stair of the six that led to Gowan's front door.

"That's Gowan, all right." Ringan shook his head. "Damn! I was hoping we'd get here before him. Ah well—he'll know we were stuck in traffic."

Gowan Camborne, six foot five in his bare feet and with a head of chestnut hair just beginning to show silver around the edges, uncoiled his length and bulk, and met them at the foot of the stairs. If he was upset about having been kept waiting, there was nothing to be heard of it in his voice, or in the enthusiasm with which he greeted them.

He cut through Ringan's apologies. "No, no, don't say you're sorry, there's no need, none at all. Stuck in traffic, were you? Of course you were, it's summer in Cornwall and the place is chin-deep in caravans and tour buses, and every inch you drive, you risk pranging someone in a banger with Swiss plates. Ringan Laine, by God, mate, would you look at you, all lean and healthy looking! How'd you manage to stay looking so young?"

He enveloped Ringan in a warm hug. Penny, watching the men, felt something move in the pit of her stomach. It was unfamiliar to her, a sensation, a feeling she could give no name to; all she knew was that her nerves, responding to some unknown stimulus, had somehow sounded an alarm, and that Gowan Camborne had somehow triggered it.

It wasn't the man himself, surely; that didn't seem possible. He was just what Ringan had said he was: charming by nature rather than by design, with the air of a serious and dedicated flirt. In fact, she thought, he was what she usually expected from musicians, or at least from her own experience with Ringan's friends and bandmates. Liam McCall, Ringan's Irish fiddler, had a similar persona to the one Gowan presented—Liam, forthright and blunt, lacked Gowan's charm but still managed to collect women like flies stuck to tar paper, no matter where he went. . . .

"Gowan, this is Penny Wintercraft-Hawkes, my significant other. Penny, this is Gowan Camborne—we go back a good long way together."

Penny had been so deep into trying to sort out what was making her uneasy that she'd missed the first part of Ringan's introduction. The realisation made her feel as if she'd somehow given away whatever advantage she had. *But that's ridiculous*, she thought. *Why would I need an advantage?*

"Lovely to meet you." She pulled herself together, offering him her best smile and her hand. She was not without charm herself; what was more, she could see Gowan was exactly the sort of man to respond to a pretty woman, charm or no charm. "Thank you so much for letting us come to stay—finding a place for the three of us would have been impossible. And what a nice house you've got."

"Were you comfortable, though?" He seemed genuinely anxious to know. "That's the main thing—I don't sleep in the guest beds, so I've no way of knowing. The house, well, that was my great-grandfather's—it's been with the Cambornes since it was built, a good long time now. And I love it, wouldn't trade it, but it's not to everyone's taste, and I know it."

"Very comfortable, thank you." He still had her hand, held lightly in one of his own. He had the longest fingers Penny had ever seen, and the most remarkable eyes, a clear amber-hazel colour that was as memorable as it was unusual. "Oh, and that piano! So beautiful. It left me wishing I was a musician."

"My Brinsmead? Yes, she's a grand old lady and a true beauty, isn't she? Love of my life, that piano is. But she's not half so beautiful as my guests."

He finally let go of her hand, and turned the full wattage of that beaming smile at Becca. Becca, who was slightly behind Penny's shoulder, seemed to press up against her back. It was as almost as if Becca was trying to hide, to somehow minimise herself. Penny, wrestling with another of those inexplicable surges of alarm, didn't stop to think how odd that was. She could see, easily enough, how Gowan could seem overpowering to a young girl.

"You'll be Rebecca, then." He was twinkling at her, holding out one hand, and Penny stepped aside. It was a simple gesture of welcome and greeting, no more than that, but Gowan managed to somehow make it mean something, investing it with something completely personal, a moment between a man and a woman whom the man found delightful. "An honour and a pleasure. Ringan tells me you've got one foot in the door at Hambleigh. Is that right, now?"

She nodded, her hair dipping forward to cover her face. Ringan, unloading totes from Pandora's boot and shaking the sand from damp beach towels, waited for his niece's reply. It didn't come; she was silent.

Ringan flipped a towel with a single hard flick of the wrist, and rolled it. He was grinning to himself. The child in Becca, or at least a child's shyness, seemed to be well to the fore. Not too surprising, considering Gowan's size, or maybe she just had no experience of this kind of interplay. And really, he thought, if his niece would just be one or the other, sophisticated young woman or nervous child, it would making dealing with her a lot easier.

"You must be a wonderful musician." If Gowan was at all put off by the girl's unwillingness to look up or meet his eye, he wasn't letting it stop him. He had a light grasp on her right hand. "Hambleigh has its pick of the best. So you're going to be working with your uncle and me, learning a few standards?"

The silence went on a few seconds too long this time. As if she knew it, Becca looked up. Her unwillingness to do so was obvious, too obvious. Her chin came up slowly, the shield-shaped face with its cheekbones and perfect features moving as if Becca herself was arguing with every muscle, willing them to do her bidding, understanding that she had to observe the niceties.

Penny, watching, suddenly felt a chilly cramp in the pit of her stomach. Something was happening here, something she couldn't put a name to, something she couldn't define. Whatever it was, it seemed to be coming out of the ether.

Becca looked up, finally, and met her host's gaze.

Gowan's breath, a quick whistle of shock and disbelief, seemed to catch in his throat. The noise was odd enough to catch Ringan's attention, and he turned around fast.

They were staring at each other, the lovely adolescent girl and the burly musician. She seemed suddenly fragile, delicate, her bones no heavier than a bird's might be. Had Gowan had the sun at his back, his shadow would have completely engulfed her.

The wave of shock, of recognition, that came off this tableau came not from Becca but from Gowan. His hazel eyes were fixed and staring, his face was slack with disbelief. Becca herself seemed almost entranced, incapable of moving her hand or disengaging the lock of eyes. She neither moved nor spoke.

"Gowan! What's wrong, mate?" Ringan, horrified, pushed the boot closed. It slipped from his grasp, slamming into place. The noise should have brought Penny's wrath down, but she didn't even seen to notice. "You look like you've seen a—"

He stopped in midword, appalled at what he'd been about to say. His gaze went to Penny, as if drawn on a line. What he saw in her face was not reassuring.

"It's—I'm sorry." Gowan seemed to realise he was still holding Becca's hand. "It's just . . ."

With a monumental effort, he pulled himself together. The struggle was visible—he stood on the warm sunny street, his muscles working. Ringan watched his old friend's massive shoulders contract, expand, contract again, as he got his breathing, and his voice, under control. A few streets away, tourists wandered the streets of St. Ives, looking for the Hepworth Museum, discussing whether a cup of tea so late in the day would ruin their appetite for dinner, snapping photos.

"Sorry. Afraid that was rude, and I don't mean to be." Gowan was staring at Becca, but somehow, Penny thought, he seemed to be speaking to someone else entirely. "You gave me a jolt. It's your eyes. I used to know someone—a girl. You have eyes just like hers."

"Oh." Becca's voice was quiet, very sure of itself. "You sound quite sorry."

It was the voice of an adult, and there was power behind it. Ringan, with a shock, looked at Penny and saw his realisation reflected in her face. Gowan no longer had Becca's hand; she had hold of his. All the control of whatever was happening between those two was under Becca's command. The quiet, assured voice went on. "What do you mean, you used to know her? Don't you any more? Has she gone away?"

"There's nothing to know." It was a flat statement. "She's dead."

He pulled his hand free. As the contact between them was broken, Becca dropped her eyes. When she spoke again, that moment of adulthood, of strangeness, was gone as if it had never been. She brushed past Penny, past Gowan, heading for Ringan.

"Uncle Ringan, I'm sorry, I'm a lazy cow! Here, let me help carry things. . . ."

They spent a pleasant dinner hour. Gowan and Ringan went out searching for some Chinese takeaway, and they sat in the back garden, eating and talking about current events, tours, Penny's most recent theatre production. Gowan had rung up some friends, musicians, who would be coming over the next morning to play and to show Becca some tunes. Becca was pleased, even enthused. There was nothing to alarm, nothing to worry about.

Yet several times during the evening, Penny found herself watching both Gowan and Becca, looking and wondering. That small chilly cramp had settled deep into her stomach and showed no signs of going away.

The following morning, Penny, with a cup of tea in hand, curled up in an overstuffed chair in Gowan's front room and settled in to watch a small group of world-class musicians teach Becca some traditional songs for her repertoire.

The sense of something wrong, something unpleasant or upsetting on the distant horizon, had abated slightly. Penny, who'd been unsuccessfully debating with herself whether or not to tell Ringan about it, had lost her option when Ringan had climbed into the comfortable guest bed beside her and promptly passed out cold. She'd barely had time to be relieved about the decision being taken out of her hands before she'd fallen into as deep and dreamless a sleep as she could remember. Whatever else one might say about Cornwall, Penny thought, something in the air seemed to make for restful nights.

"So what d'ye want to play first?"

Gowan, seated on the piano bench with his hands poised above the Brinsmead's keyboard, sounded subtly different. He looked different as well, a change that moved through his persona, the way he sat, the way he held his head. It was a difference Penny was very familiar with, on every level. After all, she was a professional actor and director, and anyway, she hadn't spent most of her adult life keeping company with a musician without learning to pick up the signals. Gowan's voice was as sociable and friendly as ever, but there was a new note behind it, a kind of force: under the simple question was an unspoken concentration which meant the thing that truly mattered to him was about to be front and centre.

"I'm good to play anything you like, Gowan." The speaker, a middle-aged Welshman who'd been introduced to Penny and Becca as Cian Williams, held his flute ready. "I'm wondering, does young Rebecca have any tunes she knows, or especially wants to know?"

"Not really." Becca, surprisingly relaxed and self-assured in this crew of adult professionals, lifted her fiddle and settled it into place. "I thought I'd leave that to Uncle Ringan. After all, he knows all the songs in the world, my mother says. I'd love to learn anything you can teach me, but I learn best if I can hear a piece and play along with it, before I start breaking it down. Is that all right for everyone? I don't mean to slow anyone down."

"It's fine for me." Gowan ran both hands down the Brinsmead's keyboard, and Penny felt her nerve endings stir. She loved music nearly beyond expression, and it was a particularly cruel joke of genetics that she'd been born lacking even the ability to hum a basic tune. "It's how I learn new tunes, as well."

"Let's start off with something simple. Gowan, give me a D, will you, mate? No, too high—can you give me something in the midrange?" Ringan adjusted a tuning peg on Lord Randall and touched the harmonics; chimes, as true as any cathedral carillon and just as effective, sang in the warm room. "How about 'Tam Lin'? It's got about a thousand verses and a nice repetitive pattern to the structure, so Becca can practice as she plays." He shot a wicked grin at Gowan. "Besides, it's a good Scots tune."

They started out by running through the first two verses, with Ringan leading in on guitar and singing. Penny, in the position of observer in this group of players, kept her eyes on Becca. It had occurred to her that despite the girl's avowed prodigy status, neither Ringan nor Penny herself had heard her play so much as a note.

"I forbid you maidens all who wear gold in your hair to travel to Carterhaugh for young Tam Lin is there . . ."

No fiddle, not yet; Becca had it ready, her bow rosined and poised above the strings. She was listening, her eyes narrowed in concentration. She looked very beautiful, and somehow distant, as if a part of her was elsewhere, or so focused on processing what she was hearing that there was nothing of herself to spare on anything else. There was no trace of the nerves that might have been expected from a child not yet legally old enough to drive a car, yet who found herself playing with the stars of her field.

"None that go by Carterhaugh but they leave him a pledge: either their mantles of green, or else their maidenheads."

The Edinburgh accent in Ringan's voice was very evident; through some alchemy, he managed the seemingly impossible feat of keeping the lyric intelligible as English while putting enough of a Scots touch to the story to give it an undeniable authenticity. He had one eye on his niece, even as his fingers, moving over Lord Randall's frets, gave the song not only its framework but its intricacy.

With the second verse, Gowan came in on the piano—he took the part of the rhythm player, punctuated with liquid little runs on the piano's treble end. That meshed beautifully with Cian's flute, and the two of them fell immediately into a call-and-response mode of moving melody lines. Becca waited, her face still holding that remote, listening look. Penny found herself wondering what cue the girl was waiting for.

"Janet's tied her kirtle green a bit above her knee, and she's hied to Carterhaugh as fast as hie can she . . ."

Becca smiled suddenly, shifted the position of her bow slightly, and drew it across the instrument's strings.

The violin, as unearthly and mournful as anything Penny had ever heard, hit like a summer storm, sweet and high and hard. The instrument's voice was the voice of the girl in the song, young Janet herself, defying all orders to do what she wished, rescuing the beautiful supernatural stranger who had fathered her child, taking on her own world and the unseen world as well to save him, hold him, keep him.

". . . Were my love but an earthly man as he is an elfin knight, I would not give my own true love for any in my sight . . ."

Penny swallowed hard. Something, a kind of response to Becca's playing, had put passion into Ringan's voice. His beard was bristling with it, and the room rang with the strength of the vocal. Penny had been listening to Ringan and his band, Broomfield Hill, play music for nearly fifteen years. Ringan himself was considered one of the greats of traditional music. But this wild, perfect cascade of sound was like nothing Penny had ever heard.

The song went on, through the tale of Janet growing big with child, refusing to name the father, going back to the forbidden fairy-haunted Carterhaugh, finding Tam Lin, learning his history, finding out from him what she must do to claim him back from the supernatural creatures who had kidnapped him.

"They turned him into a flash of fire, and then into a naked man—but she wrapped her mantle him about and then she had him won . . ."

Ringan's voice faltered and stopped, just long enough to impact the song's rhythmic progression. He was staring at his niece. The piano stuttered, picked up the rhythm again, and then quieted, and Cian's flute with it.

Becca, lost in the music she was making, noticed nothing. The violin spoke on alone, the compelling vital story being told in un-sung words that only Becca, swaying as she played, could hear. Her eyes were closed; she was completely unaware of the world.

The melody went from mournful to tense to triumphant. It swelled, hung, eased back down, and stopped.

Becca opened her eyes. The pupils contracted to nearly invisible black dots in those enormous pools of grey, then widened as she came back to the real world from whatever fairyland the music had taken her to, taking in as much light as possible in the sunny room.

"Was that all right?" She looked around, at Penny's slackened jaw, at Ringan's disbelieving face, at Cian, who was biting his lip and looked at her as if he wasn't convinced she was real. Lastly she looked at Gowan, sitting silent at the piano with his hands folded in his lap. "Why are you all staring at me like that? Did I play it wrong?"

"I don't suppose you're also an ivory tickler?" Gowan had a very odd look on his face, and something Penny defined as tension tightening the muscles. "Piano, that would be?"

"No way." Becca's grin turned her fourteen again. "We never had a piano at home and, anyway, pianos scare me—they're so big, I always feel sort of small and unimportant around them. No, I just play violin."

"Well, thank God for that." Gowan shook himself suddenly, the big shoulders rippling like a dog shaking off water. "Because if you played my instrument half so well as you play your own, you'd put me out of business. Ringan! What shall we let the girl outshine us on next . . . ?"

The next few hours were spent in as intensive a rehearsal session as even Ringan, who was famous for his addiction to rehearsing long hours, had ever participated in. Penny, who knew just how tedious rehearsals could get for those not actually playing, slipped out briefly for a walk into St. Ives town centre; she'd developed a craving for an old-fashioned Cornish pasty and gone on the hunt.

Although he would never have said so to Becca herself, Ringan had been stunned. In his view, the word "genius" was overused and mostly inaccurate; he himself almost never used it. But, as he'd stood there listening to his niece, it had been the first word—the only word, in fact—to pop into his head. Two minutes of what she'd played was enough to convince him that Becca was that one-in-a-million phenomenon, a perfect, intuitive, creative musician.

He had a moment of envy, identified immediately and banished. That was followed by an interior grin, as he imagined the dropped jaws on the faces of all those toffee-nosed admissions people at Hambleigh, when his niece played her audition. He hadn't asked her what she'd chosen for her entrance piece, and it wasn't going to matter. She could stand there and play scales in a minor key, and she'd leave half the panel weeping. There was that much power, and that much intuition, in the music that defined her.

Besides, the girl was something perhaps just rare: if the last fifteen minutes of rehearsal was anything to go by, she was also a perfect student, a teenager who loved not only learning, but who was thirsty for new things to learn. And unless the admissions panel at Hambleigh were idiots, they were going to know it.

It was Gowan who suggested that, since Becca had responded so instinctively to the themes of magic that ran through "Tam Lin," they tackle another song along similar lines. When Penny returned, munching a hot pasty from the local pastry shop and wondering whether anyone would mind or even notice if she slipped into her swimsuit and went out to Porthmeor Beach, she found them deep into working out the musical intricacies of "Thomas the Rhymer." That forestalled any desire on Penny's part to leave, since the song was one of her favourites. They were helped by Becca's familiarity with that particular song; Broomfield Hill had recorded it some years back, and that CD had been part of her bedtime music, growing up. They rehearsed the song, got it down to everyone's satisfaction with terrifying speed, and moved on to another song, a cheerful thing called "The Devil and the Feathery Wife."

The sun in Gowan's front room was giving way to the long shadows of late afternoon when Cian suddenly seemed to realise how long they'd been working.

"You know, we're thoughtless clots, is what we are, the whole lot of us." He set his flute down, looking guilty. "Here's poor Penny spent all the day watching us, when she could have been out of doors, splashing in the sea. As for young Rebecca, here, what are we doing, shutting the girl indoors on a glorious summer day like this?"

"Too true." Gowan flexed his fingers. "Ringan, a fine excuse for an uncle you are. The women are on holiday. Let's call this a day, if you don't mind. They can get their swimsuits on and still catch a bit of sun. The sea stays warm late in the summer."

Ringan grinned and set the guitar in its stand. Gowan nodded at Penny.

"Off with you, and take that girl with you. I'll walk out with you, in fact—I want to see if I can book room for a show tomorrow night, upstairs at our local."

"The Duke's Own?" Ringan slipped a stray guitar pick between Lord Randall's G and B strings. "I remember that pub. The room upstairs, that's a brilliant place to play—good acoustics and a full bar, not to mention room for a good crowd. Do you still have the Tin Miners going, Gowan? Same in-again, out-again way of jamming? Becca, how'd you like to be a temporary member? You get a share of the door take."

"Playing with you, for money?" Her face was alight. "Like a professional? Yes, please!"

"The Duke's it is," Gowan agreed. He cocked his wrists, and bent over the keyboard. "Here's one we haven't touched—maybe tomorrow. We ought to let our fiddler, here, take on a song that has no fairies or magic in it. A nice love song, maybe. Have you heard this one?"

He began to play. The tune was light and cheerful; Gowan sang, in a pleasant, slightly reedy tenor:

"My heart is lighter than the poll; my folly made me glad, as on my rambles I went out, near by a garden-side."

"It's pretty." Becca was settling her fiddle in its case. "What's it about?"

"A man who pretends to be dead, to make sure his girlfriend really loves him." Ringan settled himself next to Penny, perching on the arm of her chair, feeling Penny lean her cheek against him. He was watching the care with which Becca treated her instrument, and there was approval in his face. "Which, if I remember it right, is a lousy trick to play on her—according to the lyric, she's several months pregnant and just about your age. Personally, if I'm the girl and I find out he's pulled that on me, I wait until he's asleep and thump him one on the head with a blunt instrument. It's called 'New-Slain Knight.' "

"That sounds like a masculine version of 'Sovay,' " Penny remarked, and made a face; the savoury, tasty as it had been, seemed to be disagreeing with her. Out of nowhere, her stomach was tight and unhappy. "Except instead of the girl disguising herself and testing the bloke's love, it's the bloke doing the testing, or something. Do I know this one, Ringan? Does Broomfield do it?"

"I doubt you know it, lamb, and no, we don't cover it." He was listening to Gowan's piano, to the movement of the melody line on the Brinsmead's mellow ivories. "Fact is, I don't think I've ever tried it, so it'll be a learning experience for both of us, not just Becca. Gowan, mate, can you just run through it once, vocals and all? We can call it a day after that, but I'd like to fix it in my head."

"Sure," Gowan told him, and settled himself on the piano bench. "And Penny has it right, comparing it to 'Sovay' and songs of that kind, though I've never really given it much thought. Still, a nice harmless tune, after all the elves and loss of virginity and vengeful fairy-folk and whatnot."

He ran his fingers over a few notes, and cleared his throat. "Here we go, then—second verse. 'I walked on, and farther on, love did my heart engage; there I spied a well-faird maid, lay sleeping near a hedge.' "

Penny, who'd been hovering suggestively near the door, sat back down. This was the first time she'd heard Gowan singing on his own; up until now, Gowan's charm had been wasted on her. Ringan had called him a lady-killer, but until she'd caught the full impact of the musician rather than the host, she hadn't understood what Ringan had been talking about. At the piano, voice and chords moving together, he was in his element, his charm natural, as potent as the local mead. The easy pleasant tenor took the lyric and made a story out of it, while the piano provided a solid foundation.

"Then I kissd her with my lips and stroked her with my hand: 'Win up, win up, ye well-faird maid, this day ye sleep oer lang.' "

"It's very nice." Becca sounded a bit bored, an adolescent girl who'd rather be out swimming. Gowan shot her a teasing look, and continued.

"This dreary sight that I hae seen unto my heart gives pain; at the south side o your father's garden, I see a knight lies slain."

It came out of the air, out of nowhere, out of the pit of her own stomach, a voice as clear and urgent as anything Penny had heard all day: *wrong, something is very wrong, bad, this is all wrong.*

"Penny?" Ringan had noticed something, he was on his feet now, staring at her. Penny, seeing the room and its inhabitants as if through a thin moving mist, heard his voice. She made no reply;

there was no speech in her. Gowan was still playing, he hadn't noticed anything, he hadn't heard Ringan's words . . .

"O what like was his hawk, his hawk? Oh what like was his hound? And what like was the trusty brand this new-slain knight had on?"

"Penny? Are you all right?"

That nice flute player, what was his name, he was gawking at her as if she'd just dropped in from another planet, but it didn't matter, they were all of them a thousand miles away . . .

"Aunt Penny! What is it? What's wrong?"

It was Becca, her fiddle put neatly back in its case. She was closer to Penny than the rest of them. Penny had no way of knowing that she was whimpering, her eyes fixed and staring, her face grey and streaked with sweat. *This is wrong, all wrong, something's going to happen, something already has happened, don't let it, make it stop . . .*

"Penny!" Ringan had started across the room, but Becca was still closer. There was wonder on her face, and worry. She laid a hand on Penny's bare arm.

Voices, a single voice cutting over a babble, a clamour of noise and anger and pain and hate, screaming, someone was screaming, and then there was silence, horrible silence, small dreadful sounds, a gasp, a choke, a gurgle . . .

Penny reached out, and fastened her own hand around Becca's arm. The skin was warm beneath her fingers, warm healthy young flesh, vibrant, alive.

. . . *na Jenna, mar pleg, Jenna, na, hedhi, na, prag* . . .

Blood, bile, agony. A surge of darkness, and then the distant horizon come too close, the very edge of blackness. The light was fading in her eyes, nothing left to see but a girl, a murderess, a beautiful girl with enormous sunken grey eyes staring down at her. She was holding something, the child's long elegant fingers letting loose of it, was it a stone, a heavy stone, it was coming loose of her fingers, crashing down to the earth in silence as the girl's hands, empty now, went to her mouth, everything was in slow motion, there was no air, her throat was useless, darkness light, oh Jenna, why . . .

The last thing Penny was aware of was meeting Becca's eyes, and a single coherent thought, her own, slicing through the noise and the mess that contact with the girl had raised in her.

She's hearing it. Whatever this is, whatever happened here, she's hearing it with me.

Three

Then I kissd her with my lips
And stroked her with my hand:
"Win up, win up, ye well-faird maid,
This day ye sleep oer lang."

"Are you sure you're okay?"

It was very late, and Penny and Ringan, both wide awake, lay side by side, not touching, in Gowan's comfortably overstuffed guest bed. Sleepless, they'd watched the moon come up, spilling into the room, flecking the ornate lincrusta panels and the accumulation of several generations of Camborne knickknacks with a watery light. The small room, with its steeply pitched ceiling and its uneven floor, was too warm for complete comfort, even with the windows cracked open at the top, and they'd opted for the top sheet as their only cover. The decision to remove the heavy duvet, which had been neatly folded and set aside, had not required a word of discussion.

"I think so." Penny's eyes were scratchy, and her voice was thin and tired. "I suppose so. I just—I wish I knew what that was, Ringan, you know? Or where it came from, and why."

"So do I." Ringan rolled over and faced her; the need for reassuring human contact was suddenly overwhelming, and he reached out to touch her cheek. "I'm not overlooking the fact that whatever that was, it happened because someone played a song. It seemed to, anyway."

It was a question, and he paused, waiting, but she was silent. He blew out his breath.

"Penny, look. I don't want to push. I know you probably aren't ready to talk about it yet—all right, that's fine. Take your time. So long as you're all right—are you all right?"

"I'm fine."

It was a lie. She wasn't fine, not at all. Her eyes were burning, counting the same shadowed bumps on the ceiling for the umpteenth time since she'd climbed into bed for the night, what felt like half a century earlier. This was ridiculous; she was going to have to sleep sometime. *Come along*, she told herself, *just close your eyes. Do it. Either look at whatever that was, face it straight on, or else make up your mind to ignore it. Staying awake forever isn't an option. You've got to get some sleep. Just take an option and get on with it.*

It was no use. She simply didn't want to close her eyes. The problem was, every time she'd tried it, that sense of someone else's fear came back. The shock of a girl's grey eyes looking down at her, storm-coloured irises disappearing into blackness and dawning horror as something hard and rounded and heavy slipped from the girl's spasming fingers: they swamped her, threatening to drown her. It wasn't a vision, it was a reality, inarguable, impossible to dismiss: she'd been staring up at a girl who was looking down at her with Rebecca's eyes, choking on her own blood, her own lack of breath, knowing that the girl had just killed her.

And Rebecca had seen what Penny had seen. She'd shared it.

Stop thinking about it, stop, just stop, close your eyes and let go of it, you have to sleep . . .

Damn, she thought, *damn and double damn*. It wasn't going to happen. Until she looked at this thing, faced it, tried to make some sense out of it, she was going to be afraid to sleep. She wasn't sure why, either—it simply didn't make sense. After all, she thought, this was hardly the first time she'd tried to process a bit of music and come up haunted, unfairly having to deal with memory and fear and loss that weren't her own.

It's different this time. You know it is. And maybe you'd best pay attention and make sense of why it's different.

She lay still, trying to focus, as bone weary as she could remember being. She'd done two-performance days during fifteen years as an actor and a producer, days that had begun before sunrise with makeup and costuming decisions and moving scenery flats around intricately designed stages, and ended twenty hours later with her falling exhausted into a stupor. But this was new; she was drained with tiredness.

She wasn't sure what was different about this or why she was afraid to look at it. She didn't know what it was about those few moments in Gowan's parlour that was making her want to push this one away from her with both hands. All she was sure of was that something about that screaming unintelligible voice, those wide eyes, those long pale fingers holding the thing that had come down on her throat, killing her, taking away her breath and the light of life in her eyes, had hit her on a level she hadn't known she possessed. And how could the girl do that, to a—

Sleep. That was it, of course it was. That's why you're afraid to sleep. Oh, God.

"Penny?" Ringan was upright, pushing himself off the feather mattress with the flat on one hand, staring at her. "Penny, what in hell? Talk to me, lamb, please. I know I said I wouldn't push, but I can't—"

"I was sleeping." She was looking at him, through him, seeing nothing. They were at eye level—Penny was unaware of having sat up. And there it was, clear at last, the reason she was afraid to close her eyes. "I was asleep. I was all the way down, deep as you can get, dreaming. And she hit me."

"What . . ."

"She hit me." Words, not English, terror and hate and rage and the sour taste of something that might have been madness pooling up in that voice, spilling out over her, over the sleeper who had been so dreadfully roused. . . . "Ringan, she had a stone, a stone with sharp edges, and she hit me with it. She brought the damned thing down on my throat, and I was asleep. I woke up and she'd killed me. She'd crushed something in my throat. I woke up just long enough to know I was dying. And then I died."

"Jesus." Ringan's voice shook. If he lived to be as old as Abraham, he would never get accustomed to this, never be able to deal with what it did to her. That he had nearly died himself not so long ago as his own ancestor, nearly been taken to the same hideous death on the rack, under the less-than-tender care of Henry Tudor's pet executioner, only made it worse. He knew now what she was going through, just how bad exposure to the unseen world could feel. "Penny, who? Who was it? Who are you talking about? Do you know? Was there anything—"

"No. Nothing. I haven't got the faintest idea who he was, who she was." Knowledge was there, and comprehension. Forcing her exhausted eyes to stay open would solve nothing; it might even make it worse, weakening her, in case anything else happened. "Ringan, give me a minute, all right? Please? I have to look at this, and I don't want to, but I have to try. Just—be here, in case anything happens."

He was quiet. She took a deep breath, reached out to rest a hand on his sheet-covered thigh, and let her eyes close.

In fact, the darkness behind her lowered lids was, for the moment, quiet enough. It seemed that if she wanted to bring those moments of the afternoon back, to see and hear them again, to somehow gain control of whatever had happened, she would have to take the initiative and hunt for them, conjure them. It was the last thing on earth she wanted to do.

Watching her, Ringan found himself holding his breath, biting down hard on his impatience and a sense of urgency. What had happened to Penny was bad enough in its own right, but the moment of recognition, of understanding that Becca was seeing and hearing whatever bizarre taste of hell Penny was undergoing, put a new edge on the situation. That edge was honed to intolerable sharpness by his own sense of responsibility toward his niece.

His memory brought up the scene in Gowan's living room, sharp and clear, the moment when Penny, her right hand closed hard around Becca's bare arm, had lifted her free hand to her throat and spoken. She'd said something, gasped something out, a short choked stream of language. The words themselves had been low, garbled, impossible to make out. They'd been nearly lost under the sudden clamour of reaction, the horrified concern from Gowan and Cian.

One thing Ringan was certain of: whatever language she'd been speaking, it hadn't been English. It hadn't been anything he recognised, except for one word.

Hours later, remembering what he thought might never leave his awareness entirely again in this life, Ringan felt his skin move on his bones. He'd been trying for hours to convince himself that he'd heard wrong, but he'd heard what he'd heard, and he knew it.

Penny had said something, a word, speaking it as though her throat was drenched in her own bright blood. She'd spoken as if she were choking, as if she could bring forth nothing but pain and reproach and regret, one word only that had been a question she didn't have enough life left in her to vocalise. Whatever else she'd been trying to say, in whatever the language had been, one thing, one word, had come out clear.

She'd said a name, a woman's name: *Jenna*.

The name itself meant nothing to Ringan. It was the pain in Penny's voice, the shock of disbelief on her face, the horror, the sense of betrayal that had coloured that incomprehensible speech, that had carved themselves into the dark places where bad dreams lived.

Ringan's hand, resting lightly on Penny's closed hard. She didn't feel it; she was retracing the steps of where she'd been that afternoon, trying to pinpoint the precise moment when something in her head and heart had opened and provided a conduit for her to see a pretty young girl with a stone in her hand bring it down with all her strength across the exposed throat of a sleeping man. She was probing, pushing herself, trying to find the trigger that had put her into the mind and heart and body of a man being murdered.

Man? She kept her eyes closed, questing, propelling herself back and down into the darkness. *How do you know it was a man she killed?*

It had been a man, that much was certain. She'd been in him, had *been* him, had felt his body and spirit react to that dreadful reality as he'd woken from the calm of sleep into the cataclysm of sudden violent death, deliberately handed out. Body, soul, spirit, she'd felt the essential maleness of him. And she'd felt something else, as well: the disbelief in him, coming from one source only . . .

"Oh God." A cold sweat was chilling the nape of her neck and her bare shoulders. *The girl, her eyes, the stone, why, why had she done this, how . . . ?* Her nails dug into Ringan's thigh, straight through the light sheet. "Ringan? Oh God, I'm sorry, darling. Did I draw blood?"

"Never mind about that. No worries, it's fine, I'm fine. It's you I'm worried about." His skin was in fact stinging, but he ignored it and slid his arm around her, pulling her close. She was shivering, wracked with long tremors, and her teeth were chattering. She didn't seem to notice. It was ridiculous, and he fought down the familiar hated pangs of his own helplessness. "Penny, lamb, you've gone parky—completely cold. And you're shaking like an aspen with St. Vitus' dance. Here, cuddle up to me—a good snog ought to help drive the chill off. Right, that's it, good. No, don't talk yet. Just get warm again."

Pressed against him, grateful and quiescent, she gradually relaxed. He felt her flesh warm, coming back to normality in the shelter of his arm. The shaking eased and, at last, stopped entirely.

"You saw something, didn't you?" He'd been stroking her bare arm; the stroking continued, rhythmic and soothing. "Remembered something?"

"Yes. What he felt. What he understood, what he knew." She rubbed her cheek against his shoulder. "Ringan, I don't know who he was, or why it hit me, or even what caused it to happen at all, unless it was that song Gowan was singing. I mean, it's usually a song. But whoever this man was—he loved that girl. What he felt, his only thought, the only thing that was clear—"

She stopped, swallowed hard. Ringan said nothing. There was no point in prompting, or pushing. He knew her well enough to

48

know that, just now, she was wrestling with what had happened, sorting out what she'd seen, trying to make sense of it. She'd tell him when she was ready, and not before.

"Ringan, it was betrayal he felt." The moon was down, and the soft wash of pearl across the china dogs and souvenirs from trips to London and the oversized mahogany headboard had moved on, leaving the room a shadowed, stuffy cave, in nearly total darkness. There must have been a shift in the tide, Penny thought, for the air in the room to be that strongly laced with the smell of salt water.

"He had no idea why she was doing that to him." She kept her voice even, steady. "Not the first clue. All he had was a sense of betrayal. It was huge, overpowering, it just buried anything and everything else—he didn't have room to feel anything else. He woke up, he met her eyes, those big grey eyes of hers, and he knew she'd killed him. But he didn't believe it, he *couldn't* believe it." Her voice faltered. "How could he, when he didn't know why? He loved her. He didn't understand."

Ringan said nothing. The bewilderment in Penny's voice brought the pain she'd felt into the room as a tangible thing. It didn't matter who the dead man had been, or when he'd died, or where. Shock, bewilderment, betrayal, she'd felt them all, as a dead man's proxy.

The realisation of something she'd said came almost as afterthought. "Penny—listen. What did you mean about her eyes? You said something about her having big grey eyes."

"She did." Penny shuddered. "For a moment, there was a bit of him and a bit of me and we seemed to have got ourselves crossed up. It was really nasty, Ringan, really unsettling—I wasn't sure if I was seeing the girl with the stone or Rebecca, or both. But the face I saw—that *he* saw—that wasn't Becca. They didn't look at all alike, not really, except for them both being right around the same age, and of course the eyes. Their eyes were really similar. Ringan, what is it? What did I say?"

"I'm not sure."

There was something, information he felt he ought to remember, something about grey eyes and Rebecca, but he was sleepy now; a long intensive day of playing music had been capped by the horror of whatever had come through Penny, and exhaustion had finally caught him up. He wasn't alone, either—Penny had already snuggled back down under the top sheet, cheek against the pillow.

He yawned, a jaw-cracking gulp of the air that tasted so strongly of the sea. Through the window, the hush of the late tide against Porthmeor was distant, yet steady. Something, grey eyes, who had said something about Rebecca's eyes? Whatever it was, it was staying maddeningly out of reach. And what about the song–what were the lyrics?

It was no use. His brain had gone silent, refusing to function. "Pen, I'm ready for some kip—truth is, I don't think I'm actually awake. Let's talk in the morning."

It had been a long time since Ringan had stayed as a guest under Gowan's roof—so long, in fact, that he'd forgotten about Gowan's love for cooking up and serving a full breakfast. Coming downstairs at half past eight, Ringan stopped as he reached the bottom floor. He'd caught the smell of food: eggs, fish, coffee, other scents he couldn't identify, all mingling together and acting as a siren's song.

"Wow." Penny, at his heels, stopped and sniffed. "This place smells like some corner of gourmand heaven. Well, heaven for a farmer, or someone else who has a job that works best off enough breakfast to last all day."

"Farmers, or tin miners, or pilchard fishermen," he agreed. His stomach had begun tingling, a talkative rumble that seemed to be telling him to get on with it. "I just realised, we didn't really get supper last night, did we? Not much appetite."

"No, and I'm starving to death. That food smells blissful. Ringan, are you planning to come and eat? Or shall I just go find a watering can and sprinkle your roots with it?" She gave him a small push and edged around him. "I swear I smell hot pasties. Aren't you coming?"

They found Gowan in the kitchen, wearing an apron that, while it would have been outsized for a smaller man, seemed barely adequate for him. Sometime during the past hundred or so years, one of Gowan's ancestors had decided to sacrifice a portion of the enormous back garden for extra floor space and added an extension to the house. As a result, the small kitchen, which had once opened only to the dining room, had acquired a second doorway leading out to a screened-in sunroom.

The sunroom had been turned into a kind of alfresco second dining room, equipped with a rectangular dining table and four wooden chairs. It was a beautiful space, framed in glass and mellow wood; it had the sense of spaciousness and greenery that came with eating out of doors, while offering the warmth of the house and protection from the elements.

"Oh, how beautiful!" Entranced, Penny looked out at the fruit trees, the primroses, the flowering vines along the fence that marked the boundary of the Camborne property. "What a gorgeous idea, turning this into a breakfast nook. I have to say, I'd probably eat all my meals in here—this room must be sensational at night, when the stars are out. And when it's raining, it must be amazing in here. Good morning, Becca. Are you all right? You look tired."

"Good morning." She sounded as tired as she looked. Ringan, pulling out a chair and watching his niece settle in opposite him, found himself wondering if she'd closed her eyes the previous night. There were deep shadows under her eyes, and her mouth seemed to want to droop. "I'm okay. I just—I didn't sleep very well. I guess maybe I'm a little nervous about tonight. Are we—is that happening?"

"*Eah,* child, that it is. And your having nerves, that's understandable, but no worrying for you, young Rebecca. You'll do very well, very well indeed, and it's only three songs, the ones we did yesterday, with your uncle right there to help you along. And *myttin da* to you both, Penny, Ringan. A beautiful day out of doors, or looks to be." Gowan, who had stripped off the apron and hung it on a hook just inside the sunroom's door, set a platter down in the centre of the table. *"A vynn'ta kavoes neppyth dh'y dhybri?"*

Ringan blinked. "Gowan, if you're going to speak Cornish, I'm off. You know damned well I know about three words of the language. How'd you like me speaking Lallans back at you, mate? A little tit for tat?"

"Now, don't be cheeky, Ringan. I'm just after young Rebecca here getting the tone of it—after all, no one learns languages better than a musician. I was asking if you'd like something to eat, that's all." He reached for a slab of bread. "Mind that plate, it's hot. Here's fresh pilchards and scrambled eggs—there's toast browning up, and coffee. Pasties will be out in just a few minutes. I'm hoping you're hungry. Breakfast is the main meal here and always has been—when your day begins at sunup, and you're eating your midday pasty half a mile down a tin mine, you want something to go on with."

"Tin miners?" Ringan exchanged a grin with Penny. "As to being hungry, if I wasn't before, I would be now. No way to not eat, not with the house smelling this way. Becca, does Robbie let you have coffee at home? You look as if you can barely hold your eyelids open. . . ."

He stopped.

Grey eyes.

There it was, the memory, the thing that had refused to declare itself as he'd drifted off in the small hours the night before. Gowan, holding Becca's hand—or had it been the other way around? What had he said?

I used to know someone—a girl. You have eyes just like hers.

Ringan opened his mouth and closed it again. Penny and Gowan were talking, discussing a film that had been shot locally a few months ago; Penny knew most of the cast of the film, and Gowan was being his usual charming self, sharing amusing stories of the Londoners' adventures in the Duchy of Cornwall. Penny was

52

laughing, holding her own, offering insider anecdotes about the temperamental leading lady, being nearly as charming as Gowan.

Ringan was familiar with Penny's technique; he'd been watching her do it for years. He was usually highly appreciative of it, but this morning the conversation flowed around him and went unnoticed. His mind was moving around, trying to pinpoint things, to somehow put the oddness of yesterday into a context that made some sort of sense.

Gowan hadn't mentioned yesterday's post-rehearsal incident, not a word. He hadn't said anything during the evening, not as Penny had gone shakily up the steeply pitched stairway, with Ringan at her back, and curled up, dizzy and sick, eyes wide open, trying to recoup. He hadn't said anything beyond asking if she was feeling better when she'd come down again. He hadn't said a word to Ringan, either. No curiosity, no wanting to know, no concern.

And that was very unlike Gowan. The man matching stories with Penny, plying them with food, anxious to make sure everyone had what they needed, that was the Gowan Camborne Ringan had known for more than half his life. Even with nothing wrong, he was famous among his circle of acquaintance for his genuine warmth as a host and a friend. So why had Gowan said nothing?

Ringan, not realising it, had speared a small salty pilchard. If Gowan's behaviour yesterday had been peculiar, Becca's had been even odder. Gowan wasn't the only one who should have been all over what had happened. Surely, Becca ought to be saying something; Ringan had seen her reaction as she put her hand on Penny. He'd watched the easy rose colour drain from her cheeks, seen her pupils turn the deep grey that surrounded them to nearly black as they expanded with the shock of feeling and hearing the same horror that Penny had felt and seen.

Yet she'd said nothing, not last night and not this morning. The main thing on her mind seemed to be her nerves at playing her fiddle in front of an audience of strangers for the first time. And that was ridiculous. A self-absorbed adolescent she might be, but she wasn't insensate.

You have eyes just like hers.

Penny, in the dead hours of the night, had still been so affected by the memory of the experience that she hadn't wanted to close her eyes. Yet Becca, without Penny's armament of past experience to fall back on, didn't even seem to be thinking about it. It was as if it had never happened.

There's nothing to know. She's dead.

"Becca?" He hadn't intended to say anything, not yet. This wasn't the place or the moment, this cosy pleasant meal among friends and family. Yet he couldn't stop himself; the words wanted out. "We need to talk a bit, after breakfast. Not about tonight—about yesterday. All right?"

"Yesterday?" She raised her eyes and stared at him, and something locked down hard in the pit of his stomach. There was nothing but bewilderment in her face. It looked to be genuine, not a teenaged girl trying to avoid something unpleasant. "I don't understand. What do you mean, talk about yesterday? About us rehearsing, you mean?"

"I think he means about what happened after that." Penny was watching Becca's face, her mouth tight around the corners. "That little episode I had, that we had, after Gowan played that last song—what was it called?"

"*New-Slain Knight,* that would be." Gowan spoke from the doorway. He'd gone to the oven and come back with toast and an oversized plate heaped high with warm pasties. The room smelled of bread baking and meat sizzling, a strong savoury aroma. "We're not doing that tonight, unless we can get it down at speed—even Cian doesn't know it well enough to play. I'm thinking we can maybe add it if we rehearse it early. After all, it's not a tricky song, nice simple structure and melody, and I'm happy to sing it."

"Fine. Whatever," Ringan, staring at his niece, replied automatically. "Always up for a new song in the repertoire."

Gowan turned his attention toward Penny. "But you've reminded me, I have to apologise, for not making sure there was nothing I could do for you yesterday." Nothing, no hint of shadow, no hint of anything at all. Ringan glanced at Penny and met her eye, seeing his own thoughts mirrored there. Gowan, Becca—it was as if they'd completely blocked out what had happened. "Thing is, my mother had the same problem, and she couldn't bear people fussing over her. All she was good for when that happened to her was a long lie-down in a dark room. But really, I should know better than to think everyone's the same."

"The same problem?" Penny blinked at him, wondering what he was talking about. Surely his mother hadn't been susceptible to sudden visions of dead people, reliving their deaths? "Gowan, you're certainly forgiven for whatever it is you think needs forgiveness, but honestly, I haven't got any idea what you mean. Not a clue. What are you apologising for? What was wrong with your mother?"

"Migraines, of course." He reached for a pasty. His voice was normal, unshadowed by anything but a remembered sympathy for a woman with a headache, and perhaps surprise at Penny's slowness to understand. "Mam used to get them sometimes, real head-splitters, she called them. She used to practically hallucinate, the pain would get so bad. I remember how she used to want to just turn the lights off and have herself a sleep. You looked just like that yesterday, white and played out."

"But that wasn't a migraine." Ringan had set his fork down. *There's nothing to know. She's dead. You have eyes just like hers.* "Penny doesn't get migraines."

"Was it not?" Gowan sounded surprised. "What, then?"

"A visit from a dead man."

Penny heard her own voice and closed her eyes for a moment. *Right*, she thought, *that's torn it.* She couldn't turn back now; having said that much, she was committed. And Gowan and Becca were both staring at her, mouths slack.

"I don't get it." Becca suddenly sounded very young, and the Scots in her voice was noticeable. "What do you mean?"

"Exactly what I said, Becca." She folded her hands together in her lap; they wanted to clutch something. Somehow, no matter how many times something like this happened to her, it was always a shock and it never got any easier. That this one had felt somehow different, that her reactions had somehow left her with a sense of holding her breath while waiting for the next shock, was something she hadn't yet had the chance to look at. "It was me sharing a moment with a dying man, a man who was going through his own murder. It's not surprising you thought my head was aching, Gowan. It was, believe me. But it wasn't a migraine. It was a visit from a dead man, and it's happened before, too many damned times. Just—not quite like this."

Her voice had moved upward, higher than usual. Ringan reached out, and touched her hand.

"You should tell them, lamb." He met her eye. There was trouble in his own look; her last words had not been lost on him. "Tell them. They ought to know. It's better if they do."

She told them, giving them not only everything she remembered from the events of the previous afternoon, but the history of what had led to her own susceptibility as well. As she spoke, she found herself wanting to watch, not Gowan's face, but Becca's.

And there was nothing to see there, nothing beyond interest and bewilderment, with what was probably a healthy dose of scepticism: *Are you having me on? Is this all a joke?* If the girl was remembering that moment of shared darkness, she was making a superb job of hiding it.

"My God." Gowan's pasty had grown cold on his plate, as he listened. "That's—ghosts? It's ghosts you see?"

"Yes, I do, and don't ask me what it's like, because it's hell, and I hate it." Her hands were tight in her lap, fingers laced together hard. "It's not something I want any part of. Unfortunately, I don't get a choice. Lucky me."

The silence stretched out. Becca broke it:

"You're having us on, aren't you?"

"Are you seriously asking me that?" Penny's hands wanted to unclench, clench again, ball into fists, tear something. She kept them hard and tight in her lap. "You? Because if anyone ought to know just how serious I am, it's you, Becca. You saw it yourself yesterday. You felt it yourself."

"I don't know what you're talking about." Her head was tilted, her eyes wide and clear. There was nothing to be seen in her face beyond bewilderment. "What do you mean, I felt it? I just thought you had the migraine."

"Right." Penny got up, too fast, not paying attention; she bumped the table hard, sending coffee and tea moving in cups, and crockery chattering. *Get out,* she thought, *sort this out, is Becca lying or has she just wiped it from her mind? Or am I out of my own mind?* "Okay. Right. Whatever you say. Have a lovely rehearsal, everyone—I'd just be in the way for that, and anyway, I want to be out of doors. I'll see everyone later."

Four

This dreary sight that I hae seen
Unto my heart gives pain;
At the south side o your father's garden,
I see a knight lies slain.

"A very good evening to all of you, and welcome to the Duke of Cornwall's Own. For those of you who've not been here before, this group of disreputable types up here are my mates, and we're the Tin Miners. Oh, and I'm Gowan Camborne. And from me to you, *Kammbronn a'gas dynnergh!*"

"What a pretty language Cornish is." Penny, sitting at a table in the front row with Rebecca, felt her shoulders move slightly as Gowan moved his hands up the keys, a dancy cascade of the piano's highest notes. "Was that his own name he said?"

"That it was." At the table to Penny's left, Lucy Williams, Cian's wife, had overheard the question. "He was just welcoming everyone to the show personally. *Kammbronn a'gas dynnergh* just means 'Camborne welcomes you.' It's also the name of a town not far away, so Gowan was having a little joke with the tourists in the crowd."

Penny nodded and smiled. Lucy, small and placid, seemed pleasant enough, albeit with what Penny had privately labelled a pronounced didactic streak. Penny, herself a theatre director and used to being the one giving information and orders, didn't generally do well with being at the receiving end of instructive types. Still, Lucy was already proving a good source of information about everything remotely

Cornwall, and, after all, Penny had asked the question, even if she'd really meant it as nothing more than an idle observation.

"Give us a minute, two minutes maybe, to tune up, and we'll have some music for you. Makes me happy I don't play guitar—this way, at least I haven't got to be tuning up all night long." Gowan's voice rang easily out over the crowd. Ringan, adjusting a tuning peg, shot Gowan a look and sounded a resonant harmonic on his D string. Cian piped the same note on the flute, synching the two instruments. Ringan said something, lost in the wash of crowd noise and onstage tinkering. Gowan grinned.

"And we've got a treat for you tonight." Gowan lifted a hand and pointed towards Ringan. "A couple of fine musicians sitting in, special guests: first one up is Ringan Laine on guitar and vocals. Just a little something to make tonight stand out when it's done."

There were hoots and cheers as some of the crowd realised who Ringan was. "That's Ringan Laine of Broomfield Hill, and a damned fine group they are, if you haven't heard them. Don't be after taking my word on it, though—if you'd fancy a listen, you can buy their brand-new CD at the table next to the bar, only ten quid. Don't be shy, now. Dig into your pockets . . ."

Lucy Williams, meanwhile, was still talking, instructive and self-assured and right on the edge of annoying, modulating her voice in the manner of a woman accustomed to making herself heard under any circumstances. Since she was a teacher of small children when she wasn't doing what she was doing tonight, which was or-namenting the front row of her husband's gig, she had no trouble at all. Penny, who despite her own fame and success in an entirely different artistic field had spent her spare evenings for the better part of fifteen years sitting at front-row tables watching Ringan play, mentally referred to this inevitable aspect of a relationship with a musician as the 'oh please, not that same damned song again' syndrome.

"It really is pretty. Cornish, I mean." Becca couldn't seem to sit still. Her fiddle, resting in its case, was already onstage, tuned and ready for her use. She was twitchy, moving in her seat; Penny thought that if her gleaming mass of hair hadn't been pulled back off her face and clipped down hard, Becca would have been chewing on it. If the severe hairstyle was supposed to give her the look of an adult, it was failing miserably. There was something touching about her obvious nerves—they were a dead giveaway of just how young she really was, talent or no talent.

Penny, returning to Gowan's house earlier after a couple of hours of wandering St. Ives, had found the rehearsal done with, and a plan for the evening's show in place. The band would warm up the crowd with five songs, then bring Becca onstage for the trio of songs they'd rehearsed. Becca, after an intensive session of matching her fiddle to the other instruments, had seemed calm enough, but her tranquillity was deceptive, a thin and transparent mask. She had good reason for the nerves. It occurred to Penny, as it had already done to Ringan, that not only had Becca never played in public before, she would be playing as part of an ensemble after a childhood of mostly solitary practice. Penny, who thrived on live performance and without a shy bone in her body, was aware of strong sympathy. This had to be terrifying for the child.

"Gowan says Cornish is just as musical a language as Gaelic is." Becca didn't sound terrified, just distracted. Her eyes were aimed at the stage. "He says the drummer is playing a *crowdy crawn*—I thought it was called a *bodhrán*, but Gowan says no, not in Cornish. I wonder if it's tricky to learn? The language, I mean?"

"Haven't got a clue—I don't speak a word of it. Excuse me, I'm off to the loo before they really get started. Your uncle gets shirty if I disappear on him midshow. Here, Lucy, watch my seat, will you? Ta."

Onstage, Ringan was fastening a capo at the third fret of the Martin's neck, and the houselights were flickering. Lucy slid across to take up both Penny's chair and her own. She'd overheard Becca's question and was too obviously gearing up to answer it at length, with all sorts of educational details. If Becca resented being lectured, she was hiding it nicely; Penny, weaving her way between the packed tables and the standing crowd at the back near the bar, glanced behind her and saw the two heads close together. *Good,* she thought. Maybe Lucy's calm would settle the butterflies that were undoubtedly in full mad wing-beating mode in the pit of Becca's stomach.

The upstairs bar had been doing a brisk business since the first people had wandered in, if the end result—a queue of women waiting to use the single loo—was anything to go by. Waiting her turn, Penny heard the catcalls and applause from the crowd as the Miners, with their current lineup of Gowan, Cian, Ringan, and a sixtyish bodhrán player whose name Penny could neither remember nor pronounce, swung into their first song. By the time she finally emerged, the band had worked their way through the opening number, "Lamorna," and both the show and the audience were heating up nicely.

Penny stayed where she was. The crowd at the back, those who'd either come too late to nab a chair or who wanted to stay as close as possible to the bar, was dense enough to make navigation tricky at best, especially while the band was playing. Penny slipped off to her right, waited for Ringan to glance up from the tricky duet he was playing with Cian, and lifted a hand. He saw her and nodded twice in her direction. It was an old signal between them, familiar and comfortable, and Penny found herself grinning. She was definitely in "musician's old lady" mode tonight; Ringan knew she was out there and he could get on with playing.

The Miners finished "Lamorna" and moved on to the second song, also a Cornish traditional, a song with the peculiar name of "Little Eyes." Gowan sang this one, leaning into the vocal, the piano setting up the rest of the instruments.

Penny, edging her way back to the bar, got herself a glass of the local mead. It was wonderful stuff, strong with honey and lemon; with long experience of the local brews to be found at country pubs, Penny was mindful of the strength behind the soft taste. She sipped it slowly, paying little attention to the music, splendid as it was. Somehow, standing alone at the back of the crowd, she'd managed to detach herself from her immediate surroundings to the point where her mind could focus on what had been bothering her since the conversation over breakfast in Gowan's lovely greenhouse room.

"I dreamed a dream the other night." Gowan's voice was mellow, powerful, effective. ". . . The strangest dream of all . . ."

Penny closed her eyes, letting the moment she'd been trying to forget come back, in full dreadful clarity: A man, desperate for one last breath through a crushed windpipe. The need to breathe, the expectation of aid, the disbelief and loss of both hope and will when his eyes met the eyes of the girl who was killing him. . . . She felt a tremor move down her back, weakening her legs for a moment.

"I dreamed I saw you kissing her behind the garden wall . . ."

She took another mouthful of mead. Around her, the audience was nodding appreciatively, swaying with the music. Becca must be getting edgier by the moment, Penny thought, with only a few songs left to go. Odd, very odd, that Ringan had so completely ignored the most obvious aspect of the incident in Gowan's front room: the fact that it seemed to have been triggered by a song. Ridiculous, in fact. If anyone out there had reason to drop everything and take a good hard look at the song they'd been playing when Penny had got hit with whatever it was she'd actually seen, it was Ringan. Yet he'd said nothing, done nothing. She was damned well going to ask him why; the topic might not be the most pleasant way to end up a nice night of live music, side by side in Gowan's guest bed, but damn it, she wanted to know.

It made no sense, none of it. Ringan's shrugging off of the fact that a song—a song about a death, no less—had triggered something that they both knew was supernatural in origin, was ridiculous. Rebecca claiming she'd felt nothing unusual, that was complete bollocks. While it was possible that she'd blocked it out, she'd known exactly what Penny had been feeling and seeing. Closing her eyes, Penny could remember the sense of electricity, of shock, moving between her hand and Becca's bare arm. She could still see the horror in the girl's eyes as it happened.

And the song itself, what was that about? There was no murder in there, no violent death. Her ramble around St. Ives this afternoon, more of an escape from Gowan's house, had included a stop at the local bookshop. She'd had a stroke of luck there—they carried the current reprinted edition of the collected Child ballads. She'd found the song easily and copied down the lyrics, memorising them as she might have memorised a juicy bit from a play she wasn't familiar with and didn't expect to actually perform. And the lyric was just what Gowan had claimed it was: a sweet song about a man who tests his very young lover's feelings by pretending to be dead. There was nothing in those lyrics about genuine death, nothing at all . . .

. . . *Na Jenna, mar pleg, Jenna, na, hedhi, na, prag . . . no Jenna, please, Jenna, no, stop, no, why . . . ?*

She said something out loud, incoherent, not knowing—whatever it was, it was lost under the wash of music from the stage across the room. She set her glass down. Luckily, she was still near enough the bar to support herself against it. She suddenly needed all the support she could muster; the room seemed to be moving around her as vertigo hit, hard and fast.

"All right, then, are you?" The barmaid, young and slim and with a tray full of bottles and glasses balanced expertly between hand and shoulder, had seen her swaying and slipped between a mob of other patrons. To Penny, the walls seeming to fade in and out around her, the query sounded alien and fuzzy, nearly incomprehensible: *Allarathen, aroo?*

"Fine," Penny said, and managed a smile. It was a lie. She wasn't anything close to fine. Onstage, the band had finished "Little Eyes" and moved on to an English traditional called "Bruton Town." Ringan was singing lead, putting power and strength behind both lyrics and guitar. Penny, shaken and disoriented, heard none of it.

What had she just heard? Words, yes, the voice she had heard as part of her own thoughts the day before. The anguish in that voice, the power of the dying man's shock and despair—it was mind-boggling. Was it really possible that Becca had felt nothing and was neither lying nor blocking out? That Penny, herself so caught in those dying moments of someone whose language she didn't even speak, had completely misread what she'd seen in Becca's face?

"And now—right, hang on a minute, please. Quiet! *Taw taves,* will you? Hush, *hedhi,* hold your noise a moment!" Gowan's voice, amused and resonant, brought Penny back to earth and back to herself. "Can you be after showing some respect for our next guest? Her name is Rebecca Eisler, and she's as likely a fiddler as has ever stood onstage at the Duke's. Young Becca comes all the way here from Edinburgh, so we're lucky to have her doing a few tunes with us tonight. A warm welcome, if you please. Becca, *flogh,* come up here."

Cheers, calls of encouragement, some in English, some in Cornish. Penny, still dizzy, thought for a moment about trying to get back to her seat and offering Becca the support and encouragement of her own physical presence in the front row of tables. But the thought was daunting, and even as she weighed it the barmaid leaned over the counter and lifted an eyebrow at Penny's empty glass.

"More mead, then?"

After that, Penny stayed put at the back. Lucy Williams was right there, after all, a nice solid little figure, offering all the support necessary. Besides, Penny thought, if yesterday's rehearsal had been anything to go by, Becca would be so lost in the music by the time she'd played eight bars of it that she'd have forgotten the outside world entirely.

They gave Becca the minute or two she needed to get settled on her stool, pick up her fiddle and bow, and get ready. Then Ringan nodded at his niece and went straight into "Tam Lin." Gowan and Cian timed their own cues perfectly, the bodhrán player providing the base.

The music caught Penny as it usually did and pulled her in. When Becca came in, two verses earlier than she had during that first rehearsal, the shift in the audience's attitude was palpable. They'd been expecting a competent teenager, most likely a relative of someone in the band or the bar. What they got first took their breath away, then knocked them off their feet and off their balance. A good portion of the crowd were old fans of the Miners. They'd been coming to see Gowan and whoever he had with him on any given night for the better part of twenty years. They'd seen musicians come and go, integrating with Gowan, playing awhile, moving on. They'd seen some legends of the field sitting in for a night or two. This was the first time they'd heard anything like Becca Eisler.

The applause, when the song ended, took Penny's breath. It was foot stamping, murderously loud, shaking the bottles on the high shelves behind the polished wooden bar. It was a tribute to something well beyond mere quality.

And Becca handled it perfectly. She ducked her head slightly, a gesture resonant enough of shyness to give away her extreme youth. She thanked the crowd, mouthing it only, smiling, dropping her eyes.

They went on to "Thomas the Rhymer," taking it down new musical paths, letting the fiddle talk to Cian's flute. The bodhrán was stronger now, more relentless, setting a rhythm around which the more mobile instruments could play. And play they did, the piano soaring, the flute dancing, the fiddle wailing like one of the lost souls on the road to Elfland, the guitar stitching counterpoints to everything, including Ringan's vocal. The audience joined in at the chorus—"Come along, come along with me, Thomas the Rhymer!"—bringing themselves into the show at the invitation of the band, becoming, for just a few dizzying moments, a part of the band themselves.

"Okay." Ringan, getting his breath back, slid the capo back on Lord Randall's neck. Penny, beginning at last to make her way back to the front of the crowd, recognised what she thought of as Ringan's 'good night' tone of voice, and looked at her watch. With a shock, she realised that the band had been onstage for the better part of ninety minutes without a break. "This is the last song of the evening—no, no groaning, mates, how do you think *we* feel?

Anyway, it's a cheerful little thing about how to trick Lucifer with chicken feathers and droppings, just the ticket to send you all home with. Our thanks to all of you for coming out, and can we have a round of applause for the band? We've been the Tin Miners, and we'll be back here tomorrow night."

Penny reached her seat, slipping around people standing beside their own tables, passing their empty glasses along as the barman signalled time. She nodded absently at Lucy and sat down. She was watching the stage, a faint crease between her brows.

The Miners finished the show with a flourish, and someone flicked the overheads off and on in the time-honoured signal that the show was actually officially over, there would be no more music, no encore was in the offing, it was time to go home. The crowd, mellow and pleased and, in a gratifying number of instances, with a Broomfield Hill CD from the now-empty table in their hands, headed for the doors and out into a summer night as warm and soft as creamery butter.

The band and their immediate circle of friends and family stayed behind, putting their instruments away, unwinding, relaxing in the quiet room. Conversation eddied and flowed. Someone had opened the windows to air the place out, and below the usual mixture of alcohol, sweat, perfume, and tobacco, the smell of the sea was strong and clean.

"You all right, lamb? You're looking peaked." Ringan's beard was bristling, and he had a gleam in his eye. Normally, Penny would have been pleased to see it; it was an old sign the night wasn't over, at least for the two of them. Tonight, however, she barely noticed.

"No, I'm fine. I've got a headache, that's all. Nothing a good sleep and some aspirin won't fix."

The headache was real, a nasty thumping behind her eyes. It had come on only over the last few minutes—perhaps, Penny thought, as payback for two full glasses of mead. She massaged her temples, her lids half-closed. Ringan was looking at her, and below her lashes she was watching Becca.

The girl, completing the odd circle of watchfulness, was staring at her uncle. There was something wrong with her face, with her look.

It took a moment for Penny, blinking and slow and trying to think through the starburst that was burgeoning behind her eyes, to identify what she was seeing as raw hatred.

Soft air, a breeze so sweet it might have been the very breath of the summer itself, a faint tang of salt. Unsure of whether she was dreaming or waking, Rebecca Eisler was certain of one thing, at least: she could smell the sea.

Above her head, the sky was a crisp clean blue. Small clouds made their way south toward Brittany, riding the prevailing wind. The sun fell on her face, warming her.

Okay, Becca decided, *so I'm dreaming.* She shifted in the narrow guest bed in Gowan's third bedroom. The bed was comfortable, and she'd fallen into it within minutes of their arrival back here after the show at the Duke's Own. She'd been as tired as she could remember being in her life—even brushing her teeth had taken more energy than she really had to spare. Making music in front of people, getting paid to do it, maybe that was the kind of thing that made you want to sleep and sleep and sleep . . .

Dreaming, she thought, *okay, dreaming's good,* and snuggled her cheek deep into the feather pillows. It was nice, and rare enough, that the real world and what she'd always thought of as the night world came together, and in a way that felt blissful at either end.

In the way of people with one foot on either side of the barrier between sleep and wakefulness, Becca was in that state of quiescence in which her mind, undisciplined by any need for interaction, wandered randomly from subject to subject. Moments from the evening just past jostled against each other: a line of music Cian had played in a minor key that would sound wonderful on the fiddle, the desire to go back to the seafood restaurant they'd tried their first night in Cornwall, the weird little moment of nausea she'd felt just before they'd left the Duke's. Aunt Penny had looked ill, and small wonder, if she was having a migraine. Becca remembered the small stab behind her own eyes, the sudden movement in her stomach, the thought that she was about to disgrace herself by throwing up as a reaction to her first-ever performance for money.

But the nausea, as well as the headache, had been momentary, fleeting, nothing at all, and the evening had ended with nothing to sour the memory of her triumph. She'd played before a crowd, and they'd not only paid to hear her, they'd cheered for her. Besides, unless she really was loopy with sleep, she was pretty sure she'd heard Uncle Ringan tell the audience that they'd be back tomorrow night, and maybe she'd better ask him about that in the morning, because if some of the same people came back again, they'd not want to be hearing the same songs over, would they? And of course, there was Gowan—he was so cool, even if he was sort of old—but there was something about him, she couldn't pin it down, so sleepy, maybe she ought to just let go and breathe in the smell of the sea and let herself relax into . . .

Jenna?

She turned her head. Now that was just silly, she thought, as silly as the sudden cramp at the pit of her stomach. It was silly that she should be reacting at all, because why would she respond to some imaginary dream-person? Anyway, it was only her father calling her, Hywel, and he was a good and kindly man who doted on his only daughter. Besides, he wasn't her father at all, she was miles deep and dreaming away the night, only this one felt a bit too real for—

Myttin da, flogh.

Far down in the uneasy part of Rebecca's sleeping instinct that still dealt in real-world symbols, something rippled. *Flogh.* Surely, someone else had called her that, and not so long ago, either. She hadn't known what it meant, not then—but of course she knew what it meant, that was more silliness and more oddity. It meant *child.* He was her father, Hywel Camborne, and of course she was his child, but time was he stopped calling her that, or time would be, soon, unless she was sore mistaken. Really, she was of an age, thinking of marrying and bedding, and he would soon need a different endearment.

But someone else had called her that, a man, and she was no child of his, nor wished to be. There were other things she maybe wished she might be to him, but not his child, not now, nor ever so.

Her father was asking her now: did she wish to go to the fair? All the rest of the family was to go, except the baby, her infant half-brother, Pasco. Hywel himself would lead the outing, and even Jenna's stepmother, the Lady Elyor, had said she would accompany them. At that, the girl knew a moment of wanting to roll her eyes, to be snide, biting down hard on asking her father if his goodwife meant to put aside her endless nameless illnesses for the day?

But she said nothing and was glad she'd held her tongue, for her father had not done with his plans for the day: her brother Perran, he told her, was eager to see what might be available in the way of decent horseflesh. This being the time of the summer fair, there would be horses in plenty, and bargains could be had. Perran, said his father, had it in his mind to buy himself a new mount, the old grey he'd ridden these many years having grown tired at last. And Perran had suggested that his little sister, too, might have a new mount, so that they could ride together, as they'd done in years past . . .

She cast her eyes down, long black lashes falling to cover what the eyes themselves might reveal. *Modesty,* she thought, *that is the best way, best and safest.* It would not do to let her father see what only God had her blessing to see, the feelings that were like to come up in her face at the merest mention of her brother Perran, the heir and the hope of the house. It wasn't safe.

And here was her father, asking her once more, *A vynn'ta mos? Do you want to go?* And here she stood, young Jenna, looking at the toes of her shoes, at the green summery earth beneath her feet, wondering if he, or her stepmother, or anyone else, could read what she felt, and praying that none might ever know. Not even Father Maban had heard one word from Jenna, and he never would. If that meant she must burn, then burn she would. . . .

Rebecca muttered something. The words, under her breath and articulated as little more than the exhale of a sleeping girl, were lost in the feather pillow, the quiet bedroom, the deadness of the hour. In some concrete and anchored corner of herself, she was growing bored with this dream. Why was she dreaming about some stupid girl in a garden in Cornwall anyway? And why was she so certain she was in Cornwall?

Ny vynnav, she told her father, scuffing the toes of one soft little leather shoe, feeling with a very undreamlike clarity the small smooth stones on the path beneath the hem of this ridiculous dress she was wearing. It was a pretty colour, though, she had to give it that, soft and silky and the colour of the clutch of eggs she'd once seen in a robin's nest, the year they'd nested in the apple tree outside her bedroom window in Edinburgh. *Na vynnav mos.* No, thank you, she didn't want to go. It was hot, she told him, and she was tired. Kept to herself was the thought that it was better, far better, if she stayed well away from anywhere her brother Perran chose to go. And of course, Rebecca realised, this was Cornwall, because they were speaking Cornish to each other, and anyway, this was where they lived, the Camborne family, Cornish to their heels and the ends of their hair, with cousins from Tintagel to the Lizard, from St. Ives to Penzance.

But her father, it seemed, had not done with her yet. He had another inducement to offer his darling daughter, something more to tempt her from her solitude and boredom, that she might change her mind and sample the sometimes rowdy pleasures of the fair within the safe circle of her family and acquaintance. Word had come from the manor at Ancell: the Cann family was hopeful of meeting them at the fair, including, Hywel said with a heavy playfulness, young Cador. Hywel's voice was indulgent, a bit sly; really, Rebecca felt, if he'd been talking to a son instead of a daughter, he might just have jabbed her in the ribs with an elbow.

But Jenna's eyelids stayed lowered, and her gaze stayed down. And if her father heard, or even sensed, the movement of the breath shortening in her lungs as she heard Cador Cann's name, he was wise enough not to show it.

Becca, deep into sleep, didn't feel her own body tense and then relax. She slept, the dream becoming fragmented as she lost touch with the symbols of her waking world. Indecently long black lashes lay across her cheekbones, the soft pillow pushed against her by one hand, its fingers calloused at the ends. After a while, the fingers relaxed, and Becca, deep in dream, began to move.

One wall and a doorway away, Gowan Camborne was also dreaming. Unlike his young houseguest, he wasn't smiling.

It had been a long time since he'd had this nightmare. Once, ten years or so ago, there had been a very bad patch, a stretch where he'd spent most nights forcing himself to stay awake to keep the dream at bay; wakefulness, never a favourite state of being for Gowan Camborne, had been the only way to avoid nights that felt like the dressing room backstage in Hell. So recurrent had the dream been, and so persistent, that he'd reached a point of being able to tell when the dream was beginning, no matter how deep asleep he might be. From there, it had been a fast step to training himself to wake up immediately.

What had brought it on again, after nothing more traumatic than a splendid and very relaxed show at the same club he'd been calling his home turf for nearly a quarter of a century, he didn't know. All he knew was that for whatever reason, he was standing in the cool shadowed hallway of the house that had been in his family for as far back as land deeds had been granted and records kept, his heart thumping, hearing his name being whispered from upstairs. . . .

Oh, no, he thought, and twitched. *Let there be none of that. I'm not after having this dream, not again, sweet mother not again, why now. . . .*

It was no use. Here he was, at the dream's inception, just as it had been every time during the bad days: he was standing alone in a house that suddenly seemed full of shadows, of movements in corners, of his own name, whispered in a girl's voice, just a girl, not something to fear, not some giant spider sitting in a web spun across his bed, she was calling him but how could he hear her if he was downstairs and she was upstairs whispering away like a chilly wind, how . . .

Gowan. Come up to me. I've been waiting for you. I've been wanting you so long, come to me. Gowan?

Silence. He thought, as always, *Where is my mother? Mam, are you home, for the love of God don't be home.* His entire body hurt with willing himself to stay down here, with his hope that his mother, with her migraines and her aches and her bad heart, was anywhere but here, in her own house. And his lungs hurt worst, from holding his breath.

He exhaled and then inhaled again. There it was, that smell, that salt like a brush of the far horizon across his lips: the sea smelling so strong. The house was an echo chamber of soughing waves and a whispering woman. She wasn't a woman, though—just a slip of a girl a good fifteen years his junior. It was stupid, him being so frightened. There was nothing to fear, certainly not the girl herself.

But of course, this was the realm of dream, where all debts are burned into the blood and all memory is unforgiving. And Gowan Camborne, with a debt he could never hope to repay or atone for in this life, stood planted at the foot of his own stairway, his legs made of seawater, held in place both by guilt at what he had caused and by terror of what he would find up there. The genuine sickness in his sleeper's fear came from already knowing what he would find there.

Gowan. Gowan, Gowan, Gowan. I love your name—it's so cool. It's from King Arthur, right? Like Gawain and the Green Knight? I love saying your name, Gowan Gowan Gowan. Come up to me, don't let me go. That woman, that girl you used to hang out with, the one who played with your band—she didn't mean anything to you, right? Gowan? Answer me, damn it, damn it!

One leg was moving, bending to take his weight as he moved toward the dream-stairs that seemed so long, so steep, with the top landing so far away. The other leg followed, bearing his weight; he felt as if every bone in his body weighed half a hundredweight.

He heard the creak in his dreaming mind, almost theatrically ominous, as he set his foot—it was always the right foot, and why he remembered that was a mystery in itself—on the first riser. He was whimpering under his breath, bleeding internally with his unwillingness to follow the dream to its conclusion.

No. Damn it, no!

The words, clear in his mind, came out as a garbled half shout, muffled by the overstuffed pillow and his own arm. Across the hall, Penny stirred and turned over, one eye opening a fraction as she registered something from the waking world of night: a footfall in the dimness, a door opening and closing.

Gowan come up to me come up I need you I love you . . .

He began to shake, trying to rouse himself. He had never once gone the full length of the dream, never once allowed himself to get beyond the point of climbing those stairs as the whispering grew strong and rang around him like a carillon of church bells, beyond the point of opening his own bedroom door, of seeing what was waiting there, the rope, the naked girl, her eyes half-opened in death, seeming to watch him with dreadful awareness as her wasted flesh stirred and danced in the salt-scented wind that blew in from the sea. . . .

Dreaming, on the stairs. But something creaked, clicked, creaked again. The door to his room, opening and closing.

And suddenly, disoriented and on the verge of screaming, Gowan was awake, his eyes wide open in the darkness. This was no dream—it was night, not the late afternoon of his nightmare. But she was there. There was a girl in his room, a young girl with her eyes half-open, fixed and staring, enormous grey lamps, and a waterfall of black hair.

Gowan screamed. It was only in his mind, heard by no one but himself, but it served to wake him all the way, bringing him back to full awareness, pushing away the idea of a succubus or a revenant. In that breath of time, feeling his nightmare and this impossible moment of reality collide, he recognised the girl in his room.

It was Becca. And a bare moment later, there was Penny in the doorway behind her.

"Shhh." Penny slipped past the girl and got in front of her. Becca's face, slack and unseeing, was a mask of herself: smooth, blank, bloodless. Macbeth, Penny thought, the Lady, moving through the darkness of her husband's stolen digs, propelled by guilt. The line, one of the unluckiest in the English language and to her mind one of the most chilling, came fully into her memory: *Her eyes are open. Aye, but their sense are shut.*

Unlucky or not, it fit. Becca was an uninhabited shell, and this emptiness, this movement with no waking awareness to propel it, was something Penny had seen before.

"What . . ." Gowan, about to climb out of bed, remembered that he slept nude and stopped where he was. His voice was thin, just above a whisper. His heart was stuttering, seeming to slam against his rib cage. "What are you two doing in here?"

"I heard her door open and close, and I heard her walking." *Infected minds to their deaf pillows will discharge their secrets . . .* "I thought she was going to the loo, but she turned the wrong way."

"I don't—"

"She's sleepwalking." Penny stepped back, watching Becca. Her own voice was normal, if low; it reflected nothing of how rattled she was. She'd been only a few years older than Becca was now the first time she'd seen this, and, even now, if she brought the memory back fully, it had the power to leave her skin moving on her bones. "My sister used to do it, sometimes, when she was Becca's age. There's nothing you can do except stay out of their way and steer them away from danger areas."

"Jesus." Gowan slid out of bed, wrapping the top sheet around his waist. The dream, the nightmare he'd hoped was over and done with, was still too close to him, fresh and dreadful; the living girl, with those eyes that were so familiar and had shaken him so thoroughly at first meeting, was as unnerving as any ghost or dream-lover could have been. "Excuse me. Give me a minute, will you?"

He slipped into the bathroom attached to his room, letting the sheet fall, finding his pyjamas and getting into the trousers. It took him three attempts to knot the cord belt of his robe; reaction had set in, and his hands, so sure on the piano's keyboard a few short hours ago, were uncoordinated and fumbling.

He came back into his bedroom to find it empty and his door still standing open. Barefoot, shivering despite the warmth of the night and the flannel robe he'd pulled on, he put his head out into the hall, just in time to see Penny pulling Becca's door shut behind her. She saw him and put a finger to her lips in the classic gesture meaning *quiet*.

There was no conversation; without a word spoken, Penny headed for the stairs, with Gowan at her heels. Turning right as they reached the ground floor, they headed for the greenroom.

"I need a drink." It was the first thing either had said, and Gowan's voice reminded Penny of a huge bell with the clapper muffled; it would have been impossible to hear it more than a few feet away. Certainly, there was no chance of waking Ringan with it. "Whiskey for me. You?"

"Yes, please." Penny, remembering the days of Candida's school tests and the odd unfocused wandering that would take her sister to stand at the end of the hallway, reaching toward the curtained window embrasure as if reaching for a book, kept her own voice low. "She's probably down for the night. I remember our family doctor telling us that repeat episodes in the same night are quite rare."

He disappeared into the kitchen, leaving the lights off, finding two glasses and a bottle.

"Here," he told her, and filled both glasses to the halfway point. "*Sowena*. Bottoms up. Cheers."

She sipped the whiskey, taking small mouthfuls, letting it burn its way down and in. It was potent stuff, and Penny, who wasn't much of a whiskey fan normally, found herself savouring it. Gowan, on the other hand, drained his glass in one shot, shuddered, and reached for the bottle again. "Sorry," he muttered. "I got a fright, seeing her there."

"Yes, that was fairly obvious." The room around them, lovely in full sun, was exquisite in the dead hours, dappled with stars; the surfaces of furniture and flesh alike were alive with moving shadows of tree limbs responding to the touch of the night breeze off the sea. She levelled her eyes at him. "Gowan, what's going on in this house?"

He was silent, neither speaking nor meeting her stare. The silence stretched out, Penny giving him time and room. After a bit, she spoke again.

"This won't do, and we both know it." Her voice was no louder than it had been, but it was stronger and firmer, the voice of someone with no intention of letting the subject or the issue drop. Startled, he looked up at her across the table. Dark eyes met hazel, and the hazel dropped first.

"All right." He set his glass down. Everything about him seemed wilted, somehow; the effect, oddly, was to make him seem even larger than he was. "You want the story? I'm after warning you, it doesn't make for pretty hearing."

She said nothing. He reached for his glass, but changed his mind, and drew in a long breath.

"There was a girl." Leaves on the trees in the Cambornes' garden rustled across the glass roof. "An American girl—Jenny Wilbury. She came to see a show we did at the Duke's Own, the Tin Miners, that is. She was with her mother and brother—she was fourteen, maybe fifteen. They were on holiday. This was back in the eighties."

Penny swallowed hard. Twenty years ago, Gowan had been thirty or thereabouts. The idea of him getting involved with an adolescent girl was doing unpleasant things to her stomach.

"*Na, na,* that wasn't the way of it." Even in the dimness, her face had given her away. "I was involved with a musician in the band, a woman called Lowenna Maddox. I just noticed Jenny in the crowd—she was a young beauty, but young's the word, too young for me. I remembered her, though—truth to tell, even if she'd not been so lovely, I'd have been hard put to forget about her. There was an incident."

"What sort of incident?" That she immediately believed him, believed that he wouldn't have pursued a child so young and vulnerable, was oddly reassuring. "What happened?"

"She and her brother, they got into a scuffle. Right there·down in front they were, at a table. We were in the middle of a song, and they began to beat at each other, fists flying, a serious row. I never saw how it began, but their mam got each one under the elbow and took them out of there. I remember . . ."

His voice died away. Penny watched him tense, relax again, and reach for the bottle.

"They were half out the door, and Jenny looked back at us." His lips seemed dry. "At Lowenna. I'd not seen such hate in a face, never. That old saw, about if looks could kill? I was damned thankful they couldn't, that night."

"You saw her again, though?"

"Sure and I did, near five years later. She came back to Cornwall; she was at university in Exeter, she told me. I was playing in Penzance with a few friends one night, and I looked up and she was there, sitting at a table and watching me with those eyes, just as she'd done before . . ."

"Right." Penny touched the back of his hand. The situation was bizarre, she thought; Ringan and Becca were fathoms deep upstairs, and here she was, getting sozzled with a middle-aged musician who obviously had something in his past he wouldn't mind gouging out of his memory with a handsaw, if that was what it would take. "Breathe. Even in this light, I can see you've gone gummy looking. What happened to her, Gowan? I mean, I'm perfectly willing to listen to the whole thing if it'll ease your mind to tell me about it, but what I really want to know is why I got hit with whatever it was that hit me after that rehearsal, when you played that song about the dead knight. And going on past history, I'm betting it was something that happened in this house. So tell me, please—what happened?"

"She hanged herself." The hand beneath her own was hot and unpleasant to her touch. "From the ceiling beam in my bedroom."

Gowan Camborne was no actor, and it was clear to Penny that he wasn't trying for effect. The words were simple, unadorned. They were also dreadful, as stark and cold as a graveside vigil.

"We had an affair, you know?" Something gleamed on Gowan's cheek, the faint track of tears, touched by the moving starlight and the waning night. It wasn't far off morning, Penny thought, and let her hand stay where it was, resting on her host's. "She was near twenty then, maybe the most beautiful thing God ever created for this earth. She loved me, she said. I don't know about love—for sure she wanted me, and me, I was glad to oblige. I could scarce keep my hands off her, day or night."

You have eyes just like hers . . .

"She looked like Becca, didn't she?" The words were clear in Penny's memory. *There's nothing to know. She's dead.* "Grey eyes and black hair?"

"Enough to be her sister, or her ghost." As if he'd suddenly re-alised his own tears, he wiped his free hand across his cheeks. "My mother was alive then. We shared the house, she and I did. She hated Jenny, had no use for her at all. I was just glad it wasn't Mam who found her swinging, though. She was an old woman, only a few years off her dying, and she'd suffered enough over the years, with those headaches."

"What do you mean?" Penny's senses were tingling, sounding a warning. There was something here. "Who did find her?"

"I did."

"Oh, dear God," she whispered. "Gowan—"

"She'd stripped herself naked and run a rope over the beam." His voice was dead flat. "I'd no notion she was even in the house that day, none at all—Lowenna Maddox was back in town to see her brother, and I'd been visiting. I came upstairs and found Jenny swinging. Her eyes were open." His voice shook suddenly. "Look-ing at me, glazed over. And her mouth was open. The doctor said a person's jaw goes slack when they hang."

There was nothing to say, no words, none at all. Penny's hands had woven together; from somewhere out in the garden came an incongruous trill of birdsong.

"I dreamed about that for years after it happened. Over and over and over again, that bloody dream." He was speaking louder now, faster, as if under a compulsion. "Days were, I thought I'd never be rid of it: her voice, whispering my name as she'd whispered it when we'd—" He stopped. "Never mind. But that dream, that damned dream—the house would be sunlight and full of her whispering my name, and I'd know what was waiting for me upstairs in that room, always, her swinging from that beam. Young Jenny, calling to me. And I couldn't not go."

He got to his feet. Clumsy and uncoordinated, his thighs banged against the table, sending the now-half-empty whiskey bottle rocking and clattering.

"I'm off for a try at some rest. There's rehearsing again in a few hours, and it's nearly day now. Another gig at the Duke's tonight, and that means young Becca needs to learn another tune or two." He laughed suddenly, a harsh cold laugh edged with a bitterness that seemed as unlike Gowan as anything could be. "Becca with the grey eyes. There must be a song in there somewhere. Good night to you."

He was gone, heading upstairs before she could reply. Following slowly, she made her way back to bed. The birds were in full song now, filling the dawn with sweetness. It was only after she settled herself back next to a deeply sleeping Ringan that Penny realised that Gowan's story had left the biggest question untouched.

The dead girl in Gowan's room, tragic though her story was, had nothing at all to do with what had happened to Penny. The eyes she had looked through, the crushed throat, the sense of betrayal, had belonged to a man.

Five

O what like was his hawk, his hawk?
Or what like was his hound?
And what like was the trusty brand
This new-slain knight had on?

"A fine evening to you, ladies and gentlemen . . ."

The houselights at the Duke of Cornwall's Own flickered once and went down. Hoots, cheers, catcalls.

"We're the Tin Miners, and I'm Gowan Camborne . . ."

It was, Penny reflected, just like last night. There was Ringan, snapping the capo in place on the guitar's third fret. There was Cian, checking his rosin. There was Gowan, talking it up behind the piano, hamming for his local audience, welcoming the crowd. And here she was herself, parked at a centre table in the front row, with the irritating Lucy Williams at her left elbow and Becca, who seemed to be not nearly as nervous as she'd been the night before, at her right.

". . . welcome to the Duke's Own, and from me to you, may I just say, *Kammbronn a'gas dynnergh. . . .*"

It was going to be fine, Penny told herself. It was all right. They were away from the house, with its unnerving effects and its dream-inducing history and the shadow of a dead girl swinging slowly from a creaking beam over a man's bed as he stood there thinking he could hear her voice, whispering his name. This was a private room in a public house, packed with cheerful fans; just a crowd of music lovers, selling out another capacity house. There was safety in numbers.

Everything was all right. Nothing would happen. There was no reason for her head to be thumping, for her nerves to be singing like hot wires, for every sense she possessed, not to mention at least one she'd have given a lot to be rid of, to be on high alert. So why was she so damned edgy?

". . . if you were too lazy to get yourselves down here last night, you missed a treat . . . special guests for you tonight . . ."

Onstage, Ringan fumbled with the capo, dropped it, and muttered something as he stooped to retrieve it. His beard was bristling. He looked distracted, Penny thought, and small wonder; he had quite a lot to think about. While Penny had said nothing to Rebecca yet about her nocturnal visit to Gowan's room, she'd told Ringan everything that had happened while he slept. After all, he was essentially his niece's legal guardian for the rest of this holiday, and he had the right to know. More than that—he *needed* to know.

But the timing of that discussion had been unfortunate. While the rest of the house had been nightwalking or dreaming or drinking whiskey in the glassed-in kitchen room, Ringan had slept deep and long. He hadn't come downstairs until everyone else had nearly done with breakfast, a bare fifteen minutes before Cian and the bodhrán player were due to arrive for rehearsal. They'd managed a good morning kiss, before Penny pulled him aside and gave him the situation, in as brief a form as she could manage. There'd been no time for real discussion, and certainly no time for a confrontation with Becca.

". . . but your staying away, that was its own punishment. Of course, if you were lucky enough to be here for last night's show, you already know what to look forward to—one of the best young fiddlers you're likely to hear . . ."

Becca, in black jeans and a lightweight black shirt, looked ridiculously beautiful. She also, somehow, seemed far more adult than she had the night before. There was something in the outfit she wore, in the way she'd scraped her hair back in a casual ponytail, that reminded Penny of someone. A young Audrey Hepburn, she thought, that was it; there was that devastating combination, deceptive fragility on the surface, all toughness and heart underneath.

Becca also looked to be the only member of the Camborne party who was even remotely at ease. The small pouches under Gowan's eyes, generally a signal of nothing more than his fondness for beer, were puffed with lack of rest. Penny, looking at him as he nattered in a lively back-and-forth with the crowd, thought his entire face looked swollen and sagging. He was definitely showing his age tonight. Ringan, while physically rested, was taut and edgy. And Penny herself, aware of small jagged wires of pain threatening just behind her temples, felt as if she hadn't slept in days, and might never sleep again.

". . . and here we go!"

They'd rehearsed all morning and into the afternoon, as well. Penny, who had about as much of Gowan's house as she wanted to deal with just then, had given the rehearsals a miss. Deciding that if she stayed indoors she'd be cranky and unhappy by nightfall, she waited for a break in the musical discussion, asked for the latest time she could reasonably be back if she wanted a shower and a change of clothes before the show, grabbed her swimsuit and a tote full of sunscreen and bottled water and towels, and drove out to the shore at Penzance. With a small beach umbrella shielding her exposed back from the worst of the sun and her pricey wristwatch set to beep an alarm at the proper time, Penny dozed in the heat and did her best to recoup.

Even with the much-needed rest, the headache that had been simmering in the background ever since last night's show refused to budge. It was there, ominous with small movement-triggered jolts of electric pain, when she woke up to the superheated air of midafternoon. It was there as she gathered her various belongings and headed back to the car. The headache seemed to intensify as she gentled Pandora through the stop-and-go tourist traffic along the crowded road to St. Ives. It was infuriating, Penny thought, as she parked the car and locked it. She'd never got headaches before, not unless there was flu involved. Infuriating, unusual and unwelcome. It was also worrying, and it could stop any bloody time now.

That she'd walked in on the tail end of a serious disagreement among the Tin Miners was obvious from the moment she let herself in and peered around the doorway of the front room. One look at Ringan's beard, jutting and warlike, would have given it away, but the signs of discord were visible on everyone's face. Cian and his bodhrán-playing friend both looked extremely uncomfortable, and Gowan's cheeks were flushed, his lips compressed. There was no way of telling whether Becca had been there for the quarrel, whatever it had been in aid of; enquiry had elicited the information that she'd gone upstairs to shower and change. Penny, who dealt with the tender egos so common in the theatre on a daily basis, was just glad she'd missed this one. . . .

A crashing chord on the piano nearly sent Penny out of her chair. It took her a moment to realise she'd come perilously close to dozing off; the band was into their third song of the evening as a quartet, and Becca, beside her, was stirring in her seat. Penny, who'd decided to save the mead for another day and stick to something less potent, sipped her cider in the dark and washed down aspirin. The Miners had opened their set with the same two songs they'd done the night before, but this third one was one they hadn't done and which Penny couldn't put a name to, a lively instrumental march of some sort that seemed to lean heavily on a rousing call and response between piano and flute. It had a decidedly military feel to it, and Penny made a mental note to ask Ringan what it was called.

Becca, who'd been watching the stage and listening intently, suddenly turned to Penny. "That's me up next. I'm with the band on four songs tonight—two new ones. We worked them out while you were out—it got dodgy for a bit; Uncle Ringan didn't like one of Gowan's choices, but—wish me luck?"

Becca's tone was plaintive, and the request made the girl a child again. Penny found herself oddly touched. There was no way to read whether Becca was genuinely nervous, but no reason to assume she wasn't either. "Of course. Honestly, love, you don't need to ask me that. All the luck in the world, of course. If this was my patch instead of Ringan's, I'd be telling you to break a leg, but really, all things considered, I'd rather you didn't. I just wish I knew some Cornish—their word for *cheers* would be useful."

"That would be *sowena*." It was Lucy Williams, of course, right there with the information. Penny forced down her irritation and managed a smile. How in the world did Cian live with being lectured like a first-former day in and day out? And Lucy, serene and oblivious, was still explaining. "Or you might say *yeghes da*. Really, though, *sowena* is a better choice, when you consider that—"

"I'll stick with the first one, Lucy, ta. Too many choices just confuse me." Penny kept her voice pleasant, but it was tricky. All the alarm bells, the nerve endings that had jangled and then quieted, were sounding, loud and clear. What had Becca meant, about Ringan not liking the choices? "*Sowena* it is, then, and best of British luck, not to mention Cornish and Scots. Whatever you need. And I think—right, here comes your cue. You're on."

There seemed to be a number of repeat attendees from the previous night in the audience; Gowan's introduction of Becca brought friendly cheers of recognition and admiration. Looking slender and frail in her unrelieved black, the girl nodded at the crowd, took up her fiddle, poised the bow above the strings, and waited.

Penny settled herself against the chair's hard back and watched the band. While she'd apparently been right about the band's having argued earlier in the day—after all, Becca had confirmed that herself—they weren't showing any signs of dissension now.

They opened Becca's participation in the set with an instrumental piece unfamiliar to Penny. It was light and cheerful and charming and, as a painless way to ease Becca into both the music and the onstage camaraderie, it was close to perfect. They went from that straight into "Thomas the Rhymer," clearly with the intent of switching the order of the set list around and providing a sense of variety for the repeat audience, even if the songs were mostly the same. It was a masterful version, beautifully done and as well structured as it had been the night before, but it was clear to Penny that Becca, at least, was still getting warmed up.

By the time they finished "Thomas the Rhymer," Becca had hit her stride and was ready for "Tam Lin." She seemed more at ease with her environment tonight, and it showed in her playing; being onstage was becoming a part of the girl's comfort zone. That was just as well, Penny thought, since there were clearly concert halls, complete with adoring fans and music cognoscenti asking stupid questions, in Becca's future.

". . . Were my love but an earthly man as he is an elfin knight, I would not give my own true love for any in my sight . . ."

The fiddle hit the break, wild and perfect, and Penny jumped. Beside her, she caught a movement, as Lucy Williams began to sway with the rhythm; Penny saw the appreciation there. Rather to her own surprise, Penny found herself beginning to like the woman.

But the music had taken hold of Penny, good and hard. There was something in it tonight that she identified as urgency, and that urgency was coming almost entirely from the fiddle. Becca was skirting the edge of her own limits, taking a few musical chances tonight that she hadn't taken before: letting her fingers move faster, going to places higher on the fiddle's neck, risking the chance of a wrong note, willing to roll those dice to see if she could somehow tap even deeper into the power that made the song what it was.

"They turned him into a flash of fire, and then into a naked man—but she wrapped her mantle him about and then she had him won . . ."

And here was Ringan, understanding what his niece was doing, coming in full throttle on guitar, Lord Randall's beautiful full-bodied tone holding the pulse of the song steady. She was riding the music, and he held the ground, giving her the room she needed for that wild unearthly exploration of sound and story. More than that, he was responding to it; his vocal was audibly strengthening, gaining power, as the song moved toward its climax. The entire band, Penny thought, was basically sweeping the road clear for Becca to move along.

And move she did, eyes closed to better map the territory of inner sound, unconscious of her support network, letting her flying fingers and poised bowing hand take the listening crowd down that road with her. There was no conversation in the darkened room; there was no space for it. Every inch, every corner, every movement of air, was full of music.

". . . And then up spake the fairy queen, and an angry queen was she—'Woe betide her ill-fared face! An ill death may she die!' "

Becca drew her bow across the fiddle, a long wailing chord. So strong and long was the sustain that for a moment, her skin crawling, Penny thought she heard a human voice calling out from the fiddle's strings. Cian responded, synching the flute to the howling echoing cry of the fiddle, waiting for Ringan and Gowan. They came in together, guitar and piano, matching up to Becca, to Cian, to each other. Penny saw the concentration in Ringan's face as he turned to the microphone for the final verse, and saw that same concentration reflected in Gowan's.

"Had I known, Tam Lin, she said, what this night I would see, I'd have looked him in the eye and turned him to a tree!"

A short burst, four bars of emphatic sound, and silence. The song was over.

The crowd was on its feet, cheering and stamping in a firestorm of appreciation. The applause was the kind of accolade any live performer might consider himself lucky to get once in his career; for a performer whose career had yet to begin, it was astonishing.

Gowan, leaning into his microphone, said something that was lost in the tidal surge of sound. In the end, he gave up and sat back on his piano bench, watching the crowd.

From her seat, shoulders suddenly hunched hard, Penny was watching Becca. Something other than the music, something that wasn't merely the girl's reaction to live performance, was different tonight. Last night, she'd acknowledged the applause with shyness and a mouthed *thanks*. Tonight, she was silent, expressionless, her eyes apparently unseeing, registering nothing. What in hell . . . ?

Something at the base of Penny's spine had gone tight and anxious.

The girl looked for all the world the way she'd looked in the dead hours of this morning, walking without awareness or conscious will into Gowan's bedroom. Her face was completely immobile, a mask of herself, a lovely effigy.

"Thank you, *meur ras,* we all thank you—if we can have a bit of quiet, please—all right then, I'll just say it: hold your noise!" Gowan, pitching his voice to carry, waited for the laughter. "We're after playing you an old tune now, something I've known since back when I was all the way too young to set foot in the public, downstairs. This is one my mam used to sing sometimes, when she thought I wasn't listening. It's a favourite of mine, but we've had three tries at it and no more, so if we cock it up, you'll know the reason why."

Hoots, banter, comments. It was all perfectly normal, as basic to a show of this sort as the scrape of chairs or the clink of pint glasses. Penny, a cold sweat pooling at her hairline and her nerves as taut as one of the fine strands on Becca's bow, heard the back-and-forth repartee as a dull roar, a background throb to her own sense of immediate dread. *Something, what in hell is all this, something's going to happen, this is all wrong. . . .*

"It's a nice little love song, a bit of a change from the doomed lovers and the fairy-folk, all right?" Gowan ran his hands along the keyboard. He was talking to the crowd, but his eyes were elsewhere; his gaze was locked on Ringan. "A very old tune—I took the melody from an old woman who was playing it in a pub up the coast near Tintagel, on a dulcimer, of all things. It's about a young man testing his pregnant girlfriend's love for him, and it's called 'The New-Slain Knight.'"

Wrong all wrong something's wrong oh God my head . . .

"Penny?" Lucy Williams had a hand on her arm. "Mercy, dear, you look terrible! What's wrong? Can I get you something?"

Penny made a noise in her throat. Voices, was it the crowd around her or Lucy or had the singing begun, the room was full of salt water, the air reeked of it, she was going to be sick, stop it . . .

A dance of notes off the piano, matched by the bodhrán. Ringan, coming in a fraction of a second later on Lord Randall—even his fretwork sounded clipped, a bit terse. Cian's flute, sounding high and sweet, like the birdsong that had flooded the glassed-in room that morning, during the waning minutes of the night's darkness . . .

My a'th kar, my a'th pys, mara pleg, na wra henna Perran, a'm kerydh . . .

Penny screamed. The scream was in her mind, kept there by instinct; nothing of it escaped to form sound. But Ringan's head jerked suddenly and, through the mist of wet salty air that seemed to be muffling everything around her, she saw his face change. And beside him, Becca began to sag at the waist. . . .

I love you, I'm begging you, oh please, don't do that Perran do you love me . . .

She was out of her seat, moving on legs she couldn't feel, frantic and claustrophobic, cutting through the crowd. Somewhere outside there was clean sweet air and silence in her head, silence, no stabbing pain and no high desperate girl's voice asking questions and making demands in a language Penny herself should have no way of understanding . . .

She stopped outside the door, at the top of the stairs. For a critical moment, the roaring in her ears and across her eyes cleared enough to let her see her own danger: a full flight of steeply pitched stairs, narrow and worn, as old as the pub itself. Two steps forward or perhaps three and she would have fallen, tumbling down like a rag doll, breaking ribs and legs and maybe her neck.

She sat down hard. Closing her eyes, she put her head between her knees, willing the upsurge of nausea away, trying to remember what she knew of yoga and relaxation. After what seemed to be hours, she got the sickness in her stomach under some sort of control. *Breathe,* she thought, and let her hands, which had been clutching her own knees, relax.

Behind her, the door to the main room clicked open and shut again, as someone came out.

"Penny?" It was Lucy Williams, kind and anxious. "Can I help you up?"

"Lucy." Penny looked up at her. It was nearly back to normal, easing up. The air was just air, the normal smells and sights and sound of a pub. True, something seemed off with her hearing, but at least the voice in her head had stopped, and with it the sense of disorientation. "Tell me something. You speak Cornish. What does 'perran' mean?"

"It doesn't. It's a proper name, a boy's name. Piran is the patron saint of Cornwall." If Lucy found the question peculiar, she said nothing. "Here, let me help you up. You're needed."

"What?" She was on her feet, grateful for Lucy's supporting hand cupping her elbow. "Why?"

"It's your young friend—Rebecca." She stopped, reaching for the door, and suddenly Penny understood that there was nothing wrong with her hearing, that the music inside had stopped in mid-song, replaced by an odd quiet. "She's had some sort of seizure."

"Wake now, my lovely girl, my darling. Wake, I say. It's overlong you sleep."

Blue sky, soft green grass, the smell of salt in the air. Becca, her head in someone's lap, opened her eyes and looked up into a very handsome male face.

"Wake now, Jenna."

"I've woken, Perran." His voice was as fine as his face, Becca thought, deep and sure, one step over the line into arrogance. A very dishy boy. She wondered who he was.

(Becca, oh damn Ringan she's all the way out no wait did she just say something)

That sounded like Penny, Becca thought, only she couldn't actually see Penny anywhere, so maybe it wasn't her, just another part of this weird dream that kept coming back, like a bad plot on daytime telly. *Serial dreamer,* Becca thought, and swallowed a giggle.

She sighed, feeling the dream body ripple, and gave a long sigh, part pleasure. Below her head, strong thigh muscles stirred, and she realised there was a hand, a strong masculine hand, supporting the weight of her neck and skull. The cute boy had called her Jenna, so yes, of course, she was dreaming again, this time with her head— Jenna's head, someone's head, both their heads—in the cute bloke's lap.

Nice, Becca thought. She was relaxed and lazy, unwilling to move. Whoever this Jenna person was, she at least had a very hot boyfriend. And the hot boyfriend had a very nice lap in which to rest her head. . . .

What was it he'd said, though? Something about sleeping too much? *This day ye sleep oer lang.*

Somewhere at the back of her awareness, Becca knew a momentary unease. She'd heard that recently—but who had said it? A song, and hadn't she been playing her fiddle, locking up the fiddle to a man with a flute, to her uncle's guitar, to a man with hazel eyes and strong sure hands on the piano?

"An you be awake, Jenna, sit up, then."

Hazel eyes. He was looking down at her with those eyes, eyes so familiar, Camborne eyes. *Gowan,* Becca thought, *that's who has eyes just like that,* but this wasn't Gowan; those yellow-tinted irises were set into a face with bones so strong, they might have come from the *moengleudh,* the quarry up in the hills near Truro. And he was young, much younger than Gowan. Bones like a *menhir,* and everything young and fine about him. Surely, though, it was unseemly, to have her head in his lap this way? Unseemly, too, to allow his hands to rest on her?

She'd been right about his hands. He had one cupped beneath her head where it met the long stem of her neck, supporting its weight but also controlling her; it held her where she was, where he wanted her. The pressure was light, but it was there. Becca was acutely aware of it, even more than she was aware of his other hand, stroking her arm in long sure touches.

"I've done with sleep, *broder.*" Brother? This was her brother? Surely that couldn't be—a brother wouldn't touch a sister the way this boy was touching her, and anyway, she was an only child. Who was he . . . ?

(Ringan is she waking what's happening her lips are moving)

"Must I tell you once more never to call me that again? Has it not been said often enough, clear enough?" His voice was suddenly cold, and the hand that had been stroking her arm had clamped down on her wrist, hurting her. Beneath her head, the strength in his hand was suddenly ominous. "For what we've done, I'm no brother to you, Jenna. Let that be understood between us, now and always."

"Perran, *na wra henna,* stop it, you're hurting!" Becca, sleeping, was suddenly frightened. There were sensations here, feelings of flesh and spirit, that she knew nothing of, had no experience to deal with, no internal language with which to express it. She knew about hormones, and all of that—her mother was a doctor, and they'd had The Talk, as she and her friends called it, early on.

But no one had told her what it felt like, that flesh-to-flesh contact. And no one had told her how it could suddenly go dark, how whatever it was that felt so good, that left her wanting more of his hands, wanting him to never stop, could change in the blink of an eye or the use of a single word, get painful and terrifying . . .

(Ringan hang on to her no I don't know how to wake her and for heaven's sake don't try just let her come out of it oh God she's thrashing hang on to her just hang on)

"Of course." The hold on her wrist became that softer, gentler touch once more, but it was too late; there would be a bruise. Becca had a moment of intuition, as disturbing as it was inarguable: Jenna would cherish that bruise, gloat over it, rub it in secret. How she knew that was beyond her, but know it she did.

"I wouldn't hurt you, my pretty Jenna. How could I do such a thing, when I love you with all my heart and body? You'd not make me hurt you, would you?"

She said nothing, searching his sun-washed features for something, anything, to see what she might trust about him. The dream was very weird, Becca thought, but the weirdest thing was that she couldn't seem to tell who was moving. Someone was, that was for sure, but she couldn't feel her own legs, her own feet. What she could feel didn't seem to have anything to do with her.

Blue sky, scudding clouds, the smell of salt blowing in from the sea. There was rain coming, harsher weather, but it would be a fast storm and soon over. She could wish that whatever was happening to her, whatever had come with Perran's silent visits to her bed-chamber in the dark hours, those painful ecstatic disbelieving encounters, would be a fast storm and soon over.

She knew better. She hadn't bled at her accustomed time, and it was two cycles now, she who was as regular as the tide. The sight of food, even the good fresh pilchards and the rich clotted cream from the farm close to town, sickened her. She'd managed to keep it from her father, from her stepmother, from Perran himself, but there would be no hiding it, not after another fortnight or so had passed. This storm was a nine-month storm, and soon she would feel the strike of its lightning.

"Our father comes. Rise up, girl!" His voice had gone sharp and angry. For a moment, it seemed the lightning had come early; he pushed her suddenly free of his lap, sitting up, getting to his feet with the speed and grace that meant perfect physical health, putting an arm's length distance between them. *Obey,* she thought, *my father must see nothing,* and she struggled to get to her feet.

Sickness, a deep angry bile that seemed to burn her chest and the base of her throat, rose hard and fast in her. She choked it down somehow, but there was no controlling her legs, no controlling the terrible painful spasms. What was happening to her . . . ?

(She said something I think it was in Cornish Gowan Lucy what did she say did you hear that Ringan hold on I think she's coming out of it)

Pandra hwer genev?

Becca, her head in her uncle's lap and her trouser-clad legs shaking and kicking, opened her eyes.

"Oh, thank God." Penny's face, white and drawn, seemed to run into slackness, and her voice was limp. She looked old, Becca thought. That was just totally wrong—she hadn't looked like that a few minutes ago. And what was she doing lying down anyway, with her head in her uncle's lap?

This was ridiculous. She'd been playing music. They'd all been playing music—"Tam Lin" and "Thomas the Rhymer," and that love song thing Gowan had insisted on them learning. So how had she fetched up stretched out like some stupid fainting girl in a Victorian novel, with everyone staring at her as if she as some sort of freak, or—

"Are you all right then, *flogh*?"

Hazel eyes, looking down at her, kind and concerned. Gowan, of course, not Perran, not the boy in her dream, her brother. He had those hazel eyes, but this was Gowan, older, kinder, the lines of his face softened, a bit blurred by time. It wasn't Perran.

"Becca?"

Out of nowhere, there it was: the memory, in its entirety. The boy with the strong bones, the full lower lip and thin upper one, looking down at her, but they weren't in her father's garden, they were in her bedchamber, it was new moon and she'd risen up and let him in he'd put his hands on her and his mouth on her oh God and she'd let him, there would be no forgiveness for her, not from her father or from God either. A child, there was going to be a child, two cycles, what was she going to do—

"Sit up, Becca. No, do what I tell you! Sit up, and drink this." Ringan's voice, sharp and clear and heavy with adult authority, cut across Becca's panic. She had no way of knowing that she'd gone white, no way of guessing that her uncle's tone was deliberate, designed to do just what it had done: snap whatever was holding her.

She sat up. For a few dizzying seconds, she couldn't place where she was or why it felt so different. Then she realised: she was in the private upstairs room at the Duke's Own. The difference lay in its emptiness. Before she'd fallen asleep, or whatever she'd done, it had been packed to capacity. Now it was empty, denuded of its audience, of everyone who wasn't a member of the band or the band's family.

"You drink that." Penny had pulled up a chair. She looked, to Becca, to have aged somehow in the breath of time that had passed since Becca's last clear memory. They all looked older, somehow,

94

older and tired and drained. "It's cider. It's good for you and it tastes wonderful, so drink it and for heaven's sake, don't tell your mother, all right? You're a few years off being legal yet for drinking this, and she'd strangle Ringan if she found out we'd fed you booze, but you need something." Penny thought for a moment. "Come to think of it, so do I. Where in hell's the barman?"

"Downstairs, I imagine. Here, you can have mine." Lucy Williams, apparently unshaken, handed her glass to Penny. She sounded completely normal. "It's just white wine, nothing much, but it ought to make you calm down. And I don't much fancy it anyway. And Rebecca, dear, Penny's quite right—you should drink that down. Come along, now."

Becca took a cautious sip and promptly made a face. It was the classic look of a child trying something for the first time, getting something she hadn't expected and didn't like, and trying not to spit it straight out again. Ringan, watching his niece with one arm behind her in case she sagged, thought the face made her look about six years old. But she hadn't looked six years old during that faint, or whatever the hell it had been. There had been a few moments where the look on her face had been so purely sensual, so redolent of an adult sexuality abundantly satisfied, that he'd felt something uncomfortably akin to a sense of decency outraged.

This was his niece, his sister's only child, and she was barely fourteen years old. Whatever had just happened—and that it was somehow connected to that bloody song Gowan had insisted on them doing, Ringan had no doubt at all—had been as shocking to Ringan as seeing a family member making love might have been. The idea that he was responsible for a child's safety made the impact of those few moments even worse.

"Tastes nasty, does it?" It was Gowan, at a slight remove from the circle around Becca. "Never mind, you're too young to appreciate the local cider. Give it some time and you'll be after asking for it every time you walk into a pub."

Gowan wasn't meeting Ringan's eye. Becca, taking the cider in tiny sips to make it through even a fraction of the oversized glass of what tasted like death to her, wondered hazily what was going on between them, then remembered the quarrel over the song choices, back at Gowan's house. It seemed so far away, and so long ago, it might as well have happened in another life.

"It's all right, really. I feel much better now." She was suddenly embarrassed. She'd always been quiet, valuing her privacy. Being the centre of attention, an option her physical beauty had always offered her, had never been her cup of tea; fainting like a stupid schoolgirl was just about as bad as she could imagine. It was completely humiliating.

She took another mouthful of the cider, imagining what she must have looked like to all those people, watching her from the crowd. Had she said anything? Or had she just fallen, gone flat out? And what about—

"My violin!" She was standing, swaying on her feet, frantic and dizzy. "Did I drop it? Where is it? Oh God, my mother will kill me if—"

"No, it's fine." Penny had an arm around her. The girl felt overly warm, clammy to the touch, heat coming from her in waves. "You didn't fall, exactly—you sort of sagged and went down on both knees, and the violin slid out of your hand. The bow bounced a bit, but there was no damage—Cian looked to make sure. It's nice and safe, back in its case. The bow's been put away, as well. Becca, sit down, will you please? You've got a fever or something. You're absolutely cooking with heat."

"I don't feel very well." It was true. Her stomach was roiling, in an uproar, and her skin was crawling. Why was everyone staring at her? "I—I'm sorry I ruined the show. I didn't mean to—look, I'm really sorry, but can we please go home? Please?"

"Of course we can." Penny got one arm around the girl, and met Ringan's eye. The unspoken message, along with the nearly invisible shake of her head, was clear enough: *This is not the place to talk to her. Wait a bit.* "Good thing this town is so small. I wouldn't fancy having you walk too far at the moment. Gowan, give me your house key, will you? I'll take Becca back now, and you lot can pack up your stuff."

"Right." Ringan's beard was jutting. She was right, of course she was, but that didn't make his impatience any easier to deal with. He was worried, and upset, and very close to being completely off his balance. Becca was his responsibility; his need to know what had just happened to her was urgent, and hard to shelve, even for a moment.

But Penny was right—this wasn't the time or the place to ask her about it. No matter how many of those odd moments of adult awareness she might have, no matter how dark the circumstances provoking those moments might be, his niece was still a child, and a frightened child, at that. No matter how tricky it might be to push aside his need to get control of the situation, her own needs came first.

"Sure and I will—here's the key." Gowan tossed it across to Penny. "Ringan, shouldn't you be going back with the women? If you'll trust me with Lord Randall, I'll put your gear away for you, and bring the whole works back with me."

Ringan, Penny, and Becca walked back to the Camborne house in silence, under a speckled indigo canopy of sky. It was amazing, Penny thought, how living in the city could erase the memory of what the sky held—wheeling constellations, stars a bit apart from the others, enormous reaches of ink-black emptiness between the light of enormous gas giants flickering thousands of light-years away—when the lights of a million windows and storefronts and moving cars weren't there to blank them. Down here, away from London, the night sky was a thing of wonder.

They passed small crowds of tourists, some of whom looked at Becca with curiosity; Ringan, making passing eye contact with a few of them, thought they looked familiar. They'd probably been in the audience tonight. Small wonder they'd done double takes when they'd walked past Becca . . .

Gowan's house was cool inside, and quiet. Ringan let the front door swing shut at their backs; he'd thought Becca might go straight for her bed, and was prepared to dig his heels in and demand a conversation, but the girl surprised him by turning and heading for the garden room. He lifted a brow at Penny, and she nodded at him; clearly, Becca was willing to talk without prompting or bullying.

Ringan, looking at Penny, felt a sharp pang. Her bone structure and colouring had always made guessing her age a puzzle. Adding to that was her profession. After years spent onstage, using makeup with an expert hand to turn herself into a teenage Juliet or an elderly Jocasta, the line between art and artifice had blurred. Had he not known her as well and for as long as he had, Ringan would never have guessed her as being two years shy of forty.

But something in the situation with Becca was taking a high toll on Penny. Ringan didn't know whether it was the strength of the voices in her head or the strain of watching over a sleepwalking teenager and getting sozzled with their host over predawn stories of suicide. Whatever it was, Penny was looking tired and pulled down.

"Uncle Ringan?" Becca's voice, quiet and tentative, jerked his attention back to his niece. "I think I need to tell you about what happened, okay?"

Penny had already filled Gowan's electric kettle and was putting leaves into a tea ball. The smell was pungent and strong and blessedly everyday. She plugged it in and came to sit at the table between uncle and niece.

"We're right here, love." Penny took Ringan's hand in one of her own and took Becca's in the other. Ringan gave Penny's hand a quick squeeze. Something about her emphasis on the connection between the three of them brought an odd lump to his throat. "We need to know what happened. Are you sure you're up for talking about it? Good. Because soonest is best."

Becca nodded. The hand Penny held was limp.

"All right, then." Ringan had caught sight of the clock on the kitchen wall; another twenty minutes before Gowan got back, maybe less. He kept his voice as matter-of-fact as he could, not sparing the time to wonder about the source of his urgency to get as much information as he could get before Gowan came home. "Tell us what you remember, or what you think you remember. And don't leave anything out, all right? No matter how small, or how silly, or how irrelevant it seems to you. Because if we've learned anything from going through this rubbish before, it's that everything's important. Penny, that kettle's on the boil—let's get a pot on the table. Talking's thirsty work."

Becca told them everything. Halting at first, stopping for small mouthfuls of scalding tea, she was visibly uncomfortable and wanting to pull back on those moments where she'd touched on Jenna's own moments of intimacy. Penny, in particular, was aware of her own surprise; it was easy to forget how young Becca was, how inexperienced. Gradually, however, the story began to gain speed and fluency. When she finished talking, less than five minutes had passed and she'd already emptied a full cup of tea. Her shoulders were shaking.

"Tell me if I've understood you." Penny had recaptured Becca's hand. She had no idea whether the girl was finding the human contact as comforting as Penny herself was finding it, and she didn't care. The story, patchy and halting as it had been, had been disturbing, and not only because of Becca's difficulty in dealing with it. Hearing it, especially under this particular roof, brought Penny back serious echoes of the man she'd felt die, in agony and betrayal and disbelief. And that girl he'd loved—had that been Jenna?

"This girl—Jenna, you said her name was—was pregnant," Penny said carefully, "And this boy, this Perran—he was the father?"

"Yes." The reply was nearly inaudible. Becca wasn't meeting anyone's eye, and her hair, released from its confining elastic, swung free to shield her face.

"He was her baby's father. But he was her brother?" Christ, Ringan thought, what an ugly little mess for Becca, naïve and quite certainly virginal, to get slapped with. "That's what you meant. Right?"

She nodded again. Her teeth were sunk into her lower lip.

"Oh, baby, I'm so sorry." Penny's voice was warm, vibrant, clearly angry on Becca's behalf. As a tonic, it was just what the girl needed; Ringan saw her flash a glance at Penny, her face startled and then grateful. "Look, Gowan's going to be here any second, and there's something I want to know before he shows up, if you can tell me. It's important, so think before you answer, all right?"

"I will." It was nearly inaudible. As if surprised at herself, Becca cleared her throat and repeated herself, loudly this time. "I mean, I will."

"Did you get the sense that he loved her?"

Ringan opened his mouth and closed it again. He wasn't sure what he'd been expecting Penny to ask, but whatever it was, this question wasn't it.

"Not really." Becca closed her eyes a moment, bringing those moments back, watching through a pair of long-dead eyes as their owner tilted her head back. looking up into his face, into his eyes. What had Jenna seen there? Becca had no touchstone, no language, for what had moved the girl whose eyes she had seen through. She found herself struggling to explain. "Or, maybe. It was—it was complicated. He was more just possessive, I think, and as if he knew he could hurt her if he wanted to. Sort of like she was his property, or something. As if he liked having control of everything, especially her. You know?"

"Bloody abusive wanker." Ringan spit the words out, and then bit his lip, as his niece turned to stare at him. There had been venom in his tone, and rage. "Sorry. I've got an attitude about blokes like that. And for heaven's sake, his baby sister! What was he thinking?"

"Nothing at all, most likely." Penny was watching Becca. "Here's another question, also important. What about the girl, then? Did you feel she loved him? Or was that also complicated?"

"Yes. No. I don't—she was afraid of him, a little bit, I think. But she was also remembering, about when he went to her room . . ."

Her voice died away. Penny took a breath and finished the sentence for her.

"She was remembering, and she'd liked what happened, and she was feeling guilty about it, and that was messing up her feelings about him. Is that the way it was?"

"Yes! That's it exactly." She stopped for a moment. Something had moved in her memory, something about the girl and the visit to the fair. "There was something else, though—she was thinking about someone else, too. I think she had a boyfriend, or something, maybe a fiancé, someone who wasn't her brother. I remember that from the dream I had about her last night. Her father was teasing her about it, about how this boyfriend would be going to some fair, or something, and didn't she want to go along to see him. You know? But I don't remember his name, just that she got all pink and short of breath when she thought about him."

"She had—" Ringan stopped. He'd heard the click of the front door. "Right, never mind, that's for later."

"One more question. Just one." Penny had heard the front door as well, and she was speaking fast. Ringan's eyebrows went up; it seemed he wasn't alone in his own unexplained need for getting information in hand before Gowan got back. "Who were they, Becca? Do you know?"

"Cambornes." The answer came at once; she tilted her head, and Ringan, who for a moment had thought she was listening for voices in her own head, realised she was hearing Gowan's footsteps, the gentle thump of Lord Randall's case in the hallway. That need, that sense of settling things before they were interrupted, had infected all three of them. "I knew that straight off. The first dream I had, when I was sort of separated from what was happening, going in and out of it the way you do in dreams, and I knew I was dreaming, but I was studying her, mapping out what she knew and felt—it was only for fun, really. Her father's name was Hywel or something, and she had a stepmother called Eleanor whom she didn't much like—she was a bit snarky about that, in her thoughts, sort of rolling her eyes when her father said her stepmother was coming to the fair, wondering if she'd stop pretending to be ill all the time. And their name was Camborne."

"Hello?" Gowan came through the kitchen doorway. "My God, would you look at you people, having brilliant notions in the middle of the night? I'd have thought you'd all have been sleeping by now. Is there any tea left in that pot, then? And did I hear my name just now?"

"No worries—I'll make a fresh pot. I think we're all going to be up for a while yet." Penny got to her feet and faced her host. "Sit down, Gowan, please? We need to have a talk about your family history."

Six

His hawk and hound were from him gone,
His steed tied to a tree;
A bloody brand beneath his head,
And on the ground lies he.

"Is this true, what you've been telling me? Be straight up with me, now. Is it?"

It was two in the morning, and the lights were still burning in the Camborne kitchen. They'd been talking for the better part of two hours, trying to make sense of what had been happening, trying to pin down or put physical identities to Becca's dream family. Despite the lateness of the hour and the long night behind them, no one was feeling the pull of sleep.

"Gowan, that's the third time you've asked that." Ringan was hovering at the edge of exasperation. "I understand you not wanting to believe it, but it's the same answer as the first two times, and the answer's not about to change any time soon: of course we're being straight with you. Now could you stop asking the same pointless question over and over, and give this some thought? Because we need to know who these people are—I mean, were."

"Sorry." Gowan, who was clearly yearning for a beer, had stayed with tea. Penny, when he'd first reached for a bottle, had pointed out that if anyone in this discussion needed a clear head, it was Gowan, since he was their only source of actual facts. She'd been rather forceful about it, and Gowan had stayed with tea. "But I've told you what I know, and that's also three times, now. Hywel, well, that was an old family name, it's true. We're like to have had least one Howel or Hywel in the family, likely more than one. It's a common enough name in the duchy, not just in the family—Christ, you take a look at any history of Cornwall and you'll be finding men named Hywel from Helston all the way up to Bude. If you mean, do I know of any particular bloke called Hywel, I *have* thought, and the answer's still no."

"Damn." Ringan, tired and edgy, suddenly smacked the table with one palm, sending the cups chattering. "Damn, damn, damn!"

Gowan shot Ringan a sympathetic look. "I know, I know. Frustrating. Jenna, now, that's also common as primroses in March. And I know I never heard a word in all my life about any ancestress called Eleanor."

They were all quiet. Gowan, seeing the near despair on Penny's face, turned to Becca. "I'm sorry, *flogh,* truly. But it would help if you could tell me more of what happened than just their names."

"Becca, look." Ringan turned to his niece. "I've got a notion that might do us some good—it worked once before, when we were trying to pin down dates. Penny's sister-in-law Tamsin used the computer—I told her everything I could remember about what a girl in a dream I'd had was wearing, and Tamsin entered it into some sort of search thing, and bob's your uncle, there it was, a nice little portrait from just the period we wanted. We would probably never have known where to start looking without that. Gowan, do you have a computer?"

"That I don't. But Lucy Williams, now, she does, and a bit of a reputation for being a wizard at it, locally. I'm sure she'd be willing to let us use the thing, and show us how to look things up in the right way."

"I'm sure she would." Penny, for the life of her, couldn't keep the dryness out of her tone. Lucy Williams, the ever-helpful, missing out on a chance to lecture an essentially captive audience endlessly on the subject of Cornish history? Not a chance. Still, if it was going to help sort this mess out, Penny herself would be the first one at the Williams' front door in the morning. "Ringan, what did you have in mind? What were you thinking of asking her?"

"Well, when we tried this before, we went with wardrobe. Tamsin went straight for the colour of the dresses the girls I saw were wearing; she said it was a question of dyes, about what was available to which social class of people at the time. The dress our murderess was wearing was a very rich, very bright shade of blue. And according to Tamsin, that meant they were posh and well-to-do, because that bright blue dye was pricey, and the poorer or even the middle classes wouldn't have had the dosh to buy it. Becca, what is it?"

"Blue! Bright blue!" She'd jumped in her seat. "That was what Jenna was wearing—a blue dress." She was suddenly animated. "I could draw it for you—I know I could. I'm decent at sketching."

"Are you, then!" Gowan headed for the kitchen, and began rummaging in one of the drawers. "Here, wait just a moment, and I'll find you something to use. Right, tablet and coloured pencils— the paper's small, but this should be enough. Here you are, young Rebecca. Draw away."

She sat still for a few minutes, pencil in hand, trying for the picture in her memory. There was nothing there—only a blank space.

Try closing your eyes, she thought, *that's the best way to bring it back.* The force of the thought that followed—*but I don't want to go back there*—was shocking in its intensity. She could remember the cold power and control in the young man's grip on Jenna's wrist, remember the shameful sense of pleasure the girl had felt, remember the heat of the sun as it fell on her face and her throat as she lay with her back in the warm grass of her father's garden, her head in her brother's lap, her own arms crossed at the wrists, lying in the folds of fabric, lovely summery blue that fabric was, it probably hushed and rustled around her feet whenever she walked, whenever she ran—

"Becca?"

Her eyes popped open. She hadn't remembered closing them, but the picture was there now, waiting to be set down, waiting to be made use of. And closing her eyes hadn't hurt her at all—she could do it whenever she liked, and it would be all right.

She bent over the pad and began drawing.

Fabric, soft as—what, silk? It didn't matter—she couldn't draw what fabric it had been anyway, so why worry herself over it? It was more the way it had looked, how much of that blue softness had been gathered discreetly over Jenna's legs and ankles, leaving the soft little slippers showing, but no more. Whenever those long-ago Cambornes had lived, it had been a time where girls were supposed to be modest.

Becca, too young to genuinely appreciate the dark subtlety of the ironic, was nevertheless aware of a stab of something that might have been outrage at a distant hypocrisy. Really, she thought, the whole modesty thing was just stupid, especially since the nice modest girl was apparently having it off with her own brother.

Sketch, fill in a line, an angle, a curve.

The colour, now—that was going to be tricky. Was there a pencil in Gowan's little notions-store box that came anywhere near? Not really, no—at least, not in the depth of just how blue it had been. For a moment, disheartened and distracted, Becca found herself wondering how even the world's great artists could possibly get across a blue that meant summer. Ah well, this would have to do for now, and maybe Lucy Williams would know what Becca was trying to do, or at least know where to look online for that full palette, that spectrum of shade and tone. Lucy sounded as if she knew pretty much everything. . . .

"Nice. Good." Ringan, who had pulled his chair alongside, sounded appreciative. "That's coming along very nicely, Becca. What about the top of it, though? Did you get anything about the sleeves, or the neckline? Was it on or off her shoulders? And what about her hair, Becca? Was she wearing it up, or was it just hanging loose?"

She closed her eyes again. Her own feet in the soft little slippers, the warm dry ground below her, the folds of skirt—and hair, black and lustrous and long. It was there, all of it, in her memory's eye.

"Down. Her hair was down. It was loose. Like mine, really, very heavy and black. My mother always calls it Laine hair—she calls the colour raven's-wing. I think she might have had something on, a little hat or a cap or something. I remember, well, weight. But I have no clue what it might have been, sorry." She thought for a moment. "Her shoulders, I don't know—I mean, I don't think I could see the shoulders, or maybe I just wasn't looking at them. I'm not sure—I can't draw them. I'm sorry. But I did see the sleeves—they came right down onto her hands. Pointy. Like this."

An arm, a hand. Becca, who'd been taught to draw but had never really been interested in doing it, found herself surprised at just how cleanly the sketch was coming out. The girl was there, on the page. No head, of course, just the dress and the shoes and the hands, but still, there she was, Jenna Camborne. Faceless, it was true, but with the bright blue dress and her brother's baby in her belly . . .

"Was the sleeve embroidered that way?" Penny was sitting close at Becca's drawing hand. "Really?"

"I guess." Now that was weird, Becca thought, she couldn't even remember having noticed anything like that in her dream, much less having drawn it. "And the top of her dress—what's that part called?"

"The bodice, you mean?" Penny was staring at the drawing. "The upper half?"

"Bodice. Okay. Well, that was different from the skirt part. It had a pattern, sort of like my mother's drapes in the front room at home, all bright and shiny. I know the word—I just can't think of it." She lifted one hand to her mouth, a moment too late to stifle a cavernous yawn. "I'm sorry. I think I'm almost asleep. Anyway—whatever that word is."

"Brocade, that would be." Gowan had settled across the table, resting his chin in one hand, watching the family group across the table. It was impossible, Penny thought, to read his expression. Did he believe any of this, or was he simply humouring them? "So you've got a girl, supposedly right round your age, in a long blue skirt and a top looking like your mother's best curtains, and with pointy sleeves. Her name is Jenna, she's carrying her brother's child, and she's supposed to have been part of my family. Am I after having that right, then?"

"Yes." He was trying to be snarky, Becca thought, and felt colour rising in her cheeks in a wash of anger. Maybe he thought this was funny, but she couldn't see any humour in it anywhere. After all, he wasn't the one who'd passed out and made a total twit of himself in front of about a hundred people, and he wasn't the one who'd had whatever that vision was that Penny had suffered through, either. "You're after having that right. Every word of it!"

"Sorry. I wasn't trying to upset you." He'd caught the bite in her voice. "But it's a bit much to swallow, especially if you think on the fact that I've never heard one word of anything like this, not even from my mam. And she was all about the family history. Trust me, she'd known anything about this, she'd have rattled it off at me day and night, every chance that came her way. Christ, she'd probably have had a shelf full of books, ten different people telling the story, with fancy little illustrations, and she'd have written one herself. It would be one of the great stories of Cornwall. But the truth is, she never said anything, not a word."

"Jesus, Gowan, don't tell me you had one of those, too?" Ringan, whose own mother was as knowledgeable about the Laine family history as she was off-balance and histrionic, felt a twinge of sympathy. "I didn't realise your mother was one of those. So's mine—she's half off her nut on the subject of the family tree. But we have this problem, and we need to fix it. Something here, something to do with your family, had a go at Becca. Penny's felt it, seen it, heard it. Becca went for a stroll while she was sound asleep last night, and there was that little mess tonight. So I don't think rolling your eyes over it is going to solve a damned thing. And I've got the feeling it needs solving, and fast."

"Why?"

Ringan jerked his head. It was Becca, the pencil in her hand, her eyes at him. Her head was tilted. "I mean, why does it need solving and fast? Why don't we just not stay here? I mean, I've read ghost stories. Won't going away make it stop? If there's a ghost here, and I'm not here for it to be sympathetic or whatever with, and Aunt Penny's not here acting like a battery in a torch, wouldn't that take care of it?"

"I don't know. It might—but it might not, either," Penny said gently. "When it happened to me at my theatre, she'd got her hooks so deep into me, she was able to use me to leave the street where she'd died. So I don't know. Simply packing up our swimsuits and sheet music might help, but we can't risk it."

"No, we can't." Ringan's beard was at full jut. "But it seems to me there's two things we can do. I say we give this drawing, and all the information we've got, over to Lucy Williams, and let her see what she can dig up in the way of information. Hell, she might even be able to bodge up something in the way of a solution. And while she's doing that, we can be nice and elsewhere, I'm thinking maybe up to Tintagel or something, for a day or two of swimming and sunning and looking at standing stones and castles and whatnot. Penny, lamb, how does that sound to you?"

"Covering both ends? Ringan, that's brilliant!" Penny got up, yawning and stretching. "I don't know about you lot, but I'm dead on my feet. It's nearly three. Why don't we do this? We'll load Pandora up with our tats and bobs and head north up the coast, once we've had some sleep. But before we go, Gowan here will take us over to the Williams house, and we'll ask Lucy to start sniffing out details for us."

"I'll do that for you, of course." Gowan had begun loading the dirty cups into the dishwasher. "And even if just leaving the shelter of my roof sorts out this little problem for you, I'd love to know if what Becca saw was accurate. After all, it's not every day a man finds out something dramatic about his own family one morning that he had no idea about the night before."

A few hours later, with a light sprinkle of predawn rain leaving the roads slick and dappling Pandora's paintwork with prismatic specks, they loaded up the boot of the car. With Gowan in the front passenger seat giving directions, Penny drove across St. Ives and pulled up in front of a small, charming modern house at the northern edge of town.

Penny, who was exhausted, was doing her best not to show it. As accustomed as she was to minimal sleep during theatre season, this current enforced wakefulness was an entirely different thing.

It had, she thought, been a genuinely bizarre night. The last thing to happen before everyone finally got a few hours' sleep was a change in sleeping arrangements. Becca had asked, very diffidently, if Penny would mind spending the night in her room; that way, she said, if anything happened, Penny would be there to take care of her.

As Penny told Ringan, something in that plaintive, halting request had turned her from the late-thirtyish, childless-by-choice theatrical producer into the fiercely protective older sister she'd been while her sister Candy was growing up and needed her. In any case, the request and suggestion were so eminently sensible, she would have to have been not only heartless but a complete idiot to have refused the girl. Besides, sleepwalking could be dangerous.

So Ringan had trotted down the narrow hall and climbed into the narrow bed in Becca's room, to spend what remained of the night alone. Becca had curled up into a tight curl in the double bed beside Penny, falling asleep almost at once. She'd stayed there, looking exquisite, smiling faintly and murmuring once or twice in her sleep, while Penny, wide awake, watched over her until nearly sunrise before finally falling asleep herself.

"Wake up, lamb—we seem to be here." Ringan, outside the car and opening Penny's door, shot her a searching look. "Right, once we're done here, I'll be doing the driving until tomorrow, at the very earliest. No, don't argue with me! You're not nearly awake enough to cope, especially since we'll be doing some twists and turns along the road. Don't worry, I won't wreck Pandora—right now, you're much likelier to put the car into a tree than I'd ever be. Give me those keys."

Gowan had rung the Williams house before they'd left, letting Cian know they were on their way. Lucy was waiting for them at the door, Cian behind her shoulder. She stood away and let them file in.

"Good morning to you all. Rebecca, are you recovered from your fainting fit? Oh, good. Here, just wipe your feet, if you would. Would anyone like some tea, or coffee? No? Here, let's come into the front room, then."

Penny, swaying on her feet and hoping desperately for a second wind, settled into a comfortable wing chair. Taking in the room at a glance, she decided it looked precisely like its chatelaine: comfortable enough, but fussy and a bit prim. Everything seemed to have its place, a little too obviously.

She leaned back and closed her eyes. Her mind, rarefied from the lack of sleep, immediately brought up a picture: From the books in the two matched cases to the knickknacks on the tables, everything seemed more aligned than set down casually. Penny had a sudden image of Lucy, holding a flower vase or a memento from one of her students in one hand, considering every inch of the room before determining where to put what. Still the room was warm and the chair was comfortable and . . .

". . . question, if you don't mind my asking?"

Penny jumped, her legs jerking. My lord, she thought, Ringan was absolutely right, and he could damned well do the driving until she got a decent night's sleep. She'd sat down in a relatively comfy chair and immediately dozed off.

"I'm sorry, Lucy, could you say that again, please?" Lucy had asked her something, and she'd missed it. How long had they been talking while she dozed, anyway? At least a few minutes, because Lucy was holding Becca's sketch in her lap. Penny yawned, a big deep gulp of air, and shook her head. "I got about two hours' sleep last night, and I'm knackered. I really am sorry."

"Goodness. Two hours' sleep? That's not nearly enough." If Lucy minded the rudeness of having a guest nod off in midconversation, she wasn't showing it. "I wanted to ask you about something you said last night. When I came out to get you, after Becca fainted, you asked me a question. Do you remember?"

"No." It was the truth. Her memory of the previous night was oddly fuzzy, as if something had got between her waking self and whatever had moved through her head at the time. A voice, she remembered that, a girl's voice—protesting? Pleading? Whatever it was, it had been in a language Penny herself had no knowledge of, and yet she'd had no trouble understanding it at the time. Now, though, all she could bring up was the sense of it, the fear that had laced the begging voice. A kind of mist, a curtain between then and now, seemed to have fallen into place. The effect was oddly muffling. "Not any details, anyway. I just remember a girl's voice, but she was speaking Cornish and even though I remember knowing what she was saying—and for heaven's sake, don't ask me how I knew, because I haven't got a clue—I don't think I could tell you one word of what it was, not now."

"Well, if it's of any use in remembering, you asked me a question." Lucy was watching Penny's face, her gaze steady and considering. There was intelligence in that look. "I opened the door from the club room and nearly stumbled over you. You were sitting on the floor at the top of the stairs—and I must say, that was rather unnerving, because you could easily have fallen and broken your neck. You really ought to be more careful."

"Oddly enough, Lucy, I didn't actually plan on nearly falling, or tripping you up, or anything else. I wasn't really in any shape to think about it." Penny, hearing the snap in her own voice, looked down at her hands. They were clenched into fists, and she forced them open. She simply wasn't going to warm up to this woman, she thought, not now, not ever. "Really, Lucy, I wasn't trying to scare you."

"I didn't say you were. I'm simply telling you what happened. There's no reason for you to get offended." Her voice hadn't altered. There was no warmth in it, Penny thought. She was reciting a laundry list of facts, no more, no less. "You looked quite ill—your head was tucked between your knees and you were chalky.

But you asked me a question. You looked up at me and you said, what does *Perran* mean? Do you not remember asking that?"

"I—no, I don't think . . ."

She stopped in midword. There it was, that voice, those words that, now, were just an incomprehensible stream of syllables. Last night, she had known the inflection, the pain, the meaning behind the meanings. *My a'th kar, my a'th pys, mara pleg, na wra henna Perran, a'm kerydh? . . .*

"Wait." Her eyes went wide, staring, remembering. "Hang on a moment. Yes! I do remember—I could hear the girl in my head, the band was playing, I remember thinking how solid Ringan's guitar sounded, how it was giving Becca room to play, and it just came slamming into my head, her voice, asking—she wanted to know if he loved her—" Hearing her own voice spiralling out of control, she stopped.

"Penny, breathe. Just breathe, lamb, please." Ringan was out of his own seat and kneeling at her side. "Long deep breaths, all right? Lucy, I'm not Penny, but here's your answer: Penny didn't mention any of this last night while we were talking it over. Becca told us this ancestress of Gowan's had a father called Hywel and a stepmother called Eleanor or something. She told us that the girl had a brother called Perran, and we had a good long talk about how the girl was pregnant, but Penny, you didn't say a word about hearing his name. What in hell is this, then?"

"I've only just remembered, that's why." They were all staring at her, Cian and Lucy, Becca and Gowan, who had been silent since their arrival. Ringan had got hold of her hands, and he was rubbing, as if he thought she might be cold. "Literally—I'm remembering it now, but it had gone missing on me. Lucy, yes, I asked you what a Perran was, and you told me Perran wasn't a what, it was a who, a man's name. The patron saint of Cornwall, right?"

"Indeed, and that's right: Piran, our name saint is." It was Gowan, breaking his silence. "And I'll say it again, I never heard of any of these so-called ancestors of mine, but that's maybe by the way. So Becca had whatever it was last night, and you had it as well, at the same time? Is that the way of it? Or was it a separate thing, do you think?"

"Not separate," Penny told him. Ringan's hand, covering hers, rubbing her fingers, was very comforting. "But you know, that doesn't really take us any farther down the road toward sorting this out, does it? Not one bloody step. All it really does is add a layer of confirmation to it: Becca sees it from inside Jenna's head; I catch the echo or the shock wave or whatever the hell it is and get knocked on my arse."

Her voice was startling in its bitterness. Ringan, swallowing hard, kept his hand where it was. He was just as tired of this happening to Penny as she herself was; it was, he thought, possible that he minded even more than she did. But right now, it was his niece he had to be concerned about.

"You're right—it doesn't seem to add anything new." Lucy tapped Becca's sketch with one hand. "But I do have the starting point, and that's something, at least. Period dress isn't a strength of mine, but there are other teachers at my school, and I'm sure not all of them have gone off on holiday to escape the summer tourism here. I'll see what I can find out for you—it may take me a day or two, but I'll be as quick as I can about it. No dawdling, and a sort of general call for information. All right? Will that do?"

"Yes. And Lucy—thanks." Ringan was on his feet. "Here, let's get Penny's cell phone number into yours so that you can ring us up as soon as you know anything. I've got one as well, but I'm still fumbling with it. So ring Penny."

"Lucy?" Something had moved in Penny's mind, a thought, a connection. "Listen. If you can pin down the time period from the clothing, can you also ring Gowan and tell him? Gowan, that's all right with you, isn't it?"

"Sure and it is, but why?" He was watching her face. She thought that his natural bent toward automatic flirtation with any woman who crossed his path had been put forcibly on the back burner for the time being. "What's in your mind?"

"We have a girl, young, pregnant, in a blue dress, name of Jenna."

It was there, at the edge of her sleep-deprived thought processes, tantalising and dancing just out of her mind's reach. She spoke slowly, puzzling through it. "Becca says she was a Camborne, and I'm betting the house that she's spot on. If Lucy can find out an approximate era, you can check into your own family, and that'll be good. You've got family records you can sit down with, don't you? Because there's one thing I was forgetting, something I have to look at."

"Aunt Penny—what is it?" Becca was watching her now, as well. *Echoes,* Penny thought. It was so close, the thing that had been eluding her. "What's wrong?"

"Nothing." *Got you,* she thought. "Nothing at all. But I've just realised what's missing in all this. Jenna, Perran, all that? It still doesn't touch what happened to me, that first day in Gowan's house."

"Excuse me?" Lucy actually looked fuddled. That had to be a first, Penny thought. "I don't think I—"

"The same thing happened to me, that second day, the first day Becca sat down and rehearsed with them." *Got you, got you, got you.* It ran through her head in a continual loop. "I heard a girl's voice screaming, saw big grey eyes, black hair—I heard that name, Jenna. Except that what I heard, what I saw, that was through a dying man's eyes. She'd just killed him, crushed his throat with a stone while he was sleeping. And his last thought, his dying thought, was heartbreak, betrayal. He had no idea why she'd done it to him. And she was horrified at what she'd done. I could see it. I could feel it."

"Good lord." The exclamation had been startled out of Cian. "Is that what was happening? I remember thinking you looked very seedy all of a sudden, but I had no idea—"

He broke off in midsentence, as if realising how absurd the statement was. Ringan, who had tightened his hold on Penny's hand, ignored the interruption.

"It happened during a song." Criminal, Ringan thought, he'd been damned near criminal in his stupidity in not putting two and two together. There was no excuse for it, none at all. He'd been seven flavours of idiotic, not connecting the dots. They'd been through it before; how could he have missed it? How in hell could he have let Gowan push the song into the set list? "We weren't even playing it, not as a band, that first time—Gowan was running through it on the piano, remember? 'The New-Slain Knight.' And then last night, Becca and Penny both getting nailed with whatever the hell it was, that was during the same song. I didn't want the damned song in there, but at least now we know where the starting point is. We need to find the truth behind the lyric, and we need to find it soon."

"But it's harmless!" Gowan smacked one hand on the occasional table beside him, sending small ornaments chattering against each other. "There's nothing in that song to be causing this, not a damned syllable. What's more, the song has nothing to do with my family. This is insane, d'ye know that? The lyric to that one, it's just a charming thing about a pair of lovers. No one really dies in there. The bloke whips off the disguise and they have a good long snog and then they live happily ever after, them and the baby she's—"

He stopped, cutting the word off in midbreath. Ringan was nodding at him.

"You're catching up, are you? So am I, and it's damned high time. I ought to have seen it. A young pregnant girl—what Becca's been feeling and seeing and getting lost in. A dead bloke, what Penny saw. A genuinely dead bloke." He got to his feet and pulled Penny upright. "We need to head out, if we want to sleep in a real bed in Tintagel tonight—the bed-and-breakfasts are pretty full this time of year. Pandora may be a luxury car, but I'm damned if I want to doss down in the back seat. Gowan, I'm not much of a gambling man, but I'll lay you a tenner that whatever Lucy finds out about these ancestors of yours will have something to do with that damned song. And another tenner on the table, right now, that the story behind the story isn't harmless at all."

Seven

O what like was his hose, his hose?
And what like was his shoon?
And what like was the gay clothing
This new-slain knight had on?

Late that afternoon, having left their gear at a small guest house on
a winding road at the north-western edge of Tintagel, Ringan and
the two women wandered down the hill for a look at the ruins of
King Arthur's Castle and a much-needed dip in the sea.

Rooms for the night had been just as difficult to find as Ringan
had predicted they'd be. At the first seven places they'd tried,
they'd been greeted at the door by friendly yet apologetic innkeepers, all singing a version of the same song: *sorry, all full up, no vacan-
cies, tourist season at the height, booked months in advance, very tricky,
have you tried something further inland, no, likely nothing at Bossinney or
Treven either, sorry, good luck to you, have a nice visit . . .*

The fruitless hunt for a comfortable bed and a roof over their
heads had left Penny irritable and Becca visibly wilting. Just as
they'd been about to give up in despair and head away from the
coast, Penny spotted a vacancy sign out in front of a pretty cliffside
building advertising itself as Guinevere's Rest, A Guest House. Despite Ringan's dour prediction, that Version Eight of what he
called the Ever-So-Sorry Innkeepers Brigade would come out and
say *No, our mistake, that's supposed to read "NO Vacancy,"* the sign had
been accurate. According to the innkeeper—a comfortable woman
who'd held out a hand, taken Penny's credit card information, and

introduced herself as Mrs. Polgarren—the luck had definitely fallen their way, since she'd had a cancellation just that morning.

They'd booked the last remaining accommodations—two small adjoining rooms with a shared bath down the hall—in what proved to be a very pretty house. Ringan, who'd consulted on plenty of restoration projects in the neighbouring counties of Devon and Dorset in his time, cast an educated eye over the clean lines and gracious proportions, and found himself nodding in appreciation. A very handsome bit of late-eighteenth-century local work, Guinevere's Rest was, even with its silly tourism-friendly name.

Their rooms, one decently sized double and one much smaller, boasted the required beds, chests of drawers for their clothing, and jaw-dropping views of the sea. Becca, accepting the smaller of the two rooms with no apparent qualms, had stood staring out the window, apparently hypnotised into silence, until Penny jogged her elbow.

"Becca?" It was ridiculous, Penny thought, that she should be so tuned into the girl's moods. Ridiculous, but also very telling; there was simply no pushing away the fact of what any hint of that blank, absent look on Becca's face might mean, for Becca herself and for all of them. "Are you all right?"

"Oh, yes, don't worry. I'm fine. I'm just—well, look at the view! It's just . . ." She shook her head. "What's that amazing thing down there, by the sea? That huge pile of stones? It looks like a ruin."

"It is. That's King Arthur's Castle. And Merlin the Magician's cave is down there, as well." Ringan, at Becca's side, turned and grinned at her. "Cornwall is very big on the King Arthur thing—hell, we're standing in a hotel named for his old lady. He was supposed to have been born here—that's one of the popular legends. Didn't you know that?"

"No, I didn't, not a word. They never taught us anything about Cornwall at school—it was all about Scotland." She was visibly straining toward the door, suddenly reminding her uncle of a racehorse, a colt, wanting to shake the stillness out of her legs with a good long gallop. "There are people down there. Can we go look?"

"Of course we can, but let's get into swimming gear first." Whatever was pulling at Rebecca had caught Penny, as well: a need to be moving, the call of the waves soughing against the land. The windows were opened to the day's heat; through the screens, a very faint chatter of distant voices could be heard, and the smell of the Celtic Sea was strong and clean. "Because according to all the guidebooks, there's a nice little cove down there. Right now, after all that time in the car, diving into some cool clear water and pretending I'm a sea otter is just what the doctor ordered. No, Ringan, don't raise your eyebrows at me; I had a nice long kip in the car, remember? I won't fall asleep and drown as I'm backstroking in the cove. It's about a hundred degrees out there and I damned well want to swim. Come along, you slackers, let's go—this is supposed to be a holiday!"

They went down the path along Tintagel Head, moving closer toward the sea. An exquisite old church, identified in Penny's guidebook as St. Materiana's, was so lovely that they nearly lost Ringan for the rest of the afternoon. It took Penny's promise, that they'd come back later or the next day and have a good long wander, to prise him loose.

The road down to the castle was long and uneven, and led to some very steep stairs. There were no cars to cope with, no tour buses, no caravans full of would-be campers—there was simply no place to put a motor vehicle nearby. For some reason, Ringan found himself approving; it was somehow satisfying to visit a historic spot that was still so wild, so physically untamed, that even the forces of Mammon and tourism couldn't wreck it by levelling the rough spots or putting in a motor café and a car park.

The full force of the sun had begun to ease off as the afternoon moved toward early evening, but it was still very hot. Breathless from the warmth and the steep climb, they passed tourists coming up from a day out on the coast in a steady stream of humanity. Penny, returning nods and smiles from the passers-by, thought how relaxed they all seemed, how calm.

"Oh, wow!"

Startled, Penny looked up at Becca. She and Ringan, moving a bit more quickly than Penny, had reached a natural vantage point at the cliff's edge. Surrounded by the gaunt remains of the castle's lower ward, they were staring down and out toward the southwest.

"My God, that's impressive." Catching them up, Penny caught the rapt look on Becca's face. The girl looked unearthly, her black hair caught in movement, blowing away from her face in the steady breeze coming off the water. Below them was a footbridge between two impossibly craggy peaks of rock, strung high at one end and connecting lower down at the other. Below that, a cove of calm water, barely ruffled by the lap of white froth slapping its way in from the open sea on the other side, lay waiting.

"Right now, I'm just glad no one wants me to help restore the castle." Ringan was taking in the scene, mentally populating it, rebuilding Richard of Cornwall's thirteenth-century fortress in his mind's eye. "My mind's a scary place, isn't it? Gorgeous views, water, horizon, historical castle, King Arthur, the lot, and what's the first thing that came into my head looking down? How tricky it would be to get building supplies to the site, that's what. I mean, look at it! What did they use? Mules? Camels? Dragons? Levitation?"

Penny snorted. He grinned at her. "Right, so, maybe not quite as weird as it sounds—there's been something down there for a good fifteen hundred years, after all, and *somebody* had to handle the paperwork. They probably used the water for transportation. And levitation might have been on the building manifest, as well, considering that this is Merlin's country. Let's get down there. You two can have a lovely paddle in the cove, and I can wander and gawk at all the pretty stones and try to imagine what the place looked like when Tristan was hanging out there, mooning over Iseult. Come along. I'll brave that terrifying bridge thing if you will—it's not really as high off the water as it looks from here. Ladies first."

The bridge, in the end, was a good deal sturdier than it had looked from above, and they made the descent easily. Penny, dropping down on the sandy spit with her sandals in one hand and Becca right behind her, caught sight of a beautiful arch of stone, set into the base of the cliffs. Something stirred in her memory.

"Is that Merlin's Cave, Ringan? That arch thing? And is that a natural formation?"

"Yes to both, so far as I know." He watched his niece, who had pulled her light summer dress over her head and dropped it on the sand, streak for the water. "Mind Becca, Penny—she's in full mermaid mode right now. Are you going to explore?"

"Maybe. Right now, though, Becca's got the right idea—I just want to swim a bit. And good on me, for having the sense to not drag a purse along. You go have yourself a nice wander."

The water in the cove was cool, and clear enough to see bottom from a depth of fifteen feet. Penny, backstroking lightly toward Merlin's Cave with her face to the sun, closed her eyes and let the water take her along. While her body was perfectly in tune to the rhythms of the water and the breeze, however, her mind refused to relax.

If Lucy Williams was as good as her word, she would have spent a long summer's day indoors, in researcher's mode. Penny, her body adjusting to ripples in the salty shallows, wondered if she'd find anything—if, in fact, there was anything to find. Her mind was sharpening, clearing itself, focussing; the more relaxed and instinctive her body was, attuning itself to the water, the more her brain seemed to streamline its approach to the problem at hand.

What did they already know, or what could they assume? That somewhere in the shadows of Gowan's family history, a girl named Jenna had done the unforgivable with her own brother, named for Cornwall's patron saint. That the unforgivable had resulted in the unthinkable, a child born of incest.

Splashing nearby, children's voices. Penny tuned it out, concentrating, her hair floating in the water behind her.

A child born of incest. Had that happened, though? A pregnancy there almost certainly had been, or at least the girl Jenna had believed it to be so. Becca had felt the girl's panic, and that panic had translated itself to Becca's listeners to a degree of intensity that Penny had found nearly sickening. What had the girl thought? *Regular as the tide . . .*

Something travelled the length of Penny's spine, tightening her muscles. She sank a little, kicked with her feet, treading water, trying to regain her equilibrium. An easy overhand stroke put her back in the water, away from the sand. The water was a bit more talkative out here, farther into the sea; there were actual wavelets.

A girl, an incestuous affair, a disastrous pregnancy, all with members of Gowan's family. That much seemed sure. And there was one other thing: someone had died, in violence and in disbelief, his death coming at Jenna's hand. Penny, at least, was certain of that much; she had reason to be. What didn't they know?

Too many damned things, Penny thought grimly, and flipped over onto her back, backstroking lightly to bring herself closer to the land. For one thing, what was the connection? It didn't seem to be the house, or at least not primarily the house, although the old building certainly seemed to hold echoes. Both she and Becca had reacted, not only in the house itself, but well away from it.

Was it the song, then? Probably, Penny told herself. After all, it always had been the damned song, up to this point, and why would this time be any different? Gowan believed the song had nothing to do with his family, but of course that had nothing to do with anything. If she and Ringan had learned one thing over the past few years, it was that anything one might think they knew about a song's history or the validity of its lyric was probably a half-truth at best.

But there had been indications of something wrong before they'd ever played the song. Looking back at it, Becca's first reaction to Gowan, her first sight of him, had been odd, and disturbing. And that had been not only before they'd ever picked up their instruments together—it had been out of doors.

And, of course, there was another great unknown here, the one bothering Penny the most. A girl, a brother, yes. But Becca had been certain that whatever Jenna's feelings toward her brother might be, she'd sensed no real love or even fondness for the girl from the brother.

So whose eyes had those been, that Penny had looked through at a girl's horrified face? Whose throat had gurgled in death throes, choking on its own blood, desperate to draw air into lungs straining toward destruction? Who had looked up with surpassing love and tenderness and disbelief, knowing the girl he loved had taken him to this ending, not wanting to believe it could have happened, not understanding why?

"Penny! *Penny!*"

Maybe Lucy would find out something. Maybe she was sitting there, placid and a bit smug, glorying in the accumulation of facts just because they were facts. Maybe she was liking that she was being all helpful and useful, jotting down notes, ringing up Penny, ringing up Gowan. Maybe—

"*Penny!*"

Her head jerked up. Someone was calling her. Someone was screaming her name. People were shouting.

The movement of head and neck came at the same moment as a movement of the tide itself, catching her, knocking her off balance. She went under just long enough to swallow a bad mouthful of salt water. Then she righted herself, clearing her lungs, shaking water out of her eyes.

There were people in the water, looking around them, looking at each other. There were more people gathered on the sand at the mouth of Merlin's Cave. They were pointing, cupping their hands to their mouths, shouting incomprehensibly and waving their arms. Disoriented, dizzy, Penny trod water, moving toward them. Something was missing, something was off, something was wrong. What . . . ?

One figure, detaching itself from the crowd, pushed into the water: Ringan, kicking off his shoes, otherwise fully dressed. He hadn't taken the time to strip down to swim trunks.

Full awareness kicked in. Three heads in the water, four heads. A small clutch of people on the shore, panic-stricken and urgent.

Becca. There was no sign of Becca.

Ringan was in the water, pointing, yelling. Things were moving slowly, much too slowly. Her own head felt as if it weighed a thousand stone on its own, so slowly did it swivel to follow his pointing hand.

She saw black hair, a moving swirl of it. It seemed to have a disconnected life of its own, a dreadful nightmare image from someone's sick idea of a horror flick: black hair floating on the water's surface, not twenty feet to Penny's left.

No hands in the water, no face. There was only hair.

It took her no more than ten seconds to get there, kicking her legs out hard behind her, putting the full strength of her shoulders and back into it. The ten seconds might just as well have been ten centuries—her heart had gone into panic mode, every nerve screaming at her to hurry, get there, go.

She got a hand under Becca's chin and pulled her face clear of the water. She was aware, even in the shock of the moment, of the dichotomy between her actions—*right, capable, calm, that's right Pen, keep your head, you've always been able to do that in a crisis*—and her actual mind-set.

Once, many years ago, she'd been put in charge of minding her small sister, Candida. They'd gone down to the stream on the grounds of their family's property, playing as children do; Penny, always looking for ways to keep her ebullient sibling amused, had asked Candida how many of the plants she could put a name to. Candida, challenged, had picked a variety, naming them as she went, making up names for the ones she couldn't identify.

She'd got quite a sizeable handful together when she'd suddenly screamed. There had been a rat there, a water rat, sequestered safe among the tall reeds. Candida, poking about at the stream's edge, had surprised it into self-defence.

Up to this moment in her life, the memory of that day, of her own helplessness, as the rat attacked Candy, biting and lunging and glaring with its small red eyes as the child in her care screamed and bled, had been the worst fear Penny had ever had to live through. That fear had just been eclipsed.

Becca was going to die, Penny thought. The girl was going to drown, and it was her fault. She'd let her mind wander and now Ringan's niece was going to die, choking as her lungs filled with the sea . . .

But there were people in the water with them now, competent people, taking the girl's weight and getting her out and clear.

They laid her, limp and motionless, out on the sand. Ringan was out of the sea as well. Someone was performing mouth-to-mouth. A middle-aged woman, competent but urgent, was doing CPR and compression, turning the girl's head.

Penny, coming out of the ocean and feeling her heart rate spinning madly out of control, saw the sudden gush of water from Becca's lungs, spilling out onto the sand. She saw Becca's chest heave suddenly and heard the hacking sputtering cough, as Becca's lungs, cleared now of the salty weight, began to function properly once more.

She was at Becca's side now, pushing people away, bending over the girl. Becca's eyes opened and found Penny's. Her lips moved, twisting her face as she spoke.

"What?" Ringan had both arms under her, holding the girl, supporting her head. "Becca, what did—"

"*Pandra hwer genev?*" Becca said very clearly, and blacked out.

"Ringan, will you answer something for me?"

The afternoon, mellow and golden, had slid into evening, and now into night. Becca's small room had gone from soft cheerful light to lengthening shadows that made the high corners seem blurry. Now, with the onset of night and full darkness out of doors, Penny had turned Becca's bedside lamp on. For some reason, she was finding the idea of a dark room unnerving.

"If I can." Ringan took his eyes off his sleeping niece long enough to meet Penny's eye. She looked drained and exhausted, he thought, but his mind was too tired to worry at the realisation. He had no way of knowing that she was thinking the same about him.

They were both looking their age just then. Between the long drive, the physical exertions of the day, being short of sleep, and the adrenaline let-down, both adults were exhausted. Getting Becca back to Guinevere's Rest had been the sort of experience that forms the basis for future nightmares. Penny, looking back at the events of the afternoon, thought that everything had seemed to happen in slow motion. Every memory of this day that she was unlucky enough to keep was likely to come back to her as part of a series of stop-action movie sequences.

They'd had a good deal of help, of course; when faced with a child in danger, people generally rise to the occasion. There had been a dozen or so people on the sandy strip outside Merlin's Cave, and every one of them had offered their services in getting the girl safe away from the shore and back to her hotel bed. And the help had been needed. Becca, having asked her question in a language she couldn't know, had closed her eyes a second time. This time, she'd stayed asleep. She'd made it back to Gowan's after her faint, but this time she wasn't going to walk back under her own power.

People had taken turns carrying her, the last quarter-mile being blessedly undertaken by a very large, and very prosaic, visitor from Hamburg. They'd come across him halfway along the path, as he'd been on his way down to explore the castle. Instead, having heard the story, he nodded, hoisted Becca in his arms as if she weighed no more than a sack of groceries, and taken her back he way he'd just come. Ringan, who'd been edging his way along the path hanging on to his niece's feet, was panting and sweating. He was sturdily built, but he wasn't a large man by any means. His offer to buy the unknown Good Samaritan a lavish dinner was waved off, and a heartfelt thanks and handshake accepted instead.

Mrs. Polgarren, horrified but as capable and impossible to ruffle as everyone else in Cornwall seemed to be, had got Becca tucked up and got the local doctor over before Penny had even had time to brush the dried salt and sand from her hair. The doctor, a young woman with London in her voice but that same reassuring air of easy competence as everyone else here, had heard the story, asked a few intelligent questions, and checked Becca over. The girl had opened her eyes a moment, looked blankly at the stranger listening to her heart, sighed, and gone back out again.

"She'll be fine." The doctor, putting her stethoscope away, sounded unworried. "No, don't worry—this is quite normal as a reaction to shock, especially at her age. Just let her sleep. She'll wake up when she's ready. Her throat may be a bit sore from the experience, but that's normal, as well. I'll let Mary Polgarren know to have some warm broth on hand. If your niece wakes hungry and her throat is up to it, get her to eat a bit of easily digestible food—soft eggs, that sort of thing. And do ring me if there are any problems, of course. But really, I doubt we'll see any."

Four hours later, Becca was still asleep, and Penny had been thinking. They'd taken turns at bathroom breaks, each getting a hot shower. Ringan had rung Lucy Williams and got the voice-mail; the message he'd left, he thought grimly, was going to light a very warm fire under their shiny new researcher. Mrs. Polgarren had rung down to the local fish and chips takeaway, and had some dinner sent in; Penny, taking the savoury-smelling containers at Becca's door, had taken the opportunity to pull their hostess aside and asked her to translate something. The answer she'd got, the meaning of the words she'd heard Becca say twice now, had sent Penny's mind down a trail of puzzlement and led her to the conversation she had just instigated.

"Why did you agree to let Gowan do that song?"

Penny's voice was at normal volume, but it had an edge to it. She and Ringan were seated side by side in comfortable chairs that had been pulled up alongside the bed. Becca had been asleep so long that had she been still, they both would have worried. It was a lucky chance she hadn't been, because at the moment she was on her back with arms at her sides, outside the light duvet. She looked uncomfortably like a corpse.

"Let him?" Ringan had heard that edge. "It wasn't a question of letting or not letting, Pen. The Tin Miners are Gowan's band. I got a vote, but that's all I got."

She opened her mouth, thought better of what she was about to say, and shut it again. She looked about as confounded as she ever did. It was easy, he thought, to forget that Penny had virtually no professional experience as a guest on someone else's patch. She'd founded her theatre group, the Tamburlaine Players, straight out of university.

"Ringan—you had to know that song was involved somehow." She kept her voice low, choosing her words. "We'd given Gowan the history, for God's sake. Maybe he didn't believe us, not then, but even if he didn't, he couldn't claim we hadn't told him about it. And you knew. You saw how she reacted to it."

"What do you mean? She didn't react to it." Had that been a murmur from the sleeper? "Hang on a minute—that's right, you weren't there, were you? When we rehearsed it yesterday, back at Gowan's? You'd gone off to splash in the sea."

"You rehearsed it?" Penny's eyes were narrowed. "Look, I want to know about this. You're right, I wasn't there. Becca told me you and the rest of the band had a row over the set list. Was it about covering that song?"

"Of course it was. I didn't have any desire to do the song. I'm not familiar with it, for one thing, and it seemed to me that even with no other issues attached to it, having both your guest players having to learn the piece from the ground up in less than a day would be a good enough reason to choose something else. But Gowan wanted to do it, and he dug in his heels. Says it's one of his favourites. Cian likes it as well, so I was the only one not on the bandwagon. We ran through it twice—with Becca playing along—and nothing, no problem at all. She didn't react, Pen. Nothing at all."

She was silent, clearly unconvinced, and he heard his own voice flatten out, going a bit fierce. "Besides, this isn't Broomfield Hill, lamb. I'm not in charge here—I'm a guest. If we were talking about Broomfield, well, that's different. We won't be covering it, trust me. Hell, if Becca had shown any signs at all of the ghost thing while we practised it, I'd have put my foot down and told Gowan sorry, no, we're off."

"You should have." Her gaze had moved away from his and back toward Becca. "I wish you had done."

"In hindsight, yes, so do I." He pushed down the snap that wanted to tint his voice; criticism from Penny was not something he dealt well with, especially when she was right. "But that would have upset Becca, Pen. I hate having to remind you, but you aren't a musician— there are some things you won't see the same way a musician would. Besides, it was our idea to get her the public performance experience in the first place, remember? She needs that—the girl's going to be very much in demand when she graduates from Hambleigh. And she was enjoying it. You weren't there, so you didn't see. But she got into the song. She even came up with a few interesting little riffs on the fiddle, very fluid and innovative." He stopped, watching his niece turn over and away from them, snuggling her cheek into the pillow. The longer she slept, the more difficult he was finding it to resist the urge to poke her, shake her, wake her up. "Do you want to ring Lucy again? I left a message when I rang before."

"I will, in a minute." She was back to watching his face. "All right, so you didn't really have a say in it, and you didn't want to upset Becca or do her out of a chance at live performance. I can see that. I'm not trying to be a bitch, Ringan, I swear."

"No, I know. If you did want to be a bitch about it, there wouldn't be any missing it. I know you too well. And speaking of which, there's something else on your mind. Isn't there?"

"It was what she said, after we got her out of the water." Becca's lips were pursed like an infant's, and her skin was pale. Penny thought that the lines of her face, which should have been relaxed, seemed oddly tight. "That was the second time she'd said it. Did you catch it?"

"No. I knew she said something, but—wait, what do you mean, twice? What are you talking about?"

"She said something, the same thing—once back at the Duke's Own, when she blacked out during the song. After she woke up, or maybe it was when she was just coming out of it—don't you re- member? I heard her say something and I asked Lucy and Gowan what she'd said, but neither of them had caught it. She said the same thing today, once we'd got the water out of her lungs. This time, I memorised it. She said, *Pandra hwer genev,* or at least that's what it sounded like." She reached out and took the glass of water from Becca's nightstand; Mrs. Polgarren had left them a carafe of ice water. "I asked our landlady what it meant, when she brought dinner in. I suspected that if it was Cornish, she'd know."

"And . . . ?"

"It was a question." She emptied the glass. "She asked it twice, Ringan, the same question. Mrs. Polgarren says it means, *What's happening to me?*"

He said nothing. Penny reached beyond him and took the water carafe. Her throat was very dry.

"I thought this afternoon was—I don't know, an accident," she said. "That she went out farther from the shoreline than she could really handle, she got a cramp, something like that. Something normal, I mean. The sort of thing that might happen to anyone. I don't know what the official statistics are, people drowning while they're swimming in the sea, but it happens, and quite often. Nothing to do with ghosts or anything else. Accident."

"And now you don't think so?" It hadn't even occurred to him. He hadn't really thought about first causes, but now that he considered it, he realised he'd assumed just what Penny had thought: too far from shore, cramp, any one of the uncounted reasons why people swimming peacefully in calm water under an untroubled sky are then found floating and bloated, bumping horribly against a shoreline somewhere a few miles distant from where they'd started out. "Because of what she said?"

Penny nodded. "That's it. If she hadn't said that—and I wasn't mistaken, Ringan, I heard it—I'd have thought, right, damn, we got very fortunate indeed, and escaped her becoming a statistic by the skin of our teeth. But she said it. And now I think something happened to her in the water. I think something got at her."

"Then she isn't safe away from the house. Not if you're right." His jaw was tight. This feeling, the need to be up and doing, to somehow take control of an impossible situation, was hated and familiar. What was new was the sense of urgency. *Roberta's only child* . . . "Christ. Penny, look, I'm going to ring up Lucy again, and if I don't get her, I'll get on to Gowan. This is getting out of hand. And we haven't got the time to—Becca! Sorry, did I wake you?"

The girl had turned, away from her soft pillow and the shadows on the facing wall. She had rolled onto her back. Her eyes were open and fixed on her uncle. She said nothing.

"Becca?" Something in that stare was as unsettling as anything Ringan had ever seen. "What's wrong?"

"Ringan." Penny's hand had moved, without her knowledge or volition, and fastened hard on Ringan's sleeve. The words came back to her, cycling, turning around, chasing each other in a loop, a snake eating its own tail: *Her eyes are open; aye, but their sense is shut . . . infected minds to their deaf pillows will discharge their secrets . . . Pandra hwer genev?* "Wait. I don't think—"

Becca opened her mouth and spoke.

The words were a jumble, a freshet of English and Cornish and something else that Ringan, his breath stopped in his lungs, recognised as the Scots Gaelic of his own childhood. The grey eyes were empty lamps, no light in them.

"*Ny garav*, Perran, don't touch me don't let me alone *na'th karav* what's happening to me . . ."

"Oh God, oh God." Penny had hold of Ringan's arm, feeling the muscles under her fingers knotting up hard. "Ringan, don't touch her. Just—don't. She's not really here. I don't know where she is or what she's doing, but she isn't really here."

"Get away from me get away *hedhi* stop don't please . . ."

There was no intonation, no voice recogniseable as Becca's, or even human. It was words and words only, language in a cold dead waterfall, imparting only fear. Ringan, his eyes held in place by the terrible babbling and the dead grey lamps as securely as Arthur's Excalibur in its stone prison, remembered that the first time he had been confronted with someone he loved in this kind of peril, it had been Penny. Then, he had tried telling himself that he wasn't frightened. This time, he wasn't bothering.

The atonal distant voice stopped. For a moment, Ringan thought he saw something flicker in the grey eyes, awareness, intelligence, something that was essentially a not-quite-child-and-not-quite-adult person called Rebecca Eisler. It might have been nothing more than expansion or contraction of her pupils; he couldn't be sure.

Then her eyes closed once more, the heavy lids with their freight of black lashes settling back into place. Her breathing was steady and even. It had not once changed its rhythms during the outpouring of words.

"Get Lucy Williams on the phone." Penny's voice was a thin harsh rasp; he could hear the shock in it. "And hurry. We need information and we need it fast. The doctor was wrong, Ringan. I don't know what this is, but it isn't sleep."

Eight

His coat was of the red scarlet,
His waistcoat of the same;
His hose were of the bonny black,
And shoon laced with cordin.

Had Penny been able to see across the length of Cornwall, she might have taken comfort in the fact that Lucy Williams was, in fact, every bit as good as her word. The faint impression of Pandora's tyres had not yet faded from the damp street in front of the Williams house when Lucy settled herself at the computer, mentally cracked her knuckles, and got down to work.

Her desk was organised enough to reveal its owner as either a teacher or a librarian. She had a pot of tea, a notepad, and a freshly sharpened pencil at one elbow; at her other side was Becca's sketch. She had a short list ready of Internet sites that might serve as appropriate starting places for the information she wanted. A second list, in her clear handwriting, were her own notes, jotted down after her guests had gone. She had a small stack of books from her personal library, local histories of the area that had long formed the nucleus of her collection on the subject that was the nearest thing she had to a lifelong passion. She had telephone numbers of colleagues and friends, all of whom might have suggestions for her in case she ran out of leads or got stuck. The one thing she didn't have was any belief in ghosts.

It was just as well Penny hadn't asked for her belief, because the answer would have been a calm negative, touched with mild surprise at such a silly question. Had she asked Lucy why, in that case, she was willing to take on the job of hunting down answers and waste a full day of her summer holiday doing it, Lucy would have responded that belief in ghosts wasn't needed to research genealogy or period costuming, surely?

Her first look had resulted in as happy a stroke of good fortune as any researcher might have hoped for. She'd decided, very sensibly, to begin with what she had to hand: her own books. At the top of the pile was a slim volume with a pricey cloth cover. The book, barely fifty pages in length and wrapped in a dull purple fabric that had probably been chosen to subconsciously invoke a sense of importance, was a self-published bit of ego gratification dating back to the late nineteenth century. Its author, a minor cleric, seemed to have fancied himself the keeper of the unwritten history of the local moneyed families. He'd put the thing out under the name of Peter Menegue. That, Lucy thought, had to have been a nom de plume. *Menegue* meant *monks*; unless the unknown cleric had chosen his profession on the strength of his family name, the coincidence was far too convenient for belief.

Peter Menegue had apparently decided that the brevity and slightness of the book's contents needed some balancing, and he had opted to saddle it with a title impressive enough to make the book—scarcely more than a pamphlet, really—stagger under the weight. It bore the imposing title *The History, Stories and Probity of the Landed Gentry of the South Western Duchy of Cornwall: Some Facts and Discussions*. Lucy, shaking her head, flipped to the back and ran down the index. As she scanned, she found herself smiling and reaching for her pen. Whoever he'd been, Peter Menegue had been meticulous about his referencing.

There was no dearth of entries for the Camborne family. They had one of the longer sections to themselves, facts interspersed with Menegue's comments. There was also substantial cross-referencing and, to Lucy's satisfaction, a time line.

She let out a long sigh of relief. This looked to save her some time and, her own disbelief in the root cause of Becca's distress notwithstanding, time seemed to be an issue. Even if she got nothing more from this particular source than some vague gossip and a few hints of other sources to check, it still looked to have been a lucky choice.

She began with Menegue's introduction to the Camborne family. He'd written in a style all too familiar from his time period and social surrounds: chatty, slightly coy, pompous. The writing was aggravated by his clerical tendency to take small breaks for pontificating. .

The spur of that ancient and respected family, the Cambornes . . . who are local to our own township of St. Ives has a most interesting lineage that it may claim, solely apart and separate from the primary line of that family of the same name. While perhaps not yet so famous as their more famous cousins, this branch, with few exceptions, is one of men and women of virtue, devoted to the service of God, queen, and duchy. Truly, that they have prospered so well and for such a length of time and circumstance may stand as an exhortation to others of wealth and property, to not cast to one side the needs of the Church that shows the way to Heaven. . . .

Lucy wrinkled her nose, and poured some tea. Pedantic though she might be, she wasn't a fan of the late Victorians. She sipped, set the cup aside, and read on.

. . . Piran Camborne, second cousin to that Ruan Camborne who is so well thought of in the church records, first built a small manor for himself and his wife and family on five acres of land in St. Ives township, some close to the waterline, in 1288 (vide land grants, recorder). Piran, the cause of whose rift with his cousin Ruan remains a mystery, died during an outbreak of plague, which wrought great desolation and sorely distressed the community, in 1322. As shown by church and duchy records, his young son Alan, then still well short of his majority, took possession of the family land and fortune and, with the help of Our Lord, came to healthy manhood enough to keep both family and property intact and growing.

Lucy stopped and reread the paragraph. Piran? That was one of the names Becca had mentioned, a name Lucy had promised to look for. But it was also one of the most common names in the duchy, as common as David in Wales or George in England. Hywel, as common as it might be, offered a better bet. And of course, there was the girl herself, Jenna.

Over the passage of centuries, the family grew close ties with both their sheltering community and with the duchy in its entirety. Through marriage, alliances were formed with families to the north and east. Some of those families, Roche and Wherry and Penerreck, now sadly gone but for their names listed in the ancient ledgers that hold our past glory, brought fresh blood and those many benefits as may be found in such alliances.

The family fortunes remained steady, even though the three seasons of winter storms that afflicted our fair duchy from 1481 had a most deleterious effect on those who rely on crops and the bounty of the sea. The Camborne family suffered some loss, the heaviest and, doubtless, that which was most difficult to endure being the loss of the heir of the house, Perran. This tragic episode was followed, in short order, by the death of Perran's young sister, weeks before a most anticipated and advantageous wedding to the scion of the well-established Cann family from Sennen. Thus was completed a most tragic season in what had been else a long and tranquil history.

Lucy stopped. She squinted, peered, looked again. It occurred to her, with something of a shock, that she had honestly not expected to find anything, so absolute had been her disbelief in what she'd been told.

But there it was, in the not-quite-flowery language of a century earlier, and her honesty was not about to allow her to push that written confirmation away. Gowan himself had known nothing of this long-forgotten moment in his own ancestry, but here it was.

Lucy, sitting very still in her businesslike desk chair, thought back to the conversation, information ebbing and flowing among the group in her front room this morning. She remembered every word: Penny, exhausted and snappish from the lack of sleep and the voices in her head. Ringan, with his concern for the women and his obvious edginess and dislike of what they were talking about. Becca, young and extraordinarily gifted, in the grip of something she could neither understand nor cope with.

And, of course, there was Gowan. Whether or not he believed what his guests told him was happening was an open question; Lucy had always found him iffy to read. For herself, up until this moment, she hadn't actually believed a word of it. Her belief wasn't needed. All that was needed was her willingness to help and her skill. She was perfectly willing to offer both.

Was it possible? Every instinct she possessed, all her training, the bent of her own temperament, left Lucy Williams wanting to snort in disbelief. But, as she would have been the first to admit, the empirical streak ran both ways: if she was going to demand hard data before allowing herself to believe in what was before her, her own honesty would not permit her to ignore inconvenient information just because it jarred with what she wanted to believe or disbelieve.

Of course, she thought, there was always the chance that this was pure coincidence. She considered for a moment and found that particular theory fading; the long arm of coincidence would have had to be well beyond anything she could accept. Besides, there was the one fact that couldn't be covered by coincidence, no matter how much she wanted it to: Gowan apparently hadn't known and didn't seem to believe it.

Lucy, while perhaps not the most astute of women when it came to other people, had good reason to know Gowan Camborne. He'd been playing music with Cian for a quarter century. She'd sat at shows, eaten meals at the same table as Gowan, smiled and thought of something else as the talk turned, inevitably, to music. She'd had half a lifetime to reach her own conclusions about the burly piano player with the taste for pretty women. One thing was perfectly clear: there was no deceit in Gowan anywhere. He had no guile, none at all.

Gowan had known nothing of this. The information was obscure, not ready to hand. It wasn't as if the Reverend Peter Menegue had left thousands of copies of his chatty little historical conclusions lying about in heaps all over Cornwall. Lucy's copy was a rarity; even the town's lending library didn't have one in their special collection of local work. The booklet was one of several oddities she planned to donate to the local Preservation Society at some point.

Gowan, with eight centuries of family lineage behind him and a mother who'd been obsessive about the family she'd married into, hadn't known. But Penny had seen it, during whatever it was that had impelled her out of the upstairs room and left her collapsed at the head of the stairs. Becca had lived through it—so powerfully, in fact, that she'd suffered some kind of seizure because of it. And here was the confirmation, the validation, set out as a small matter-of-fact tidbit in a printed booklet.

Lucy took a deep breath and let it out again. She was distantly aware that her hands were shaking.

"All right, then." The sound of her own voice, spoken aloud in the small cheerful office with its logically arranged library shelves and tidy desk, nearly made her jump. Outside, the day had turned lovely, warmth and sunlight moving through the branches of the apple tree outside her window, dappling the desk and the floor and her light summer dress with streaks of moving shadow. "Concentrate. Where to look next?"

Carefully, methodically, she went through the volumes she'd culled from her own library. The stack awaiting reshelving grew on the far side of her desk.

But there was nothing to find. None of the references Menegue had cited were even mentioned in her own collection. It was time to take stock, and consider what she had, where to begin, where to go next . . .

"Lucy?"

She started, nearly knocking over the stack of books. Cian had stuck his around the door.

"Sorry." He sounded apologetic. "But it's gone half past one, and I'm thinking about lunch. Could you fancy something?"

"That I could." She shook her head as if to clear it. "I've hit a bump, anyway, and I need to think about this. Here, I'll make us something to eat."

After lunch, seated across from each other in the small sunny kitchen, Cian cocked his head and looked at his wife.

"Well, now." He leaned back in his chair. "You said you'd hit a bump. Would talking it out help, do you think?"

"It might, at that. The fact is, I'm feeling muddled, and I don't like it. Give me a minute, all right?"

She was quiet, marshalling and organising her thoughts. Cian, who knew his wife, waited in silence. When she was ready, she would present him with as concise a summary of the problem as anyone could want.

He knew quite well that he and Lucy were an odd mix by anyone's criteria: the freeform creativity that came from Cian's being a musician went very strangely indeed with Lucy's careful need to structure nearly every breath she took. For whatever reason, it worked, and it always had.

It took her all of two minutes to put her train of thought into order. When she'd finished outlining what she knew and what she wanted to know, Cian was tapping one calloused forefinger on the table, a sure sign that he was thinking.

"It seems to me that you ought to be starting at the point of information where the Right Rev or whoever this gent was meets what Penny and young Becca told you: a tragedy where the local Cambornes lost their eldest son, who was called Perran, and the death of his younger sister. From what you've told me about it, you've even got a nice narrow time frame to work from: he said something about there being a series of very stormy winters in 1481, or thereabouts. So isn't that your confluence, right there? Or have I misunderstood?"

"No, you're right." Really, she thought, it never failed. Cian might be scattered and disorganised nearly every minute of every day; he might be incapable of remembering more than three items on a grocery list, but when a simple fact had somehow got itself buried just out of his wife's field of vision, there he was, pointing the way back to the shortest distance between two points. She found herself feeling rather cross at herself. "And so obvious, too. How did I manage to miss that?"

"Truthfully?" He'd taken her literally. "I think it's the whole 'things that go bump in the night' aspect that muddled you. Not your cup of tea at all, Lucy, nor mine, either. People start telling ghost stories and I start rolling my eyes—I swear, it seems like half the stuff I play is about murder and ghosts, me listening to Gowan or whoever the guest vocalist happens to be going on about haunted housewives or demon lovers or whatever, and I'm damned if I believe a word of it."

"Yes, I feel the same." It was rare, she thought, that Cian opened up this way. "But you play the songs, all the same."

"Of course I do. It's music. It's what I am, and that means it's what I do. I don't have to believe the lyrics, you know. And if you'd like my opinion, Lucy, it's this: you don't have to believe it, either. Can't you treat it the way you would any other research project and just get on with it? Not let yourself be blindsided when things you can't explain turn out to be possible after all?"

"I can, and I will. Thank you, Cian. You've got far more sense than I do." Lucy Williams, undemonstrative by nature, leaned over suddenly and planted a kiss on her husband's cheek. "Well, no, maybe not more sense. I had enough sense to say yes to you when you asked me to marry you."

"That you did, and I've been glad about it ever since. No, you go back to your books, or the Internet or whatever your next step is. I'll do the washing up and put the kettle on for another pot of tea."

Back at her desk, hearing the lazy song of birds moving in the bushes outside her window, Lucy gathered her wits and her information, and decided to move from the printed page to the vaster resources of the Internet.

She began with a new browser window and her favourite search engine. A second browser window let her open a link to a teachers' resource user group she belonged to. It occurred to her that they might be useful; while scattered the length and breadth of the United Kingdom, two or three of the regular users were either in Cornwall or just across the Tamar, in the far west of Devon.

She decided to try the search engine first. For some reason that she wasn't quite ready to explore, Lucy found herself balking at the idea of having to explain to any of her online associates why she wanted the information. With the box in her first browser window blinking steadily and requesting that she enter her desired search terms, she took a deep breath and began to type.

Camborne Perran 1481. There, she thought, that was a decent starting point; there would be probably be nothing, but she could always expand from there. She hit the enter key, watched the little hourglass symbol that meant the engine was gathering information, and waited.

Your search returned three hits.

There it was again, the same flutter of disbelief in the pit of her stomach, the same momentary sense of shock that had frozen her wits in place when she'd first read Peter Menegue's note about it. But Cian, bless the man, was absolutely right, she thought: it simply wouldn't do to let herself react this way. She'd promised to get it done, and she had a very low opinion of people who went back on their word.

The first entry, nothing more than an exact lift from Peter Menegue's tract, was a disappointment. Lucy, after peering at the cached URL, moved on to the second entry. The cache on this one had a county location, and seemed to be from someone's official records: *Camborne Perran b. 1463 d. 1481 drowned, estate pass to half-brother Pasco, b. 1478, father Camborne Hywel, mo. Elyor.*

A sharp sound nearly sent Lucy out of her chair, before she realised that she'd heard her own breath, whistling into the quiet office. *Nonsense*, she thought, *this is impossible,* and bit her lip. Something came back to her, a snippet of the morning's conversation as she'd been showing her guests to the door, Cian at her back: Gowan, wishing her good hunting, saying something about the slimness of her chances of finding he had a raft of ancestors he'd never heard of. And Lucy herself, her notebook with its points and lists in one hand, waving them into the morning and on their way.

She took up her notebook, her hands trembling slightly. Becca's list, the names that the girl had remembered from dream, from seizure, from those bad moments of the past few days—where was that?

She found it at the bottom half of the second page of those notes she'd jotted down, as Penny had dozed with the dark circles under her eyes making her look her age, as Ringan had radiated a peculiar cross between helplessness and anxiety as he looked between the two women he was travelling with, and as Gowan—open, guileless Gowan—had looked as impassive as Lucy had ever seen him. It was headed with the single word—*Cambornes?*—and was followed by a numbered list: *1, Jenna = daughter? 2, Perran = son / heir? 3, Hywel = father?*

Just below that, in parentheses and in her own legible handwriting, was the number 4, followed by one word: *Eleanor?*

"Becca?"

Waking out of sleep, curled into a tight ball in a bed she didn't think was her own, Becca heard the voice and identified it as her uncle Ringan's. She made no response, partly because the movement that had caught her uncle's attention had been an attempt to swallow. It was really a mean trick on the part of the fates, she thought, to wake up out of a bad dream, or something, and find yourself hurting.

And hurting she was. The pain, stabbing and harsh, was turning her throat into something her own mother, that pragmatic doctor, might have worried about. The darkness behind her closed eyes was shot with pain. The problem was, she had no memory, not the faintest clue, of why she hurt so badly.

"Becca, do you want some water?"

"No." The word, fully articulated in her mind, seemed to have got mangled between her vocal cords and the outside world; all she heard was a tiny whimper. That was annoying, but so was this sense of hanging in darkness, of being afraid to swallow, of being afraid to open her eyes.

A hand, laid lightly against her cheek, solved that issue for her; the gesture and touch caught her unawares.

Her eyes popped open.

For a few paralysing moments, staring and uncomprehending, Becca thought something had happened to her vision. Everything was oddly limned, ringed in shadow where she'd expected light; she saw Penny, and Ringan, but behind them was a room she was unfamiliar with. She felt a clutch of panic at the pit of her stomach. What . . .

"Here." Ringan, holding a glass, set it down on the night table beside her narrow bed. "Let's sit you up—you need water. Your throat must be a mess—you had mouth-to-mouth and you coughed up half the Celtic Sea."

"Where—" She stopped in midword, her eyes going wide, drinking in the room and all the available light, placing it, placing herself in it. One hand at her throat, she pulled herself upright, and mentally answered her own question.

The guest house, that was it—the hotel with the twee name, Guinevere's Something or Other. They were in Tintagel and this was her room. But why was it dark, and why did her throat hurt, and what had Ringan meant about coughing up the sea . . . ?

"You don't remember, do you?" Penny slid over and got an arm around her shoulders. "Here, straighten up. Ringan, help her hold on to that, will you? Ta. Take small sips—it's room temperature, not too cold. We were swimming, earlier today, down by the castle. Do you remember that? No, don't talk. Just nod or shake your head. Becca?"

She was neither shaking her head nor nodding. Penny had neglected to offer her a third option, and she needed one; she wasn't sure. Something about the sea, yes, she did remember that. But not swimming, surely? How . . .

Shame, it's shame you've brought down upon us, am I to tell Jory Cann that his son's bride comes to him with a baby already planted in her belly . . .

"Becca!" Ringan, seeing the hand around the glass of water going slack, moved fast. "Here, let's set that down. Becca, no talking yet, but can you write? I know it's a lot to ask right now, but if I get you a pen and some paper, can you give it a shot?"

No daughter of mine, from this day no daughter of mine, cursed be the day you were thought of and cursed be the day your mother died in the making of you . . .

"Yes." She managed the word, hearing it as nails grinding across a slate. She felt as if she'd been gargling with shards of pottery. "Only—talk—if I have to."

"Good. And keep sipping." Penny angled the lamp toward Becca's hands. "Okay. A question—did you just remember something, just now, I mean? Yes? All right. Now, do you think it might be something useful?"

You ought to be whipped, who was it, who, I'll have a name out of you . . .

Becca shrugged. It was a gesture of total helplessness, as wrenching as it was disheartening: *I don't know, maybe nothing is useful.* Penny kept her voice level; at the other side of Becca's bed, Ringan's jaw was tight.

"Was it to do with whatever happened today? No, just write it, love. Take your time."

They moved their chairs, twisting to be able to read as she wrote. *Voice, her dad, calling her names. Pregnant, not getting married. Someone called Jory Cann. No wedding.*

"This was Jenna?" Penny caught Ringan's eye. "So she was engaged to someone named Jory Cann—no?"

Jory=father. Becca's pen was moving quickly now, the words coming easily, decorating the paper in her round schoolgirl's handwriting. *Marrying son.*

"Good. You're doing well. Here, take some more water."

Penny's mind was moving with speed, drawing scattered threads together, braiding them, twisting them, making a rope that she hoped would hold some of the weight of what had been happening. The problem was, they had no way of knowing whether what they knew meshed in any way with what the one person checking the history for them had learned—or, in fact, if she'd learned anything at all yet.

It had been three hours since Becca had opened her eyes and, staring through unrecognising eyes, had spoken words that should have not been possible for either her throat to produce or her language skills to manage. It had been three hours since Ringan had gone out into the corridor and left a frantic message on Lucy Williams's phone, telling her what had happened, asking what, if anything, she had come across.

Lucy had either not been there to take the call or had chosen to let her answering machine take it for her. Either way, Ringan thought, it was time. In exactly one week, Rebecca was due to be handed back over to her parents . . .

"I'm going to try Lucy again." He got to his feet. "Let's see if she's found anything."

She picked up the phone on the third ring. Ringan, feeling the tension run out of his shoulders and legs, realised just how much he'd been counting on hearing her voice at the other end of the line.

"Ringan?" She'd seen his caller ID. "Oh, good. I'm sorry, I had the phone off, and only just saw that you rang. I've been down at the county library, checking into some old ledgers in the special research collections. I—well. I seem to have found out a few things for you."

"Thank Christ for that." She'd sounded surprised at herself, he thought. "Do I dare hope you've got a positive identification on who these vintage Cambornes were? Because after what happened today—"

"What do you mean, what happened today?"

He gave her the story, keeping it to the bare bones. The feeling of impatience, the sense of wanting, needing, to somehow get both his hands on the situation and take some kind of control of it, was threatening to swamp him.

". . . and she's just told us something about the girl being engaged to some local bigwig's son, and having it broken off because she was pregnant," he finished. Lucy, he thought, was one hell of a good listener, despite her obvious tendency to lecture about anything that might come up; she heard him out in complete silence. "Lucy, we're going to have to tell her parents what's going on, if we can't stop this fast. That's damned near the last thing on earth I want to do. Besides, this is my niece we're talking about, and she's only a kid. So talk to me, will you? What have you got?"

"I've got quite a bit, actually." Her voice was very odd. "And I'll share it all, in just a moment, but first, if you don't mind, I'd like you to answer a question or two for me. In the first place, you did say Becca had almost drowned? That she had whatever this was while she was swimming in the sea?"

"Yes, she did. What—"

"I'll tell you, but one more thing, please. The family, that is, the name of the boy that girl Jenna was supposedly affianced to—what was their surname?"

"Cann." Becca's scrawl was clear in his mind. "No idea what the boy's name was, but the family name was Cann, C-A-N-N. The father's name was something weird—Rory, or something? No, not Rory, of course not. They were Cornish, not Scotsmen. Jory, that was it. With a J."

She was quiet. The silence stretched out so long that Ringan, his nerves already stretched, broke it with a snap.

"Lucy? For Christ's sake, say something, will you?"

"Sorry. It's just that—well, really, I suppose I might as well admit it: I'm surprised by what I found out today."

She stopped. He had a sudden mental image of her at the other end of the duchy, in her summery dress and neatly styled hair, with her calm features and the air of pedantic competence that had rubbed Penny so much the wrong way, both seriously ruffled. "I have a pamphlet in my own collection, a piece of Victoriana. You know the sort of thing, I imagine—very pious churchman, fancying himself the chronicler of the Glories of Cornwall. He had a section about the local Camborne family—they're quite distant from the main family. And I found a brief mention about a family tragedy in 1481 or thereabouts."

She stopped again. The sense of her gathering her thoughts and her courage alike was so clear, it was nearly tangible.

"It mentioned Hywel Camborne. It also mentioned that he'd lost his oldest son and his daughter in a very short time. There's a paragraph in my Victorian booklet, about how the winter of 1481 was a very bad one, with serious storms—of course, Cornwall relies heavily on our fishing industry—this was well before the days of the tin mines. And the book didn't give the daughter's name. But the son . . ."

"Perran?" He spoke gently, quietly. The meaning behind her reaction, her surprise, had just come clear to him: she hadn't believed a word of it. Lucy was a pure sceptic; it had taken her own discovery of a third party, dead over a hundred years, offering up corroboration, to get her to even question her own disbelief. "The father was called Hywel and the son was called Perran? Is that it?"

"Yes. But there's more. I found a reference on the Internet to the local Cambornes from that year—once I had the time frame to hand, the search became a good deal simpler. It led to some archival records from the land grants and estates from the end of the fifteenth century. That boy who died, Perran, was apparently the heir to the estate. When he died, the estate came to his half-brother. Apparently, the two older children were Hywel's with his first wife. But he'd remarried, and he and his wife had an infant son of their own, a child called Pasco. He was three years old or so when Perran and his sister both died."

"And . . . ?" There was something going on, he thought; she was holding something back. If he'd read Lucy properly, she had no taste for drama, none at all. If she was reluctant to share, either she wasn't sure that what she had was fact, or else she was sure, didn't want to be sure, and was badly rattled. "Lucy, talk to me. I really can't afford to waste time playing ring around the roses with the facts—too much is happening and it's happening too damned fast. What is it?"

"Pasco's mother—Hywel's second wife." The rebuke had stung; her voice had smoothed out. "Her name was Elyor. I realise that isn't a precise match with what Rebecca said—she said it was Eleanor. But it would be a logical thing for Rebecca to hear, surely? Eleanor is common, Elyor is not. I do feel that's close enough to qualify as the fourth point of five."

"There's a fifth point?" *Close*, he thought, they were close to something. He could feel it, taste it.

"Indeed there is: the Cann family. According to Menegue, a potential alliance with what he called the illustrious Cann family was cancelled by the daughter's death. You do realise, Ringan, that's one hundred per cent verification, isn't it, or close to it? We have a father named Hywel, an elder son named Perran, a daughter with some sort of tragedy attached to her, and a stepmother named Elyor. I doubt we can hope for a closer match, especially with the Cann family confirmed for good measure. And yes, I'm surprised. If you want the truth, I didn't think I'd find anything at all. I'm still not certain what's going on here, or how your niece is aware of all this, but it will certainly be interesting to find out. I've had a talk with the county archivist, and he's put me on to a woman in Helston, who apparently specialises in local collectibles. There should be more information for you, after I see her tomorrow."

They were both quiet, Lucy because she had presented her findings and was waiting for Ringan to comment, and Ringan because he was processing. *Got you*, he thought, and his hands curled into fists, his fingers, slippery with the sweat of a warm summer night, sliding on the small cell phone. They had a year, 1481, in which to look. They had a family. They had names. And even more than that, they had the one piece of the puzzle that they'd been lacking in all this.

What Penny had seen during that first horrifying incident, she had seen through the eyes of a dying man. A dying man had been absent from the mix, but that missing piece had just been found: Perran, the man who had seduced and impregnated his own sister, had died, and his sister as well. What they needed now was the truth behind those deaths, and the truth, too, behind a song that not only seemed to have nothing to do with whatever had happened in that stormy winter of 1481, but also had nothing at all to do with the St. Ives Cambornes. Gowan had been very firm about that; he'd found the song in the north of Cornwall . . .

"Ringan?" The silence had gone on long enough for Lucy's liking. "Do you think any of this might be useful? And is there more you'd like me to do?"

"Useful? Yes, of course it is. You've been amazingly fast on this, and speed was just what we needed right now. As for more, there's one thing I'd ask of you for the moment, if you wouldn't mind. Can you find us a place to stay in St. Ives? My thinking is, we need to come back down there and have a look at whatever else there might be in the way of records. St. Ives seems to be the epicentre of all this. My thinking is that we'll spend the night here and be back down there tomorrow night. And we'll need beds."

"Of course—happy to oblige." The unspoken question—*Why not stay at the Camborne house?*—was left unsaid. Lucy's belief or disbelief notwithstanding, the answer was obvious. "I'm sure I can find you suitable accommodations. I gather you feel it's—safe—to bring Becca back to St. Ives?"

"She almost died here, in Tintagel. We're nowhere near St. Ives. And that didn't stop whatever is happening, did it?" It had to stop, he thought; the prospect of trying to explain any of this to his sister and her husband, while paling in comparison to the idea of any lasting damage to his niece, was still enough to make him sick at his stomach. "Besides, I have a strong feeling that the one place she'd be most at risk is at Gowan's little digs. So we'll keep her away from there, and work like navvies to get at the truth. Her mum and dad are due back from Vienna in a week."

"Well, I'm here for whatever help I can offer. I have a decent-sized acquaintance of teachers and librarians, and quite a few of them are local. I'm sure they could help. It's simply a matter of knowing the right questions to ask." Something that might have been amusement coloured her tone. "And hopefully, they won't ask me why I want to know. Because honestly, explaining it to them would be beyond me."

"Right. Look, I ought to ring off, before Penny decides I've had an episode of my own. Oh! One more thing. You asked me something earlier, about whether Becca had nearly drowned. What was that about?"

"Perran Camborne." Her voice was suddenly quiet. "The land grant and estates archival information I told you about. It had what Peter Menegue's bits on the Cambornes didn't have: cause of death. According to the records, Perran Camborne drowned."

Nine

"Good morning to you. Mrs. Williams, is it?"

"Yes, I'm Lucy Williams." Lucy held out a hand. "And you're Ms. Casibel? Thank you for making time to see me, especially on such short notice. What a wonderful shop you've got—I can't believe I didn't know about this place until last night, and me born and bred in St. Austell. And please, call me Lucy."

According to the brass-framed sign that hung above the front door, the shop, a tiny hole-in-the-wall down a side alley in the town of Helston, was called Casibel's Collectibles. A quick glance at the front window would have left a casual passer-by wondering precisely what they were supposed to be collecting; the window display was a glorious jumble, ranging from antique china and crockery to painted miniatures and hand-woven scarves. Had curiosity been piqued to the point of going inside, a good long browse would have enabled most people to make the connection between the oddities: everything in the little shop, from the books to the china dogs to the knitted caps, had not only been made locally but dealt with the subject of Cornwall.

"It really is interesting, isn't it? I'm very fond of the place myself. And if I'm after calling you Lucy, my own name is Hedra." The proprietress took Lucy's hand in a firm, easy grip, and shook it.

"It's a pleasure to meet you. I do hope I've understood what it is you're looking for—you're needing information about some of the early members of the Camborne family, is that right?"

At first sight, Hedra Casibel, towering a good eight inches above Lucy, and with a mass of dark hair that was just going grey at the temples, could have best been described as formidable. Nearly everything about her gave off an impression of strength; from the firm mouth to the strong bones to the direct gaze, she could easily have frightened off a lesser mortal. The overall impression was softened and humanised by her voice, a mellow contralto with the easy, beautiful rhythms of Cornwall lacing through every syllable.

Lucy, after nearly two decades of teaching school to other peoples' children, considered herself essentially impossible to fluster. The problem was, she had already been thrown slightly off balance by the very oddity of the situation she was researching. Craning her neck to take a good look at Hedra Casibel's face, she was reassured by what she saw there. There was an intelligence as formidable as the rest of her, Lucy thought, but there was also kindness, and humour, and a willingness to help.

"Oh, dear, I suppose I wasn't completely clear." That, Lucy thought, was an understatement. Her interior censor, the small voice was inhibiting her from mentioning one word that might give the impression Lucy herself had any belief in ghosts. "Yes, that's it. Actually, to be more specific, I was hoping that you might have something in your Local Interest section. David Westin—the man I spoke to this morning at the county archives—recommended that I get hold of you. He thought you might be able to help me."

"Oh, so it was David who sent you along? I didn't realise." Hedra's voice, already musical and relaxed, was suddenly full of friendliness, as well. "Of course, I'm always glad to help an associate of his. He's a dear man, isn't he? Very sweet. A very old friend, and very helpful to me. Of course, the help is mutual—David has a passion for estate sales, but bless the man, he has absolutely no eye."

"So he gives you the word on where the sales are, you go along and cherry-pick the things you want to keep, and share the bits he'd like?"

Hedra, edging her way into a tiny room at the back of the shop that apparently served as her office, cast a look back and down over her shoulder. It was a perfect blend of amusement and appreciation at Lucy's astuteness, and it was as feminine as it was conspiratorial.

"Of course. And I don't charge him anything in the way of a mark-up; I don't believe in profiting from one's friends. Besides, we like very different things, so it's all after balancing out in the end, really." She settled into a very modern swivel chair behind a lovely antique writing desk and motioned Lucy toward the chair on the visitor's side. "Please, do make yourself comfortable, Lucy. Now, what's all this about the Cambornes? First of all, how far back are you looking? I've culled a few things for you, but I want to make certain I've got the time frame right."

"Specifically? The year I'm researching is 1481." The shop, despite the heat of the Cornish summer baking streets from Helston to Bude to Padstow, was blessedly cool, an oasis of shadow and calm. "I found a source on the Internet, from the county archive, that gave me some of the family's names from that exact year. So I rang up the archivist this morning—that was your friend, David Westin—and I told him what I was looking for, and he put me on to you. I do hope you don't mind me wanting to come straight here. I've got less than a week to sort this out and get as much information as I can." It felt oddly wrong to stonewall Hedra Casibel, who was clearly willing to help, but for the life of her, Lucy simply couldn't bring herself to offer up the genuine reason. "The—project I'm working on has a deadline attached."

"Well, I'm happy to give whatever help I can." If Hedra had noticed that tiny break in Lucy's speech, she wasn't saying so. "And yes, it seems I chose the right timeframe, after all. I should be clear: I'm no sort of expert on the Cambornes or on any particular local family, but I do have a fairly extensive collection of papers that either source from or cite the local landed gentry. I had a look through my personal catalogue after you rang this morning, and I found three items I think you may find helpful."

"Thank you." Lucy, looking around the small room, found herself wondering where in this extremely limited space Hedra Casibel generally stored valuable documents, especially anything old enough to need climate controls. Certainly, she thought, there was no possible nook or cranny in which to hide a collection Hedra had described as fairly extensive . . .

As if she'd caught at Lucy's thought, Hedra smiled suddenly. "The collection doesn't live here, by the way—I maintain special storage for it. The Inland Revenue lets me write that off as a business expense. Most of what I have is a good deal more recent than the period you want, but there are two pieces of documentation from the actual year in question, as well as one other thing, and they all deal in one way or another with the St. Ives Cambornes. So there's a stroke of luck. Here, do you have enough light? I'm afraid that even for David I'm not willing to let these leave the premises— they're far too valuable. Any reading will have to be done in here."

"No, I quite understand." Lucy, eyeing the short stack, was aware of a pleasant flutter somewhere along her nervous system. It was a familiar feeling and gave her notice of one of the few things that could cause that particular flutter: information, there and ready to her hand, as seen through the eyes of someone who had been there, been alive, been a witness to history.

She was not a historian. Professionally, she'd never felt justified in even laying claim to being specifically a teacher of history, although the high points of Cornish history, both social and political, were certainly part of the normal curriculum she taught. But there was something about that small pile on Hedra Casibel's desk, about what looked to be a letter written in the exquisite penmanship and faded ink of antiquity, about what might be a painted miniature covered in a preserving cloth, about the ledger bound in oiled sheep's leather that had faded over the centuries to nearly colourless, that sent Lucy's usually staid nerves off into an anticipatory tingling.

She reached out and touched the topmost item, which was the letter. She was surprised to find her every muscle tense. Suppose it verified what Rebecca had told her? Would that have to be considered proof of something, empirical evidence that would force her to acknowledge what she had never believed?

Nonsense, she thought, *just get on with it.* She lifted her gaze to Hedra's. "May I?"

"Yes, of course. I know I needn't remind you to be careful. And here—slip these on before you handle anything. This is white glove territory. I'm slowly taking photographs of what I have, but I've started at the most recent and I'm working my way back, chronologically speaking. I haven't got to the older stuff yet. These are the originals."

The letter, written in a thick sloping script in what had once been a clean dark ink, was dated, addressed, and signed. Lucy, her hands safely encased in white cotton gloves, squinted down, trying to bring the words, with their idiomatic spelling and period phrasing, into some kind of focus.

Unto my own good wyfe, Ladye Wenna Cann, beloved of herte, on this ninth day of February, my closest greetyings. I wryte in sadness, as husband, in my duty as father, with much gryfe, from the north coast wherein lie those other acres of Camborne lands.

All here is sorrow, and with a herte sore and heavy, I share that our son Cador goes from this day bereft of his bryde. Four days past did that nurse to whose duty it fell to attend Hywel Camborne's daughtyr, young Jenna, find her charge missynge from her bed. I had not seen the girl, nor spokyne with her, since I have come here—she was to her own chamber confyned, with some internal disorder.

Now she is gone. A great and diligent search they did undertayke, with many prayers spoken to Almighty God, that the maid might be found safe and well in lyfe and limb.

Such was not to be, and with heaviness of herte I give unto you, most beloved wyfe and moder of Cador in who rests all the hope for our House, such news as will make for much gryfe. Our son's chosen bride is with God, drowned in the sea—such was His will. The daughter of Hywel Camborne this mornynge was espied, her lifeless bodye floating to land where the tide did carry her, to the south and around toward Port Isaac and Padstow, by two fisher folk who had set their boat out upon the water, where swim grayte number of pylchard.

Hywel himself has fallen deep into silence, so great is his sorrow and shock at this hearynge. On this mattyr, let there be none who find blame for him, for now he has lost two children of three, and lost all that remained to him of the Lady Jenifer. That daughter whose birthynge did take her moder's lyfe hath left him, her moder unto God to follow, and he left with nowt of what he so did value. Such loss as this, son and daughter so close apart in life and death, must brynge such affliction as to overset all reason. Nor has his herte had such time as must be given to recover, his heir having died so soon before.

Therefore I do direct thee, goodwyfe, that you might give our son this word: his bride hath to the bosom of Almyghte God been taken, and he must forewith learn to love another. Let him understand in this mattyr, that no other choice is offered. Yet let him believe, goodwyfe, that his weddynge, tho delayed, will yet come with the summer, and that of all things, this will be it is first of my busyness to arraynge for his benefit.

My busyness here being so concluded, and the roads being clear, let you look for me at home again in three days time. For I would not willyngly distract Hywel by puttynge upon him the weight of care that might yet upset him, in mind or spirit. And there is no place anywhere to give me rest in more happyness than within the shelter of our own roof at Ancell, with you, my goodwyfe, fayrest among women.

God rest ye, from yr welebeloved goodman, Jory Cann.

The shop was quiet and cool. Outside, in the streets of Helston, tourists wandered, taking photos, wondering where to eat, deciding how to spend their day. Local shopkeepers sold trinkets and pasties and bottled water, reaping the economic benefits of the swarms of visitors to the warm coastal waters and welcoming hospitality Cornwall offered.

Lucy swallowed. Something about the letter, with its simple eloquent look through a tiny porthole back through the years, into a day in the life of a husband and wife who had been dust for five centuries, had affected her in a way she couldn't put a name to. Perhaps, she thought, it was a question of just how intimate the letter was; it made her feel almost uncomfortably voyeuristic. Or perhaps it was how easy they must have been with each other, something she recognised, something that made her think of Cian.

"It's an interesting letter, isn't it?" Hedra was watching her guest's face. "Very sad, too. That poor child. It does make you wonder what on earth she was doing in the sea; it's not as if splashing about out there was a done thing back in the fifteenth century. If you're curious about that last bit, by the way, Cador Cann did find himself another girl to marry—I looked it up. She came from a wealthy family near Bodmin. But do tell me—is this of any use for your project?"

"Oh, yes." There was a slight frown of concentration between her brows. Something was wrong, unexpected. It took her a moment to work it out, but suddenly, there it was, clear in her mind: *the north coast wherein lie those other acres of Camborne lands . . . her lyfeless bodye floating to land where the tide did carry her, to the south and around toward Port Isaac and Padstow . . .* "There's one thing puzzling me, though—I thought we were talking about the Camborne family from St. Ives? Because this is written from somewhere up the coast; he mentions the north coast and then he tells his wife that the girl's body floated south from where they were, and it mentions Padstow and Port Isaac. Was this a different branch of the family, do you know? A northern spur, perhaps?"

"No, this was the local branch of the family." Hedra sounded very sure of herself. "They probably owned land up north, as well—quite a few families, landed gentry with money and property, had roots deep into their home community but who had married families with property in other points around the duchy and became associated with more than one town. I suspect that would be the case here. Maybe the poor girl's mother had been from that part of the world—north coast, is it? Possibly Bude, or Camelford, or Tintagel. Good heavens, have I said something upsetting? You've gone quite pale."

"No, I'm fine." Lucy swallowed hard. "As a matter of fact, Tintagel has been mentioned in another context, in this project. It would be useful to confirm or disprove that—I wonder if it's possible. Do you think your friend David might be able to check that for me?"

"Of course." Hedra pushed her chair back and stood. "You stay here and have a nice look at the rest of the goodies, and I'll see if David's still in the office. I doubt this will take very long."

Alone in the small room, Lucy, despite having been given free rein, left the rest of the pile untouched for a few minutes. She had become aware of an interesting dichotomy, an odd split in her mind: one half was struggling to accept what seemed to be a torrent of confirmation of a specific set of facts, while the other half was frantically juggling the very existence of that confirmation with her own pragmatism, which insisted that what she had just confirmed was impossible for Rebecca Eisler to have known about in the first place.

"All right, then." She spoke aloud, breathing the words rather than fully articulating them. The situation was absurd, she told herself. It was preposterous. And Cian had been right, as usual—the best way to deal was to step outside the reality of what she was looking at and concentrate on gathering the facts, rather than judging them or debating how a teenage girl in the twenty-first century, who had never set foot in Cornwall before, could have known about them. Lucy's job was to gather the available data and organise it. Neither her belief or disbelief in the situation nor her understanding of how it might be possible came into it.

Which was all very well, she thought. But it was easier said than done. Suppose it turned out that Jenna Camborne had drowned at Tintagel? What then? Becca, swimming in the cove at Arthur's Castle, had suffered some sort of seizure and nearly drowned. Ringan had said she'd come out of it, speaking when she shouldn't have been able to speak. The girl herself, writing down her answers to her uncle's questions because the muscles of her throat were raw from choking on the same seawater that had drowned Jenna Camborne, had known about Jory Cann, known he was the father of the boy who would have been Jenna's bridegroom. And that was more confirmation that Lucy's honesty would not let her dismiss or shrug away.

She let her breath out, a long sigh of resignation mixed with determination. There would be time enough, tomorrow or the day after that or maybe never, to think about how or why any of this was happening. At the moment, she simply didn't have that luxury; time was at a premium, not to be squandered, and must be devoted to assembling those facts.

She reached out and took up the cloth-wrapped object that she'd thought might contain a miniature. Sliding it free of its protective wrapping, she caught her breath once more.

It was indeed a painting, very small and fine, formally painted on wood, its edges gilded with what looked to be gold leaf. It was in very fine condition for such old work; the cloth covering, obviously modern in origin, had a label attached to it, something that looked to have been run off on a laser printer. Setting the miniature down and lifting the cloth to the light, Lucy read the label: *Late 15th century. Subject is thought to be Pasco Camborne, aged approx. seven years old, artist unknown.*

She took up the painting, moved in a way that was new to her. It nestled in the palms of her glove-clad hands, the solemn face of a very young boy, with his stare seemingly fixed on some point just over the viewer's shoulder. Painted in the flat-faced style of the period, he was nevertheless somehow vital and lively: dark-haired, the hair smooth and cropped close to the skull. There were long vertical dimples bracketing his mouth, dimples that reminded Lucy of Penny's. What really caught her were his eyes, oversized and dark grey, the colour of the sea as it was touched by a storm on the distant horizon. . . .

"Oh, good, you found the portrait." Hedra, still carrying her cordless phone and a small notepad, had come back. "Isn't it an exquisite little thing? It's very rare to find a miniature from that period outside a gallery or a museum—that one came from an estate sale near Sennen, and I keep meaning to contact the Camborne family and seeing if they want to buy it, but I keep forgetting to do that. Oh, Lucy, I'm sorry, did I make you jump? I wasn't trying to startle you."

"That's all right." She wasn't sure she was all right; she hadn't heard Hedra come back in, and her heart was slamming. She slipped the miniature back inside its protective covering and tried to steady her nerves. "And yes, it's a charming piece of work. If you're seriously thinking about selling it to the Camborne family, I can probably be of help there. It's a family of one, these days; Gowan Camborne is the last local survivor, and he plays music with my husband, so I can easily introduce you, if you'd like. Were you able to get hold of David Westin?"

"Yes, I did, and he had me hold while he looked it up. The St. Ives Cambornes did in fact have land holdings on the north coast, between Camelford and Tintagel." She set the phone on the desk and peered at her scribbled notes. "Ah, here we go. It seems that Hywel Camborne's first wife was a Jenifer Penwythen, and came from there. The estate was part of her dowry, what she brought to the marriage. After she died, her husband inherited the property. But all that is usual. Have you looked at the register? It's fairly boring, most of it—household accounts, farm transactions, all of that. But there was one entry I thought you might want, just about at the halfway point. I've marked the place—it's that yellow slip. And by the way, I don't know if this matters to your project or not, but I got this at the same estate sale the miniature came from."

The register was heavy, but the ink used seemed to have been of the same durable quality as that used in Jory Cann's letter to his wife. Lucy, carefully slipping her forefinger between the marked pages, lifted the earlier pages free.

2nd Apryl—in accordance with Squyre Hywel's wish, those church moneys sett asyde for Monuments to their Remembrance in names of Perran and Jenna Camborne today are returned to household coffers.

"Interesting stuff, there. Isn't it?"

Lucy jerked her head up. Hedra was back in her chair. Her voice was calm, a bit detached.

"Yes. Yes, it is."

"You know, I can't help wondering who Perran and Jenna were?" Hedra had taken the clothed miniature and the letter, pulling them lightly back over to her own side of the table. "Husband and wife, maybe? Whoever they were, after having some clout in the parish, it would seem they managed to annoy someone enough to be denied headstones."

Right around the time Lucy was thanking Hedra Casibel for her help and getting permission to copy out the exact contents of both the letter and the register notation about the denial of the dead children's headstones, Ringan was requesting seating for a party of three, for a lunch of fish and the local thick soup, in a seaside restaurant a few kilometres north of Newquay.

The drive south had been taken slowly and carefully. He and Penny were equally exhausted; neither of them had wanted to risk leaving Becca alone, and they'd decided that the most sensible course of action would be to take turns snatching what rest they could. Unfortunately, Tintagel was at the height of its seasonal tourist invasion, and Mrs. Polgarren had no spare rollaway beds. Once Becca had fallen back into normal sleep in her own narrow bed, neither of them had wanted to wake her and move her next door to their room. The result had been intermittent naps for what remained of the night, sitting upright in the straight-backed chairs.

"Aunt Penny, are you all right?" Becca's voice was still raspy, and she was using it as infrequently as possible. Penny had noticed, as if from a distance, that the girl kept putting one hand up to rub her throat. "You look awfully uncomfortable."

"I'm fine, thanks." That was polite rubbish, and they both knew it; she wasn't anything like all right. Between a night in the chair and driving the coast road south to St. Ives, her neck had got a decided crick in it, and she was noticing the first ominous flutters of light on her peripheral vision that usually signalled one of her rare migraines. "Just a bit stiff, and I'm fighting off a headache. I need the loo—Ringan, can you order for me? Whatever you're getting is fine."

Ringan had opted for an outdoor table, and the restaurant's outdoor seating was perched above the water. It offered an easy breeze and a view of the ocean crashing into the rocky land that was straight out of a gothic romance novel. Penny got up and headed indoors, weaving her way between tables and hungry diners. Ringan's voice faded out behind her; he sounded just as distracted and tired as she was herself. As she smiled vaguely at a passing waiter, she heard Ringan telling his niece that she ought to stick with soft stuff, like a good soup, until her throat eased up.

Alone in the restroom, Penny held her wrists under cold running water, and splashed her face as well. Catching sight of her own face in the mirror, she paused for a moment, examining it dispassionately. It occurred to her that she looked like hell, and her lips twitched into a rueful smile. When they'd left Glastonbury for a week in Cornwall, the idea had been a nice relaxing holiday: sunning on the coast, splashing in the sea, some live music thrown in. However this little jaunt was going to figure in her memory in years to come, the word "relaxing" wasn't likely to be found anywhere.

She locked herself in a stall, just sitting, leaning her cheek against the wall. The tiles were cool, and soothing against her skin; she could feel the tic, which always seemed to accompany her migraines, beginning a steady, unwelcome rhythm just beside her right eye.

She hadn't actually needed the loo. What she'd wanted was a few minutes of precious quiet, the ability to close her eyes and come to terms with her exhaustion. She was so tired that even yawning took all her energy. Between watching over Becca, getting the story of Jenny Wilbury and her suicide out of Gowan, and waiting until dawn yesterday morning to make sure Becca was all right before she napped herself, she'd started out on the Tintagel trip already short on rest. Becca's near-death in the Celtic Sea had put the tin cupola on it. She seemed to have reached that rarefied state of awareness that goes hand in hand with sleep deprivation. The effect reminded her of how she felt on the rare occasions she drank brandy: there was a complete separation between her sluggish body and a preternaturally clear mind, a kind of detachment.

She closed her eyes, feeling the first brutal thump of the migraine, and let her mind do what it wanted. Something had been niggling, twitching under her awareness, much the way the tic was twitching under her skin. She'd been too preoccupied with the physical necessity of coping with Becca to look at it, but here it was, an equation, a question, a reason to wonder.

Whatever had happened to Becca—whatever was still happening to Becca—had something to do with that song. She flatly refused to believe otherwise; she'd sooner believe in aliens or unicorns than believe this could be coincidence. Gowan had been playing the damned thing when Penny herself had heard and seen and felt through the incredulous, disbelieving eyes of a dying man. Becca's seizure onstage at the Duke's Own had been during the Tin Miners' performance of it. There wasn't any way she was buying that as coincidence.

The door to the restroom opened and closed, and Penny heard women's voices chattering cheerfully in Spanish. She stayed where she was, tuning them out. Had she tried to stand just then, she would probably have sat straight back down again, so shaky were her legs. The migraine was blossoming like a weed.

Penny sighed, and winced with the pain of the movement. Her migraines might not be frequent, but she'd had them often enough over the years to know the pattern. She'd had the sparkle at the edge of her vision, and the hot, electric twitch under the skin. She was just now having the shaky legs, vertigo, and actual pain; next up, she thought, was the nausea and the desire to either cry or sleep, preferably both. The migraine, true to its own historical pattern, was running its usual course. There was a certain consistency to these headaches, and Penny could have set her watch to their progression and their effects on her. She wasn't going anywhere for a few minutes yet.

That song, "New-Slain Knight." Where, exactly, had Gowan got it? And why had he insisted they do it? He really did seem to have some sort of personal attachment to it, yet he himself insisted it had nothing to do with him. Nor did Penny think he was being untruthful about that. But she didn't think he'd given her the entire story, either, and Becca's safety, her freedom from whatever was happening to her, might easily depend on a simple fact that hadn't yet seen the light of day. She was going to find him, Penny thought grimly. Once they'd got back to St. Ives and settled into whatever lodgings the infuriatingly competent Lucy Williams had no doubt hunted up for them, she was damned well going to ask him.

Even that, though, wasn't the question that had suddenly shown itself, forcing her to look at it. What was bothering her was something Ringan had said about the song itself. After a row over including that particular song in the set, they'd actually played the song through, and Becca'd had no reaction. In fact, if Penny was remembering properly, Ringan had said they'd run through the song not once but twice. What else had he said? That not only had

Becca not had any negative reaction to it at all, she'd played some outstanding lines on her fiddle.

Yet performing the same song a few hours later, onstage at the Duke's, Becca had gone into some sort of fit and found herself with her head in Perran Camborne's lap. And Penny herself had reacted the day before, just from Gowan's little solo run of playing it on the piano. What was different? What had changed, between two people experiencing violent reactions to the song and the lack of any reaction at all?

You, that's what. You, and the house. Maybe just one, maybe both together.

"Penny? Are you there? Food's coming soon."

She jumped. Becca's voice, on the other side of the stall's door, was nervous even through the rasp.

"Yes, almost done. Sorry—I've got hit with a bear of a migraine and I'm just sitting it out. They make me dizzy for the first few minutes." *Get her out of here, close your eyes, look at it, see it clearly, get her out of here.* It was ridiculous, Penny thought, how normal her own voice was. She certainly didn't feel normal. "You get back to the table—I'll be out as soon as my legs want to work again. Oh, and tell your uncle to order me a bottled water, all right? I've got to take some pain meds and I'm as dry as a bone."

"I will." Becca hesitated; Penny, opening her eyes for a queasy moment, saw her feet. "You're sure you're okay?"

"Absolutely." *Is it me? Gowan's house? Both?* "I'll be out in a sec. Off you go."

The restroom door closed behind Becca. Penny, already working on the problem at hand, heard neither the girl's footsteps nor the click of the door. Her brain, still detached from the pain surrounding it, had ratcheted its way up and found another gear. She was thinking clearly and without shying away from the possibilities.

Had anything unnatural, or even particularly peculiar, happened to Becca while Penny had been elsewhere? It was a fair question. What was more, this wasn't even the first time Penny had been confronted with the issue. Jane Castle, vocalist and flautist in Ringan's band, Broomfield Hill, had nearly died while the band was playing the Arts Festival at Callowen House, the ancestral home of the Leight-Arnold family. And that had been a near-catastrophic result of the very combination that seemed to be threatening Becca now: the house itself, the song, and Penny herself, acting as a kind of supernatural switch, or battery, or something, somehow making it possible in the first place.

Penny opened her eyes slowly and cautiously. The dazzle was still there and likely would be until she got back to the table, hunted some pain meds out of her purse, and took some serious steps to knock the migraine back. Her stomach was rebellious, doing unpleasant little flips. Unappealing as the thought of eating was just then, she knew from long experience that food would help. It was time to go back and try to keep some lunch down. She just hoped Ringan hadn't ordered her anything too intensely fishy; if she got back and found clams waiting for her, she was going to be straight back in the loo.

She made her way back to the table and got there at the same time as the waiter bringing their food. Expertly juggling crockery, the waiter slid a plate piled high with different varieties of fried seafood in front of Ringan. Penny, dizzy, settled into her chair; she was carefully not looking down at the movement of the sea below them. The water and rocks suddenly seemed very far down indeed.

As she settled into her chair, the breeze caught a fragrant trail of steam from the bowl in front of her, and she sighed with relief. Ringan had got her the same soup he'd ordered for Becca, and there was a basket of lovely rustic bread, and a small plate of fresh-baked local pasties on the side. The food smelled absolutely wonderful.

"Here you are. Let's eat, shall we? I'd like to get back to St. Ives while it's still daylight." Ringan, watching Penny reach for her spoon, saw her hands were trembling slightly and lifted one eyebrow at her. They'd been together for fifteen years and more, and it was perfectly obvious to him that she'd thought of something or had sussed something out. This wasn't the moment to ask her about it, though; those shaky hands usually meant a migraine. Besides, Becca was sitting there.

He remembered sitting in Pandora's front passenger seat, trying to decide how to answer Becca's question about Gowan in a way that was suitable to her age. He'd wondered, then, how parents coped with that constant need for self-censorship; with a shock, he realised that conversation had taken place less than a week ago. So much had happened between now and then, it might as well have been years ago.

Shaking his head, he brought his attention back to Penny. "This do you, lamb? Not too fishy, is it?"

"No, not at all. It smells gorgeous. Just let me take some stuff for this damned headache, and I can really tuck in." There was some sort of alchemy in the local cookery, she thought. There had to be, because despite the headache, she was actually hungry.

She got her pills, washed them down with the bottled water Ringan had got, and tucked into her soup. There was no conversation at all during the meal; Becca's throat was in no state to allow her to chatter, and Penny and Ringan were each busy with their own thoughts. Neither of them realised that they had come to similar conclusions.

Ringan, forking up succulent mouthfuls of the fresh seafood, found himself wondering much the same thing that Penny had been asking herself about. He'd in fact been thinking about it since Penny's first reaction to hearing Gowan play the damned song he seemed so attached to. The subsequent threat to his niece had pushed it down the ladder of Ringan's attention, but he was looking at it again now, and no matter which way he turned it, he simply couldn't make any sense of it.

Was it possible that Penny's mere presence, her sensitivity to what stayed unseen for most others, had sparked something to life in a house already haunted? Yes, he thought, as he chewed on a fried prawn. That aspect, at least, was not only possible, it was nearly a certainty. If there was something waiting in the shadows for the sensitive to bring it to life, Penny was right there to do it. When it came to waking up ghosts, she had an unenviable ability to be in the wrong place at the wrong time.

That took him straight to the second part of the recipe, for every haunting he'd seen to date: the location. His own cottage, Penny's London theatre, the Leight-Arnold family's country estate, an empty patch of land on London's Isle of Dogs—in every instance, the place had seen violence, death, something. Nothing happened in a vacuum.

He speared something unidentifiable from one side of his plate and bit into it. It turned out to be a mushroom.

Right, he thought, and chewed. The bloke Penny had felt die, the pregnant girl who had taken such a hold of Becca, with her head resting in the lap of the older brother who was also her seducer—it was a sure bet they came with the Gowan house, those people, or at least with the land this particular incarnation of the house was built on. After all, it wasn't as if the ghosts had bought cheap day returns at Victoria Station and trundled down to the Camborne house for an outing. Whoever they'd been, they'd lived there. Their lives, their deaths, had been a part of this landscape, this territory, this history. And what was more, if what Lucy had found out was accurate, they looked to have died there, as well.

Up to that point, Ringan decided, it was about as cut and dried as anything so ludicrous as a haunting could be. It was internally consistent; it made sense. They had three out of three of the ingredients: Penny's presence. The location that had presumably been the original scene of whatever tragedy had triggered the haunting. And they had a song.

And that, he thought grimly, was where the whole lot fell apart. The damned song had never been part of the Camborne family's legend; Gowan said he'd learned it from an old woman up in the north of the duchy years ago. And while they knew, from bitter experience, that the song lyric rarely reflected anything other than an incomplete truth at best and a deliberately twisted version at worst, Ringan simply couldn't make the thing fit. Gowan singing the damned song should have had no more effect than Ringan himself singing it, or some girl with a zither in a bedroom somewhere in Middle America, or the King of Spain. It had nothing to do with Gowan.

Ringan poured himself some water and pushed away the yearning for a pint of cider, knowing he'd be driving the rest of the way south. He was busy running the song lyric through his mind. Where did the points touch? Where did Jenna Camborne, who'd found a sympathetic shadowy corner in Becca, match the nameless girl in the song, who'd had such a cruel trick played on her? There were places where they matched up, certainly: young girls, much of an age, and of Becca's age group, as well—and that was another thing he hadn't stopped to consider until now, the fact that adolescents had long been associated with things like poltergeist activity. So it was possible that Becca would have been at least susceptible, even without Penny being there to power up the past. . . . What else? Jenna and the girl in the song, both pregnant.

Don't forget the dead bloke in the garden.

Ringan set his fork down, not thinking. *That's right,* he thought. There was a dead man in both song and vision, a dead man in a garden. Penny had felt him, *been* him. Granted, the bloke in the song hadn't actually been dead, but that had been the trick, the claim that gave the song its name in the first place. *This dreary sight that I hae seen unto my heart gives pain; at the south side o' your father's garden, I see a knight lies slain.*

And that, Ringan thought glumly, was it, finis, the end of the line. Everywhere else, there was divergence. What was even worse, the main point where Becca's haunting seemed a perfect fit with the history of the Camborne family—with Jenna and her brother Perran—had been blown apart by Penny's vision.

If the lyric was false or wrong—if the trick had been no trick, but a genuine dead man, a knight slain in a garden—it hadn't been Perran Camborne. Perran, it seemed, had drowned. But the man Penny had felt die had been slain by that girl with the grey eyes. The lack of air in his lungs had come from the stone that she'd used to crush his throat, not from those same lungs filling with sea water . . .

I used to know a girl. She had eyes like yours.

Ringan had picked up his glass. Now he set it down again. For some reason, his senses had just gone on high alert, and his memory was working. Who had said that? Gowan, to Becca, at their first meeting, outside on the front steps of the St. Ives house that had been in Gowan's family for longer than anyone could remember, the house built on Camborne land.

A young girl, certainly unbalanced, madly in love perhaps, or maybe just obsessed with the older man, the charming piano player twice her age. And she'd died there, in the house.

"Ringan?"

She'd died there, that girl. What was her name again? Right— Jenny something or other. She'd died there, stripping herself naked, climbing the stairs to the room with the big ceiling beams, the room where she'd shared a bed with him. Penny had given him that conversation, omitting no detail that she could remember, knowing Becca had somehow been touched, knowing it might matter.

A girl with big grey eyes, knotting a rope, throwing it over the big beam, leaving an echo of herself, an imprint perhaps. Leaving him something to remember her by.

Eyes like Becca's, yes. But whose eyes had looked down at Penny, as she'd felt a man gurgle and choke the last of his earthly life away, in agony and incomprehension and disbelief? Jenny or Jenna?

It had to be Jenna, he thought. Penny had heard, thought, felt, in Cornish. Jenny Wilbury—that was it, the suicide's last name, Wilbury—was, had been, American. The girl with the grey eyes in Penny's vision had killed a Cornish man; from what Penny had shared of the experience, all his thoughts had been in Cornish.

Two pairs of grey eyes had dealt with death on that bit of land. No, three pairs—there was his niece to consider, as well. How many people were haunting Gowan's cute little cottage? How many layers of death had left a signature . . . ?

"Oi! Ringan, come back, will you?"

Penny's poke, one forefinger jabbed at his forearm, brought him out of his reverie. The waiter was hovering. Did they want coffee, tea, a look at the sweet trolley . . . ?

Out in the carpark, with Penny in the passenger seat beside him and Becca fastening her safety belt in the back, Ringan dug his cell phone free of his pocket.

"Hang on—I'll just be a minute." He was scrolling back through his recently dialled numbers, peering down at each one, his beard bristling. He'd purchased the damned phone at Penny's insistence, and he'd been using it for months now, but it still managed to make him feel a total fool, fumbling with it. He'd long since decided it was a piece of technology he was never going to really bond with; its usefulness, in Ringan's eyes, was essentially a form of détente. "I want to ring Lucy Williams and find out where we're dossing down tonight. Back in a minute."

"Hello?" Lucy answered the phone on the first ring. Ringan had the sudden image of her in his mind's eye, sitting with the phone ready to hand, waiting for it to ring. "Ringan, is that you?"

"Yes. I was ringing to check in—we've just finished lunch in a seaside place north of Newquay. Please tell me you managed to find us a place to catch some kip tonight, because if it comes down to Gowan's or the car, we're sleeping in the car. And since we both spent the night trying to sleep in chairs, I really don't want to do that. Was there anything available? And while I've got you on the line and no one's listening, have you found out anything else?"

"Indeed and I have, so that's yes to both." She sounded a good deal less placid and didactic than he'd yet heard her. Had something shaken her out of her complacency? "I've arranged accommodations at a place called the Smugglers, a small guest house here in town. I'm afraid it's going to be a bit cramped for space, just for tonight. There was only one room available—but there's an additional room that's sure to come open tomorrow morning, and I've asked her to hold it for you. Have you got something to write with?"

He took the address down. "And it's actually close to Gowan's place, just down the road, really," she told him. "Not that anything in St. Ives is all that far from anything else, but you know the area quite well."

"Ta, Lucy." Definitely less didactic; he would have thought a situation like this one, something where she had sole charge of all the information, would have turned her into some sort of robotic super-schoolmarm. Instead, she sounded just this side of flustered.

A movement from inside the Jag caught his eye, and he turned. Penny had lifted her wrist and was tapping her watch, in the classic gesture of impatience: *Mind the time, let's get on with it!* "Look, Lucy, I've got Penny and Becca waiting in the car. Penny's giving me the evil eye out the side window and my niece looks to be snoring. Can we have dinner or something, and you can tell us what you found out then? We should be down there within a couple of hours. Once we check in, we can hopefully get a bit of kip. We should be closer to being functional then. We're all seriously fried."

"Yes, let's." She hesitated. "Ringan? I do think there's one thing you ought to know before you ring off."

"Really? Something you found out?" He had his hand on Pandora's driver's side door. "I'm listening. What is it?"

"It's about Jenna Camborne. She drowned, just like her brother. But it didn't happen in St. Ives." This time, the pause was audible; Lucy, the unflappable and unshakeable, was having breathing issues. "She died in the waters off Tintagel."

Ten

O I will shoe your fu fair foot,
And I will glove your hand;
And I'll be father to your bairn,
Since your love's dead and gane.

Just after sunset that evening, a group of five people—Lucy, Gowan, and the three travellers—found themselves on a spit of land known as the Island, settling onto one of the long stone benches in the lengthening shadow of St. Nicholas Chapel.

Four of them had eaten a quick supper together. Lucy had been disinclined to go over the information she'd managed to gather; as she pointed out, Gowan was going to need to hear it as well, and she really didn't see the point in telling it twice. She seemed to Ringan to have recovered a lot of her placidity. The feeling he'd got from her earlier, the sense that she'd been shaken off her balance, had gone completely. The Lucy they'd met, the complacent school-marm who'd set Penny's teeth on edge, was firmly back in place.

"I meant to tell you, I rang Gowan after I spoke to you, Ringan." She'd finished her food, and was dabbing her lips with a serviette. "I asked him to meet us over by the chapel, on the Island; I thought I could share what I managed to find out with all of you at once. After all, you did say time was essential. Saving time seems a good idea, don't you agree?"

The restaurant, the local Chinese eat-in, was crowded; Lucy, knowing how quickly the queue of tourists could grow into an hour-long wait, had reserved them an early table.

"You're quite right, as usual." Penny had finished eating. "It was a very good idea."

Ringan bit his lip; there was no missing the ironic edge to her voice. She went on, her voice unchanged. "Thanks for finding us the digs for tonight, by the way—I'm sure it wasn't easy, finding anything at all at such short notice. But I never doubted you'd be able to find something."

Ringan kicked her under the table. It was a light kick, and she made no acknowledgement. It occurred to him, with a sinking feeling at the pit of his stomach, that his lady love was too far over the wrong edge of exhaustion to keep up any sort of facade. It was a pity, he thought, that the first thing to disappear when Penny got overtired was her patience.

Of course, it was also a pity that Lucy rubbed her so very much the wrong way. And really, however much Lucy might get on Penny's nerves, they owed her. She'd got it done, not only in the matter of a bed and a roof over their heads, but in getting what they needed: solid historical information.

"Well—I hope you're comfortable there." If Lucy had noticed that sharp, ironic edge, Ringan thought, she was making a damned good job of either hiding or ignoring it. Becca, who had slept in the car from Newquay and for another solid hour once they'd reached St. Ives, wasn't noticing anything beyond her plate; she was eating with the appetite and gusto of a young lioness. Her uncle, watching her pour soy sauce over her third helping, found himself wondering where on such a slender girl all that food could possibly be going.

"Quite." Penny sighed, a long intake of breath. "Sorry. I'm tired. So what's the plan, then? Are we walking over to the Island? It's not far, is it?"

"Nothing in St. Ives is far, not really." Lucy looked at Becca. "When everyone's finished? Good. I'll ring Gowan, and have him come up and meet us, then."

He was waiting for them when they got there. Ringan, skirting stones, spotted his old friend propped against the chapel's outer wall. For a moment, Ringan wondered if Gowan was sleeping; his long legs were stretched out in front of him, the fading sunlight just touching his shoes.

"Gowan?" Ringan got a look at his friend's face, and stopped. "Bloody hell, mate, you look like seven flavours of hell! What's wrong?"

"Wrong? Nothing, really." He straightened his back, and sat up. "Lucy was after telling me you had a near tragedy, up on the north coast. Good to see you alive and breathing, young Becca."

He looked terrible. Penny, coming up behind Ringan, thought for a moment of Dorian Gray, of a picture of Gowan that had been ageing in an attic somewhere, suddenly reaching the end of its contract. The man she'd met less than a week ago had looked youthful, vigorous; he'd been lethally charming, energetic, and damned sure of himself. Only the slight pouches under his eyes had given away both his age and his occasional taste for excess, in the form of whiskey and women.

He looked to have aged ten years in the space of two days. His hair looked lank, his mouth seemed loose, and his comfortable big-boned frame seemed to have wilted, lost its posture and its commanding easiness.

"You haven't been sleeping. Have you?"

Ringan's head jerked. There it was again, that same thing that had so unnerved him at Becca's first introduction to Gowan: his niece, for just a moment, sounded not a girl, but a woman. It was that same quiet voice, the voice of a woman with power to spare. And there, too, was that same look on Becca's face. It was close to sensual, with no vestige of childishness or innocence in it.

"Don't interrogate the poor man, Becca, there's a good girl." Penny's voice, sharp and imperative, was as brutal as a slap or a face full of cold water would have been. Voice and verbiage alike were designed to put Becca firmly back into her role as adolescent. "Gowan, it's good to see you, and please do excuse the child's manners. She's right, though—you look like a serial insomniac."

Becca went scarlet and was silent. Ringan opened his mouth,

caught Penny's sideways look and the faintest shake of her head, and closed his mouth again. The slapdown had been deliberate. Penny had seen what he'd seen, that disturbing moment of sensuality and adulthood.

"*Na, na*, there's no need for you to be making a show of it, not if you're talking about rude." Gowan sat back down again; the effort to not slump was so obvious, it made Ringan's muscles ache in sympathy. "But she's after being in the right of it. I've had no sleep these two nights past."

"Bad dreams, was it?" It was Lucy, surprising all of them. She sounded gentle. "Oh, dear. That makes for a hard night."

"That, yes." He muttered it. He was having trouble not looking at Becca; his eyes seemed drawn that way. "Ah well, talking about it won't get me a night's rest, nor anything else. But if it's talking we're doing, then I say we get on with it. Lucy tells me she's found out about some ancestors I didn't know I had, so there's me wanting to know."

"They aren't your ancestors, dear," she corrected him. "How can they be? They both died before they had children. But they were certainly family members—Cambornes, that is. Jenna and her brother Perran. Both drowned in the early winter of 1481."

There was a long moment of quiet. Gowan broke it as he got to his feet.

"We'll walk," he told them. "I want to hear about this, and I've a need to be moving."

There were other people on the Island, their hair lifting behind them in the soft wind off the sea. Ringan, his face to the water, found himself remembering his earlier stays in Cornwall, and his sense that, in some way, this small spit of earth jutting off St. Ives and west toward the sunset, had a feeling to it, one he couldn't quite articulate. Thinking about it now, he had the words ready and accessible: something about this place breathed an antiquity so great; something had been here before anyone began recording history . . .

"This place is old."

Ringan stopped so abruptly that Gowan ran into his heels.

Penny had that look on her face, a look Ringan would have given a lot to never have seen there again: her eyes were wide, yet somehow starved for light. Her shoulders were hunched into stone. He thought of it as her ghost look, and it meant she was seeing something, sensing something.

"Old? Yes, it is that." Gowan had heard the odd music in Penny's voice, the singsong cadence so different from her usual decisive contralto. "Or was it the church you're meaning?"

"All of it, the land, the water, the sanctuary from the wind above and the rocks below." Ringan felt his stomach knot up; she wasn't blinking, wasn't seeing them. *Stop it*, he thought, and aimed it at whatever might be listening. *We've had this already. Go away and let her alone, damn you.* "The little place, made from the holy stones. People with sheep grazing, and the rain lashing the ground. Bad weather."

The silence, within the group of five, was absolute. Becca's eyes were stretched, Lucy's were narrowed. People passed them by, aiming cameras, talking. Then Penny's eyes cleared, and the tension went out of her shoulders.

"Oh, damn." She knew what had happened; Ringan could tell. "Did I wander off?"

"No, you stayed right here, actually." Lucy's eyebrows were raised high. It came to Ringan, with something resembling outrage, that she thought Penny was either a liar or a nutter. "I'd say it was the modern world wandered off. Gowan, you said you wanted to know more about that brother and sister? I have quite a bit of information for you, but I can give you a very quick summary of the basic facts, if you'd like. It's been very . . . interesting, this research."

"I think we all want to hear the details." Penny was herself again. If she'd noted Lucy's disbelief, Ringan thought, or gave a damn about it one way or the other, she wasn't showing it. "Do tell us what you found out."

"My pleasure." Was that a touch of dryness in Lucy's own voice? "I began with my own library, with a late Victorian pamphlet about the local families. There's quite a lot about the Cambornes in there—you can borrow it if you want to, Gowan, but you'll have to promise to be very careful. It mentioned a tragedy—here, let me get my notebook out. I wrote this bit down. Ah, here we are. He was talking about three very bad winters, beginning in 1481: he wrote that the Camborne family suffered some loss, that being the fact that Perran, the heir of the house, had died. And he goes on to say that Perran's young sister had been lost a short time later, just a few weeks before she was supposed to be marrying the scion of a local family from Sennen."

"I don't believe it." Gowan sounded shaken. "You're after telling me they were real, then?"

"They certainly seem to have been, don't they?" Lucy closed her notebook, keeping one finger tucked inside, to mark the page. "After that, I tried the Internet, and that led me to some duchy records, in the inheritances and estates area. That listed Perran Camborne has having been born in 1463 and drowning in 1481. The records show the estate going to a child named Pasco, a half-brother. The boy was about three when Perran died; Perran had been the heir."

She waited a moment, giving them a chance to comment. No one spoke. "I'm just giving you the facts as I found them, and the next fact was the boy Pasco's parentage. His father was Hywel Camborne. His mother was Hywel's second wife." She stopped, and turned to look directly into Becca's face. "Her name was Elyor. E-l-y-o-r."

"But—but that's so close to Eleanor." Becca's cheeks had flushed the colour of old roses. Her pupils were enormous. "It's real, isn't it? I wasn't just dreaming?"

One hand went up to cover her mouth. Ringan stepped forward and got an arm around her.

"I know," he told her quietly. "It keeps happening. Last time it was all on me. Mostly it's Penny. Now it seems you're the one caught in it. And there aren't enough words, in Cornish or Gaelic or English or anything else, for just how bloody tired I am of it. It seems to get harder every time it happens."

Becca began to shake. Ringan tightened his hold.

"It's all right, love, we're right here. We're going to find out what's needed to stop this, and we're going to get you free and clear of it. You're going back to Edinburgh next week and you're going to absolutely gobsmack those toffee-nosed judges at Hambleigh. Don't worry—we're right here."

She started to cry. She wept as she did everything else, with a disturbing elegance and beauty. The grey eyes filled, tears spilled down her cheeks; she looked absolutely desolate. Penny, digging through her purse for a handkerchief, saw Gowan's face twist up.

"I'm sorry." Becca, young enough to be scornful of tears, was fighting for composure. "I just—I didn't think there was really anything there. You know? I kept seeing it and hearing it and feeling it, being her, knowing all her secrets and things, and I didn't really believe, not inside, where it matters. And now it turns out she was real, and so was her brother. And now I have to see them as real. And I don't want to." Her voice broke. "I was pregnant, right along with her. His baby."

"All right." Gowan's big voice was vibrating; twenty feet away, a group of Japanese tourists turned to stare a moment. "So there was an Elyor—not an Eleanor, but close enough for me. I'm after believing Becca heard the name she knew, not the local version. There was a Hywel. And there was a Perran, who drowned. And now it seems there was a Jenna lived, as well? That she drowned, along with her brother?"

"Not along with him, Gowan, but yes, there was a Jenna." Lucy, matter-of-fact and calm as a nun, opened her notebook again. "I don't know exactly how any of you came to know any of this, but so far, you've been right; these people were alive, once. Gowan, about Jenna—there's something odd about her death. Perran, the brother, died here, in St. Ives. I got that information from a very nice archivist called David Westin. If you'll give me just a moment—here: Perran Camborne drowned sometime during January 1481. His body was found along the coast, between here and Sennen. Jenna died in the water off Tintagel, just about three weeks later. And I hate to say it, but there are indications that her death, and possibly her brother's as well, were suicides."

"What—" Gowan was breathing through his nostrils. "What have you got about that, Lucy?"

"There were no headstones." She'd met his eye. "The church denied them headstones, Gowan. They don't seem to be buried in any of the local churches or in any of the Camborne crypts, either. I don't know that we can prove any of that, but it's certainly a safe inference. If they were suicides, they would have died in a state of sin, rather than a state of grace. Besides, there were very few classes of people who were refused burial in sanctified ground: suicides, criminals, that kind of thing. Being buried in unhallowed earth was not taken lightly back then."

"I don't like this." Gowan's hands were knotted into full fists. "Suicides? I don't like it, and I'm not convinced I believe it."

"As you wish, of course." Lucy wasn't wasting time soothing him. "But that would explain why there's no record of them in your own family documents. The information about them is available, mind you, in the council records, but I don't believe you'll find anything about them without hunting for it. They seem to have been hidden—excised, really. And that smells of suicide, doesn't it?"

"Except that we know better, don't we?" Penny stepped away from Becca. She sounded remote, distant. "That girl killed a man. I watched her do it, through his eyes. If it wasn't Perran, then who was he?"

Out of nowhere, she rounded on Gowan. Her eyes were blazing.

"I want to know something. I want to know why in hell you insisted on covering that damned song. You keep saying it has nothing to do with your family. If that's true, why were you hell-bent on playing it? Why, Gowan? You saw my reaction to it and yet you dug in your heels and refused to budge. Ringan told me. And I want to know why."

"So do I." Ringan had caught at Penny's energy. "And while we're asking questions, Gowan, I've got one of my own. Who was it who taught you the song? You said you learned it from an old woman up the coast, a sort of local folklorist type, right? Well, who was she? Is she still alive?"

Gowan was silent, four steady gazes fixed on his face. Behind them the sun slid into the horizon, in a welter of crimson and gold.

"It was her favourite song." His eyes were wet. "Jenny's favourite. She used to beg me to play it for her. My mam would shut herself upstairs, either with one of her headaches or maybe just not after wanting to bother us, and Jenny would curl up on the sofa, watching me, listening to me, and I'd sit at the piano, the grand old lady Brinsmead, and I'd play for her and sing. And no matter what, she always asked me for that one. I can still see her, hair down around her shoulders and her eyes half-closed, singing along under her breath." He stopped, and a ripple ran through the heavy shoulders. "I've been dreaming about her, these last two nights. An old nightmare, coming back to keep me awake, my darling Jenny, making me do what I'd give my all not to do."

"And Becca looks like her, doesn't she?" All the anger had gone out of Penny. Gowan's reason, so simple and so painful, was the one thing that had never occurred to her; he loved the song out of sentiment. "Damn. There are ghosts, and then there are ghosts. I'm so sorry, Gowan. That's hellish."

"It's all of that." He rubbed his eyes. "As to where I learned it, that was up in Padstow, all of twenty years ago, now. I was playing there on Mayday, me and the Miners, and I met a woman in the pub there, an older woman. We got to talking, and a good long talk that was. She came from Sennen, her family I mean. They were out of Sennen originally, down here in the south, but she'd moved north, Camelford, I think she said. She knew some tidbits about my family—nice gossipy things, from the last century. She had quite a few songs she showed me, but that was the one that stuck. It plays nicely on a piano. And—" His voice faltered. "It was for Jenny."

"Camelford?" Ringan's beard was at full jut. "Next to Tintagel? Gowan, please tell me you remember her name, because if you do, we're going to need a telephone directory for the north end of the duchy."

"Of course I remember her name. Do you think I'm daft?" The light of day had faded into the deeper colours of twilight, moving into full dark. Against the evening sky, St. Nicholas stood, ancient and serene. "Her name was Beryen. Beryen Cann."

The following afternoon, Ringan angled Pandora into a parking spot on a coast ride in western Tintagel, killed the engine, and glanced at Penny, who had been intermittently dozing in the passenger seat beside him. She was actually wearier than she'd been twenty-four hours earlier, something she would not have believed possible.

The news of Beryen Cann's existence, combined with her family name, had spurred Ringan into action. Unfortunately, the first thing to come out of it was a disagreement, as snappish and petty as it was silly, on where to go to try and hunt up Beryen Cann; Gowan's house was less than ten minutes' walk from the Island, whereas Lucy and Cian's was clear across town.

"I'm not having Becca back in your house, Gowan, not even for a minute." Ringan, in full war mode, wasn't giving an inch. "Nice house, kind of you to have us, but it isn't safe for Becca in there, and that's not up for discussion. She's not going back in there, and that's flat."

"Well, I could wait outside, couldn't I?" In contrast to her uncle, Becca sounded eminently reasonable, if rather remote. She seemed to be avoiding looking at Penny. "I mean, I don't need to be indoors, right? It's not raining or anything, and no one's going to see me sitting there and abduct me and demand a ransom or something. If you ask me, you're all being very silly, and childish."

"She's right." Penny's voice had an unfamiliar undertone to it.

She hadn't noticed Becca's sudden chilliness. "Or, you know, *I* could wait outside and *she* could go in. That would work just as well, really."

That got Ringan's attention off Gowan and onto Penny. "What's that supposed to mean, lamb? Penny for them?"

"It's something I was thinking about during that wretched migraine." It was nearly full dark; night had fallen, warm and soft, and the horizon, off to the west and out to sea, was a thin indigo line in the far distance. "Something that occurred to me—you said that when Gowan insisted on covering the song, the lot of you actually rehearsed it, and nothing happened. That is, nothing happened to Becca. She was just one of the band, playing a tune. Right?"

"So?" Ringan's hands were at his hips, his legs slightly apart and planted. He looked stubborn as a rock and ready for battle. "What's your point?"

"My point is that I wasn't there. Remember? I'd had as much as I wanted to deal with and I was sick of being the fifth wheel and anyway, your musical rehearsals are no more fun for me than my theatre rehearsals are for you. I'd gone for a wander and a swim." She yawned suddenly, a cavernous jaw-cracking inhale. "Oh, lord, sorry. I'm absolutely knackered. Anyway—you had the house, and the song, and Becca. It was all there, and what happened? Nothing, that's what. Sod all. So I think I'm part of the cause, somehow. It's as if the situation, the history, whatever it is, was the ignition switch. And I'm the key."

"That's—right, isn't it." They could hear the realisation dawning in Becca's voice, even if it was too dark to read it in her face. She was still avoiding looking at Penny, rather too ostentatiously. "Everything that's happened to me, from the first day, Penny's been there. I hadn't thought about that."

"So you're saying you think it needs all the pieces, this haunting thing?" Gowan, taking the idea at face value, was mulling it over. "Then really, why are we bothering ourselves about all this? If all you've got to do is take Becca out of Cornwall, away from anything to do with this precious pair of antique Cambornes and their incest and their suicides, and she'll be all right, why don't we just pack up and get the girl over the Tamar, and safe?"

"I don't know that." The exhaustion was there now, in Penny's voice. "How am I supposed to know? I've got no precedent for this. I do remember reading, years ago, something about how adolescents are traditionally linked with poltergeist activity, but this isn't like that. According to everything I've ever heard, poltergeists are just energy, and kids respond to that energy because it's undirected, or something. That's not what's happening here. Becca's susceptible, for one thing, and for another, this is no poltergeist. It's directed. And Becca's open to Jenna. How can I know what might stop it? Or trigger it?"

"Oh, Christ." Ringan had caught up. He sounded sick. "Please tell me you don't mean what I think you do, lamb. Are you saying you think Becca's a sensitive, as well? That this little lot has left her with whatever was left you at the haunting at my cottage?"

"Sorry." They'd walked in a circle and had come back to the old chapel, with its stone benches. "But yes, I do."

"Well, that's just lovely, isn't it?" Ringan sank down onto a bench. "That's just brilliant. After my sister Robbie finds out about this, and she and Becca's dad choke the life out of me, do me a favour and make sure to donate Lord Randall to someone who'll play him, okay?"

"I've already told you, I don't know if that's what's happening." Penny's legs were as tired and unresponsive as the rest of her; she sat down beside Ringan. "But I'm not going to pretend that I don't think it's possible. If there's any chance of shutting this down before that particular spigot gets frozen into the open position, we have to try it, surely? Outside of anything else, Becca's a musician. She won't always have her choice of which songs to play, and even if she did . . ."

Her voice died off. Ringan, bitter and angry, finished the thought for her.

". . . even if she did, she'd have no way of knowing ahead of time whether a song, any song at all, might trigger another incident like this one? With or without you being there to set it off? Right." He suddenly slammed the palm of his hand against the bench, its stones holding the warmth of the day just gone. "*Damn it!*"

Penny said nothing. Ringan got to his feet and offered her a hand, pulling her upright.

"Let's go. Gowan's house it is, and one of you, Becca or Penny, stays out of doors. I don't give a damn who goes where. Sort that out between you. But only one of you comes in."

In the end, Penny settled herself on Gowan's front stairs, while Becca went indoors with the others. Becca's opinion had not been solicited. The agreement had been tacit, between Penny and Ringan; as nervous-making as the thought of Becca under Gowan's roof again was, the thought of leaving the girl outside, alone and unattended, so close to where she'd gone sleepwalking, was simply not on. If anything was going to happen, it was far better to have her surrounded by caring adults.

Penny leaned her face against the wrought-iron balustrade and closed her eyes. She had no real worry that anything might happen, not so long as she remained out of doors. The realisation that her presence would bring Becca to danger had jolted her unpleasantly. It was a reflection on how bone-deep her weariness went that she was too tired to care. Even her suspicion that her own deliberate relegation of Becca to childhood had left Becca upset and distant had no real power to motivate her. All she wanted was to find a corner of the world with no ghosts, no music, and no complications, and sleep for the better part of a week. . . .

She sat, waiting and dozing. She roused herself when the others emerged from Gowan's house a half hour later, with a telephone number, an address, and an invitation in hand. Beryen Cann, folklorist and collector of regional music, was alive and well, and living in Tintagel, literally a stone's throw from Guinevere's Rest.

The conversation had reshaped a few misconceptions. Gowan, at the time of their meeting, had been a self-absorbed man in his twenties. What he'd perceived, and remembered, had been an old woman. In point of fact, she had been younger than his own mother, no more than twenty years his senior when they'd met at the Padstow Mayday nearly a quarter century earlier. She was now only into her early seventies, according to Gowan, who seemed surprised that she sounded much the same as she had when they'd discussed the origins of "The New-Slain Knight."

More than that, she remembered the meeting with Gowan vividly and was delighted that he'd remembered her. Yes, she told him, she had quite a lot of history, stories to share, letters and documents and told tales from their part of Cornwall, even some from her family and his. And yes, she'd be delighted to welcome him and his friends as well. In fact, it being summer and the local inns being as full as they could hold, she'd be very pleased if they'd consider stopping with her. Her house was too big for just herself anyway, she was after being fond of company, there were beds enough for all . . .

In the end, they'd all taken the trip north. Lucy had surprised Ringan by announcing that she would pack for an overnight trip and that Cian wouldn't mind. Penny opened her mouth and shut it again, wondering how soon this disastrous excuse for a holiday could be laid to rest, along with its ghosts and its side issues. She'd had a sudden picture in her head, herself penned as securely as any prisoner behind Pandora's wheel while Lucy lectured non-stop. . . .

"My thinking is that we can take two cars, and I can go up with Gowan, and come back with him as well." Lucy was looking directly at Penny. "After all, Ringan, you're supposed to be on holiday. And that would leave you the choice of not coming back down to St. Ives if you'd rather go somewhere else, once your business in Tintagel is done."

"That's a very good idea." Penny kept her voice friendly. She had no idea why she reacted to Lucy Williams the way she did; the woman had done everything asked of her, she was helpful and friendly and seemed genuinely kind and well-meaning. And yet, Penny thought, there wasn't one nerve Lucy didn't rasp against, just by opening her mouth.

But there was no excuse for bad manners, and the thought that Lucy had seen and registered her dislike flooded her cheeks with warm colour. *Come along,* Penny told herself. *You're an actress.* Just because she felt the way she did, she decided, she didn't have to let it show. Showing it was rude, and uncalled-for, and probably bad luck, as well. Besides, she had enough skill to hide it. "No offence to the Duchy of Cornwall meant, but honestly, if we can get this cleared up while we're up the coast, I'm not going to be in any hurry to come back down this way again. Not on this trip, at least. Gowan? Do you mind taking your car? Good. What time shall we meet, and where?"

They'd left from the Smugglers the following morning, loading into two cars and heading north from St. Ives before, as Gowan caustically put it, all the visitors remembered that they'd decided to forget how to drive when they left their own countries. It was a beautiful morning, the warm coastal mist that often settled on the coast roads around summer dawns burning off early. They hadn't been on the road for more than half an hour when Penny, at the wheel of the Jag, spotted a roadside cafe, signalled, and pulled off into the carpark. Ringan gave her a startled look; Becca, who had been silent since breakfast, stayed that way.

"What's up, Pen? Do you need to stretch your legs?"

"No, I need you to drive." Gowan's elderly estate wagon was pulling in behind them. "I'm sorry, Ringan. I'm half-asleep and I just can't seem to concentrate. Driving the coast road right now would be a very bad idea. Do you mind?"

"No, of course I don't mind. Here, let's swap sides." He was studying her face; there was a worried look in his eye. "Penny, are you all right? I know you got some sleep last night—I got up to use the loo around three, and you were absolutely dead to the world. But . . ."

His voice trailed off, trying to pinpoint what was wrong with her face. It came to him suddenly; she looked drugged.

"Yes, I got some sleep." The shallows under her eyes, usually barely visible except as indicators of the oversized eye sockets, were nearly as dark as the irises above them. Her lids looked swollen and somehow clogged. "I'd guess not enough, though, because I don't feel rested at all. I think I had nightmares, or something. But I don't really remember."

She sank down into the soft leather upholstery, and closed her eyes. From the back seat, Becca's voice came, still distant.

"Uncle Ringan, would you mind terribly if I went the rest of the way with Lucy and Gowan?"

"No, that's fine, if they don't mind." Gowan had pulled up beside them, and Lucy, in the passenger seat, waved Becca over. Ringan watched his niece climbing into the wagon's rear seat, without a look back at the Jag, and sighed. He'd guessed that Becca was still narked at Penny's reducing her to little-girl status the evening before, especially in front of Gowan and Lucy. He remembered how he'd wished his niece would decide whether she was an adult or a kid, just pick one and be that; he thought, ruefully, that the fates, with their usual infuriating taste for irony, had granted him his wish. Becca was acting like a sulky adolescent. Ah well, she'd get over it, and a good deal faster if she wasn't encouraged to sit in silent dudgeon around the offending adults.

Beryen Cann's house, set at the back of an oversized garden, caught Ringan's attention at once. He remembered wanting to comment on it two days earlier; in their quest to find rooms for the night, they'd driven past it more than once, and it had appealed to the period-restoration expert in him. Now, waiting for Gowan to gentle his car into a space a bit farther up the road, Ringan found himself gazing at the roof.

"Penny for them?"

He jumped. Penny had climbed out, and was stretching her arms and legs. He could hear joints cracking into place.

"I was just salivating," he told her. "Look at that roof, will you? Victorian gabling, slate tiles, and if that's not a conservatory off to one side, I'll eat a couple of old guitar picks with salt. Gowan, your friend has a very pretty taste in houses. This looks like a converted schoolhouse to me."

"If you say so. You're the expert, not me." Gowan squinted the length of the long front garden, saw the proportions of the house, and whistled. "My God, this is where she lives? The place is big enough to be a proper hotel."

Beryen Cann had apparently been on the watch for them. She had the front door open before they reached the house, a wiry broad-shouldered woman with a Roman nose and a generous mouth, as tall as Ringan, and with a silver ponytail pulled back off a strong-boned face that would have worked as easily on any local fisherman.

"*Dynnergh* to you all." Her voice, deep and friendly, was pitched to carry. She'd spotted Gowan, bringing up the rear. "Now there's a face I'm after remembering. Gowan, *koweth*, it's been so many years, I can't count them all. Come in, do. And—my God, Gowan, you didn't tell me on the phone—are you not Ringan Laine? Now this is that rare thing, a pleasure and an honour too." She held out a hand, and Ringan took it. "*Dynnergh*. Welcome to my home, all of you."

"Yes, I'm Ringan Laine." Her grip was surprisingly strong. Everything about her breathed calm and self-assurance. After the oddity of the rest of this trip, Beryen Cann made a welcome change. "And thank you, for letting us come. This is Penny Wintercraft-Hawkes, and this is my niece, Rebecca Laine Eisler. Oh, and this is Lucy Williams. She's a friend of ours; her husband Cian is a member of Gowan's band. What an incredible house you've got, Beryen. I do period-restoration consulting when I'm not playing music, and this house is superb. Was it a schoolhouse, or a local post house? It looks updated, but my first guess would be 1840s. Is that close?"

"Built in 1844, and it was the local schoolhouse, so that's a good eye you have. The family who owned it before me added rooms, up under the roof line—three more bedrooms up there." Her gaze moved to Becca. "You're a fiddler, then? There's little I like more than a good fiddle. Do you know 'Bonaparte's Retreat'? That's a fiddler's tune I dearly love. I remember I heard it first, back when I was younger than you, at a *ceilidh* near my school. We'd slipped out, me and my friend Maggie . . ."

She led them inside, down a long hallway and into an enormous sunny kitchen, talking all the time to a silent and unresponsive Becca. Penny, dropping back, put a hand out and caught at Ringan's arm.

"What?" He took a look at her face, looked again, and went very still. "Penny, lamb, what is it?"

"Becca." She kept her voice low. "Ringan, keep an eye on her, please. I know she's cross with me—I snapped her out of that unpleasant little too-adult thing she was doing to Gowan last night, and I suspect I was too sharp about it. But I don't like this. She's too quiet—the girl has good manners and this is right at the edge of rudeness. Becca isn't rude. Besides, you've seen it: when she gets upset, she goes pale and starts stammering apologies. This isn't like what I've seen of her, Ringan. Something's off."

"Damn." She was right; that silence, so easily construed as bad manners, was unlike Becca, as polite a child as he'd ever met in his life. Why hadn't he spotted it? "Right. Any ideas about what's going on with her?"

"None." She sighed, taking in air as deep as her lungs would allow. She couldn't remember the last time she'd been as tired as she was right now. "I just wish I could shake the feeling I've got, that we haven't seen the worst of it yet."

Eleven

"I will not father my bairn," she said,
"Upon an unkent man;
I'll father it on the King of Heaven,
Since my love's dead and gane."

After a dinner that to Penny seemed to consist of more food than she'd normally have eaten in the course of a week, Beryen settled her guests in the back garden, with cold drinks and stories to tell.

Of the five guests, Ringan had probably had the most interaction with serious folklorists in his day. Since his secondary line of work involved the restoration of period architecture, he was constantly dealing with local preservation societies, self-proclaimed keepers of the local history, and the occasional great-grandmother who swore that she remembered every detail of what curtains had hung over which windows in the Good Old Days. Having spent the better part of twenty years dealing with every type of historian and folklorist, Ringan would have laid odds on being able to tell a professional from an amateur, no matter how dedicated.

But it was apparent, almost at once, that Beryen Cann fell into neither of those categories. She was something else entirely: a born collector, someone with a passion for the minutiae of her immediate surroundings, a joy in the history of the place and people she loved that went as deep as her memory, and a terrifyingly accurate eye for detail. She also had the bluntness, tempered with warmth, that Ringan associated with the people of Cornwall, and it had a very useful side effect: no beating around the bush was necessary.

They could ask her anything at all and get an answer if she had one. There would be no raised eyebrows here, no wondering why they wanted to know, no need to qualify.

The summer days go long in Cornwall, at both ends of the duchy. The sun was still well above the yardarm when Lucy Williams leaned forward in her chair, set her glass of cider down in the grass beside her, opened her notebook, and got down to brass tacks.

"Beryen, I do hope you won't mind me asking, but I've been reading up on the history of Gowan's family. Very early history, I mean—the end of the fifteenth century." She seemed to have recognised a sister Cornishwoman in Beryen, someone who spoke her language. It was clear to the others that she was perfectly at ease, going straight for the information she wanted. "There's a mention in one of my sources, a self-published Victorian pamphlet, about an alliance between the Cambornes of St. Ives and the Cann family, from Sennen, one that didn't happen because of a tragedy. Is it your branch of the Cann family he's talking about? And why are you rolling your eyes?"

"Indeed, and it is my family." Beryen, completely relaxed, turned her own glass around in one hand. The liquid, a local mead, caught the fading sunlight and glimmered, deep and mysterious, against her hand. "As to the eye rolling, I'm thinking I can name that source of yours. The Right Reverend Peter Menegue, was it? Not that I'm after believing for a moment that the man was born with that name. But I have a copy of that little history on my own shelves. He got quite a lot wrong, did Reverend Peter—his section on what happened to the old ship chandlery at Portreath is absurd, and have you seen his conclusions about the Helston Furry Dance? Blithering nonsense is what that is. But he's in the right of it, about the marriage that didn't happen: it would have been a Camborne daughter wedded to a Cann son."

"Why didn't it happen?" It was Becca, speaking up for the first time since their arrival. Her disinclination toward conversation had been so marked, the adults had simultaneously and tacitly decided to let her be. "Do you know?"

"The girl drowned." Beryen swatted at an insect, hovering near her mead. Her tone was completely matter of fact. "They were actually up here in Tintagel when it happened; the girl's stepmother brought land holdings as part of her dowry when she married into the Camborne family. The Cambornes were always the canny ones, when it came to adding to their worth by way of marriage. No fools ever, your family, Gowan."

She paused for a moment; it seemed to Ringan that for the first time, she was choosing her words with care. "It's an odd thing about that," she said finally. "Them coming up here from St. Ives in the winter, I mean. The roads were in a bad state, after a season of hard storming, and there would be danger there of the roads washing out, crumbling into the sea. Travelling in the dead of a bad winter needed a good reason. But if any reason was ever given, I've not seen it."

"How—" Penny blinked at her. "Wait. How can you be sure of that? About the roads being in bad repair?"

"Well, from my family chronicles, of course." Beryen raised an eyebrow at the sudden hush. "Now, did I not mention this, Gowan? For sure, I thought I did. I've a goodly collection of documents from my own family." She grinned suddenly. "We're a clannish lot, we Canns, near as proud as the Cambornes. And me, I'm as bad as any magpie about finding choice bits to hoard."

"What sort of documents are you meaning, Beryen?" Lucy was leaning forward in her chair. "Letters?"

"Letters, journals, notes, records." She saw the eagerness in Lucy's face and shook her head. "*Na*, then, don't look so excited over it. Most of what I have goes back no more than to the end of the eighteenth century. I've little older than that, and none so old as what you're talking about. But I know every word of what I have, and there's more than one ancestor talks about that broken betrothal. It seems our family fortunes took a turn toward the down when that joining with the Cambornes didn't happen; the Canns lost much of their wealth over the bad winters, that year and the two that came after. They're legendary, those storms are, not just for me. That marriage would have been the saving of us. My own forbears were bitter over the what-if, especially when times were hardest. But it wasn't to be."

There was no bitterness in her voice; she was speaking of history, with neither rue nor regret. Gowan sighed suddenly.

"Beryen, can I ask that you show us some of what you have?" He sounded lethargic, and Ringan found himself wondering whether his old friend had suffered through another night of the bad dreams that he'd mentioned the night before. Gowan was looking sluggish, the hazel eyes dull and somehow tarnished, and the muscles of his face were sagging. "The truth is, we've got a strong need to know about that girl and her drowning, and right now, all we have are puzzle pieces. Is there a word in all your papers and whatnots that might set us right?"

"Of course. Why else did you come, if not for that?" She got to her feet. "After we spoke last night, I looked and I sorted. Everything's ready for you, laid out in my study. Fair notice—it's after being quite a tidy stack, but not everything there will have what you want. I just like to keep the sources together, so I have no worry about misplacing anything. And I'm sorry to bring us indoors and away from such a fine evening, but my papers stay where they are, safe under my roof."

Sometime toward the end of the nineteenth century, the owner of the house had decided that waste was a sin. With Victorian common sense, the oversized attic had been partitioned into two medium-sized rooms and one enormous one. A window had been added to the largest room, an oversized porthole affair with a westerly view; looking out, the tops of the ruins of Arthur's castle were visible, framed in every direction by the crashing surf.

Beryen had taken the room as her study. The oak beams of the roof had been left exposed, while the spaces between them had been insulated, keeping the room at an even temperature. The proportions were beautiful, the floors Cornish slate, mellow and functional. There were storage cabinets of heavy oak, clearly crafted by a master woodworker; there were low taborets on casters, tucked under a long refectory table running half the length of the room.

Ringan, pulling his eyes away from the view, looked around and felt a stab of something perilously close to envy. This room, calm and oversized and beautifully laid out, would have made a perfect music room. . . .

"You know, this would be a fantastic place for a theatre troupe to rehearse lines." Penny's voice was wistful. "I could just see putting the Tamburlaines up here, going over things. But of course, we'd probably never actually get anything done—I'd spend my entire life looking at that view."

"And here I was, thinking what a perfect office this was." Lucy was eyeing the long table; at one end were several small piles of papers and a few bound journals. "Twice the size of my own, in St. Ives. Shall we get started? As much of this as we can do this evening would be a good thing."

They pulled their chairs around to the end of the table, and Beryen settled in, switching on lights. Ringan, mindful of Penny's earlier disquiet, glanced over at his niece. She was looking at neither her travelling companions nor at the information they'd come to find; her eyes seemed drawn to the porthole window, scarlet now as it framed the blaze of the sun going down over the western sea.

"It's mostly that incident about the drowning you're curious about." Beryen had pulled a handful of letters, bound in ribbon, free of the rest. "Is that right? I've got a letter here, from a sort of great-grand uncle of mine, written to his wife—these are dated from January 1857. His name was Mark, and from the looks of it, they were having money worries, and he waxes eloquent about how different things might have been. I'll read, shall I? Be warned, he was very Victorian." She cleared her throat.

"My dearest Loveday—As promised, I write most faithfully, to tell you of my daily progress here in Fowey. But I am feared that you will find my news makes poor reading indeed, for we have suffered yet one

more reverse. The fishing here is scarce, and the weather bad. Of those three craft sent on our behalf to deeper waters, only two have returned. The Saint Wenna *is lost off Scilly, her ending as yet unknown; we know not whether she came to be dashed to bits against the rocks, or swallowed by the sea. Of her crew, eight good Cornish men, nothing is known, all presumed lost. May God show His blessings to them, and His mercy and compassion to their families. This fresh catastrophe could not come at a worse time for us, since we must now make recompense to their wives and children, and bear the cost of our lost ship as well. Finding these moneys will bring us in close peril of bankruptcy, so I beg you, my wife, that you may practice such economies as might preserve every penny against our days of need."*

She stopped, waiting for comment. There was none; everyone was listening and waiting. She read on:

"It comes as ironic to me, that this should befall us on the anniversary of that catastrophe at sea that so altered our family fortunes. Though I know such bitterness does no good and changes nothing—indeed, I am mindful that such may Our Lord offend—I cannot but think on what the difference would be in our family's present straitened circumstances, had Cador Cann but married the bride of his first choosing, and given his children to come that alliance with the Cambornes. But I will dwell no longer on that, for I know it serves no good purpose, and I wish to add no further weight of distress upon your heart. So expect me, dearest Loveday, only when you see me. I have no way of telling what time these visits to the bereaved may take. Yours in Christ, etc., your loving husband, Mark Cann."

She set the letter down. "And there's that. The rest of that pile is from different times, by the way—that's the only one mentioning the old story. As I say, I have them all out because I like keeping things together where they belong."

"Wow." Penny had caught a second wind; while her body was still sluggish and tired, her mind was working again, at close to its normal speed. "Four centuries later and they're still boo-hooing about it? Still saying what if? That's one powerful family legend you've got there. No, not 'legend,' wrong word. Not 'apocrypha,' either. Damn! I can't think what word I want, but you know what I mean, don't you?"

"I do, and yes, you're in the right of it. I think the word you want is 'obsession,' a family obsession." Beryen set the letter aside and reached for another pile. "You know, all things taken into account, I don't think I begrudge them. I'm the last Cann. After me, we're only history. The family fortunes began dwindling with that girl's drowning, and we never really recovered. We just hung on."

"Maybe that alliance would have been the saving of both our families," Gowan said quietly. "It's the same boat we're in, Beryen. I'm the last of us, the St. Ives Cambornes, anyway. There'll be no children. Never married and don't plan to."

"Why not?"

Heads turned. Becca, looking directly at him, had finally broken her silence.

"You want me truthful, do you, *flogh*?" He was looking back at her. "There's only ever been one girl I'd have thought to marry. And she's dead and gone. Unbalanced, maybe she was that, but they say a man only gets one woman to love in his lifetime, and if they're right, she was mine."

In the sudden hush, he turned back to his hostess. "That marriage that never happened, that might have been the saving of both our families. So don't be after thinking you're the only ones thinking *what if*, not when it comes to this. What else have you got to show us?"

"A journal entry, from about half a century earlier." She had it open, a small book bound in worn calfskin. "A two-year journal, 1810 through 1812, kept by a girl no older than Becca, here. The daughter of the house at the time—I've no idea what happened to her, but I suspect she married and went to live elsewhere. Mostly, this is about her daily life. There's an undertone to it, her complaining about the family not having enough money to buy her what she'd like, and how she wants a wealthy husband who will take her to London. A brat, and discontented with it—she's got a brother in the army, and she can hardly be bothered worrying. But there's one paragraph in here, for you: she writes, 'My *mamm* tells me the silk for my dress, that I wished to have that I might wear it to the dance for midsummer, is too costly, and that the money for it is not to her hand. I wish that girl Jenna Camborne had married into our family, instead of drowning herself in the sea; some days, I would happily walk into the sea myself, rather than be denied so many things I most desire.'"

"'Brat' is right." Lucy shook her head. "I've had a few like her in my schoolroom, and they're far more trouble than I like. But Beryen—that phrase she uses, about Jenna walking into the sea, she's talking about suicide. Is that the commonly accepted reason for Jenna's death? Because my own research led me to think that might be the case, for both Jenna and her brother."

"It is that. I've one more here that you might be interested in. I saved it for last. It's the oldest piece of family memorabilia I've got, late seventeenth century; it's written by one of the few Canns to ever join the clergy. And his name was Cador."

Ringan felt his nerves tighten. Becca was staring out the window once more. The sun was long down, the window showing only blackness. There was nothing to see outside, and a conversation inside that should have been engrossing her attention. Penny had been right, he thought. Something was off . . .

"Father Cador kept a very eloquent journal, and the family obsession seems to have caught his attention young and held it. In any case, he writes about it, right here." She paused and looked around her. Every face other than Becca's was turned in her direction. "It's longish," she told them. "Shall I read the whole thing, or just the relevant parts?"

"Whatever you think we should hear." Gowan had followed Ringan's gaze; he was watching Becca. "What does the man say?"

"It's written on Epiphany, the sixth of January 1681." She cleared her throat again.

"On this morning of Three Kings, I find myself in a most sorry state, indulging myself in melancholia when all around me is most merry. This comes in no small part from a letter from my dear sister Demelza; she and her good husband are in a great worry over some losses in their herds, the cattle dying of some sickness. They have in this new year so far lost seven head. Though she complains but rarely, even such a tranquil spirit as my sister may be worried by this, most especially as her husband is in poor health, with much to worry them."

Penny, who had closed her eyes, found herself moving along with the rhythms of a man long dust. Her professional life was centred around period drama, and the rhythms of the seventeenth century were familiar to her, and easy to get lost in. It was like a stage set, she thought, and saw the man, sitting at his own small scarred desk in whatever parsonage he'd been assigned by the local church authority, unfolding the letter from his sister, getting caught up on the family gossip and news, shaking his head over bad news, freshening his ink . . .

"Demelza asks no help of me, of course, only that I might offer her a sympathetic ear, knowing that I am not in such circumstances as to offer assistance. Yet this being January, I find that once again I fall into sadness and reverie, thinking of that poor young girl, the daughter of the Cambornes who was to have wed the man for whom I am named. It makes no appeal to my sense of what is ironic, thinking back on this, that our own name means 'bright,' or 'shining.' All glitter has gone from us.

"Lest anyone think the worse of me, I affirm that my sadness is not so much for the fortunes so disastrously changed by that event, but rather comes upon me when I think on what might have sent a girl so tender in years, so poor in experience of the world, to walk into the sea and take her own life. I find myself, too, remembering those letters from my ancestor Jory Cann to his lady wife, telling of the whispers in Tintagel township, that the girl went with child, and could not speak to her betrothed as to how she came to be such. Should that have been the truth, the weight of fear and shame of those around her might have possessed her to the point where her poor heart broke, and her wits and courage alike failed her."

Penny sucked in her breath. There it was, the vital piece of confirmation that what Becca had seen, she'd seen true and clear. And if this much was true, Penny thought, it was a good bet that the rest of Jenna's story, as Becca had told it, was true as well. And that being the case, her older brother, the heir to the Camborne line, had fathered that child on his sister.

So, she thought, they had the girl, pregnant. They had her affianced to Cador, scion of the Cann family. Then came a gap in what they knew of the chain of events: neither Lucy nor anyone else seemed to have known anything at all about Perran Camborne drowning, other than the bare fact.

Penny's own question remained unanswered. She had watched that girl kill a man, and she still had no clue who he might have been. Nowhere in the scant resources they had to hand was there so much as hint, even a breath of suspicion, that anything of the kind had happened. There was only that belief, that the girl had walked the cliff road to the sea, walked out as deep as she could go, letting her lungs fill with water, letting the sea take her, letting go . . .

Shame, it's shame you've brought down upon us, am I to tell Jory Cann that his son's bride comes to him with a baby already planted in her belly . . .

"Penny! What—"

She jerked in her chair. They were looking at her, all of them but one, she knew them, but what, who, whose voice was . . .

Tas, mara pleg, Father, I meant for none of this to happen, it was no doing of mine, no blame to me, I could not help myself, I beg you please cast me not out, Father please . . .

There was a roaring in her ears, a haze over the handsome room, a face there she couldn't put a name to, looking down on her, stone in his face, an ending in his eyes. He had looked at her differently all her life, indulgent, his only daughter, his darling girl, but now there was nothing there for her, nothing. She was on her knees to him and he cared nothing for it, and nothing for her, either.

She'd known, in her heart of hearts, that this moment must come, for there was blood on her hands and nothing to take it from her. Three weeks gone and the blood on her hands had taken her rest from her, and her will with it, sent her walking in the night, with none left to help, none to see she came to no harm.

The door was closing. She had nothing to bargain with and no heart for bargaining. She had lost it all, nothing left, only sorrow and pain and this hated child ahead, and the guilt, sweet Jesu the guilt and may the Holy Mother forgive her, only desperation, nothing . . .

No child of mine, from this day forward. No name have you, no hearth, no love of me. Get you out of my sight.

The unknown face faded, running like watery paint into a face she knew: the one who had not been looking at her, the girl who had been watching the window, the girl who was her, who had her eyes, grey shuttered lamps. The girl was watching her now, eye to eye, full on . . .

The slap across her cheek was light, not even enough to raise the colour there. But it was enough to bring her back from wherever she'd been, nausea rising at the base of her throat. *No*, she thought, and the thought was hers, clear and lucid. *I'm damned if I throw up all over Beryen's office.* Without a look around, she slid off the chair to the floor, and ducked her head between her knees.

"Breathe, lamb." It was Ringan, both hands on her, supporting her. He was on his knees on the hard floor, beside her. "Sorry I thumped you, but I couldn't help remembering that this was how you got me back, when this happened to me. Breathe—that's it, nice and deep. Your colour's coming back. No, don't talk. Breathe."

"Right." It was astonishing, how fast the pictures were fading. She had already lost the lines of the man's face in her memory, could no longer call them up. And his words, they were a jumble, because they hadn't been English, they'd been Cornish, and she didn't speak the language. What remained was the girl, the feeling of horror, of complete and total desolation. "I'm breathing." She stopped for a moment, as her side caught in a painful stitch. "More than I can say about poor Jenna."

"What?" Gowan's brows were a single line. "I wasn't after catching that. What did you—"

"So desperate." She began coughing suddenly, a thin angry congestion in the lungs, as if her body were somehow determined to purge itself of all vestiges of what it had just been through. Yet the feeling of urgency, to somehow share before the pictures and the memory were completely lost to her, was driving and undeniable, and she kept talking, the words broken by the wracking coughing. "So desolate. Her father turned her out of doors. She was literally on her knees, begging him. Not her fault, she told him—none of her doing. But she didn't believe what she was telling him. Guilty, so guilty."

She clamped her lips together, trying to steady her own air intake. It worked; she thought, with a distant amusement, that she would have the worst hiccups of her life in a few minutes, but that was far better than shaking her bones loose coughing. She lifted her head, testing her vision, hoping the vertigo was gone, seeing them all there, all watching her.

"If no one minds?" Beryen's eyes were narrowed. "Would someone be after telling me what just happened there? Did you see a ghostie, or something like?"

"Guilty?" Ringan had ignored Beryen's question. He was staring at Penny, his arm still steady around her shoulders. "Guilty of what? Do you mean she was blaming herself for being seduced by her brother?"

202

"No." It was almost gone; there was nothing there but fragments of images, tatters of the pleading voice and the implacable voice, and all that remained in its entirety was the desperation, the understanding, the guilt Ringan was asking her about. "Not that. Guilt because there was blood on her hands. I was right, that day at Gowan's, what I saw. She killed a man."

Rebecca Eisler, asleep in her room at the top of the stairs, felt herself slide into the world of waking dream, pulled there by a dead girl, and let herself go.

The fact was, she'd been expecting this. She was well aware of what her uncle thought, and Penny: they thought, both of them, that she was sulking like some stupid child. As if she'd do that . . .

She'd let them think whatever they chose, but it hurt. What hurt even more was what they hadn't seen and hadn't understood: Becca was in a state bordering on panic.

It had begun in the green-dappled glass room in Gowan's house, that fear, burgeoning like a night-blooming flower as Gowan rang the woman who'd taught him the song that had caused all the trouble. She could put no name to the fear and didn't bother trying, knowing somehow that she simply didn't have the life experience to deal with it. The fear had settled into a chill cramp at the pit of her stomach, and it coalesced into something hot and ugly when it became clear that they were going back to Tintagel.

At that point, she'd done what any sensible creature would do when it hoped to be left alone and pass unnoticed, when it was this frightened: she curled into a small ball and went as quiet as possible. The child in her was very close to the surface and hard to keep inside. Before she'd changed rides on the way north, going from Penny's car to Gowan's, there hadn't been a single moment during which she'd been more than moments away from fragmenting, dissolving into her own irrational panic, wanting to scream at her uncle: *I almost died in Tintagel, and Jenna did die there, and now you're taking me back, I'm frightened and I don't want to go,*

take me home, why can't you see that I'm scared half out of my mind,
please take me home.

But she'd said nothing, nothing at all. She'd listened, absorbing the information, taking in every word of the talk about Jenna Camborne. And sometime during the long evening, just before Penny's faint or fit or whatever it had been, Becca had looked out the window and heard a voice, a new voice, somewhere at the back of her own head. A boy's voice, coming from the air, or maybe from the pounding surf she could no longer see through the porthole window.

Then Penny had collapsed, and the voice had gone. But Becca hadn't done with him yet. While she hadn't made out a single word, she knew him. He was someone important to her, or would be. Her thoughts were random and confused, but she stayed quiet, ignoring the fuss around her, paying no attention to their explanation to Beryen. No one was minding her; they all still thought she was in some kind of bratty snit.

But his voice, oh, that boy's voice—it had been a kind of music, warm, caring, passionate, something to want. There had been love in there, and safety. Becca tuned out the adults, tuned out their insistent voices and their rabbiting on, and waited for the boy's voice to come again.

Beryen had shown them their rooms when they'd first arrived. Becca's room was at the top of the stairs; it had a bow window with a proper window seat, a big soft cushion, and an old-fashioned four-poster bed, with her violin case and bag on it. It had no bathroom—she would share the bath and loo down at the far end of the hall with her uncle and Penny, who'd been given the largest of the guest rooms, with a bigger bed than any of the others.

They'd gone to bed early, or at least Penny and Becca had. She'd felt, quite suddenly, as if she couldn't bear any more of it: the knot in her stomach, the oddness, the adults thinking she was being childish, the endless discussions of things they didn't understand and couldn't prove . . .

"Would anyone mind if I went off to bed?" She'd looked at her watch; it was early, barely ten, and she waited for someone to tell her she was being silly.

"I was about to ask the same thing." Penny managed a grin, a genuine smile that sent long dimples curving up in her cheeks. The smile was short-lived. "Beryen, I know it's a ridiculous hour to curl up with a pillow, and I hope I don't sound rude, but the truth is, I don't think I've had eight hours' sleep total over the past three nights, and of course there's what's been happening. I'm knackered, completely played out. Honestly, I just want to sleep. Becca, wise girl, has the right idea. Would you mind?"

Becca felt herself flush. She'd distanced herself from Penny, putting up an emotional wall of sorts, but there was no point in feeling guilty about that, she thought. After all, it was Penny herself who'd said that what had been happening to Becca was because Penny herself was there. It was better by far to keep a distance, better and safer.

Will you look at me, lovely girl? Look at me, into my face and into my eyes. Will you tell me that another man has got to you before me? Was it against your wish, against your will? An it was, he'll pay full sore for it.

Becca jerked, her shoulders spasming; the voice was enormous, taking up every spare cell of her brain. She looked at Penny, who'd put a hand up to her own brow, her face furrowing in pain. She looked older to Becca, not so chic, nor so in control, either. But Uncle Ringan loved her, and loved her dearly; anyone could see it, it was there in the worry in his face, the way his beard suddenly jutted, the way he moved immediately to her side. Becca had a moment of pure longing, that someone, someday, might look at her that way . . .

. . . pay, by my oath I swear it . . .

"My head," Penny said, and winced. "Damn! I think—look, Beryen, Lucy, everyone, I'm going to say good night. I think it's time I called out the heavy artillery—no, Beryen, that's fine, I don't need anything. I've got a prescription pain medicine for these. I think the last time I had to take one before this trip was over a year ago. I hate taking them, they leave me groggy and stupid for most of the next day, but they do work, I'll say that for them—"

Am I to be your babe's father in name only, Jenna? Am I still wanting to wed you, even with this? Darling girl, of course I do, though I fear my father will forbid it, an he knows. My heart is breaking with love for you. How did this happen, Jenna? Name your babe's father to me, for I think, now, that there can be no more between us, an you do not.

Becca's nails, luckily kept short, dug into her palms. Three feet away, Penny broke off in midsentence, flinching. "Right. Damn. Apparently, it's going to be one of those migraines, the ones with the flashing lights and the odd little humming in the head. I'm off for the big guns and better living through chemistry. Good night, all."

You'll give me his name, Jenna. An I love you, an I take you to wife, you come to me with land and money and a child not of my making. I'll have his name from you. There will be no wedding, else, trust me for that.

"Becca?" It was Lucy, watching her, clearly puzzled. "Did you just say something?"

"No. I mean, maybe." *Who did this? Na, then, don't flinch from me, girl. An I must take you with his seed, I'll have his name and his blood with it. . . .* "I'm going to bed, too. My throat still hurts, and I'm sleepy. Good night."

She bolted. Her breathing was coming in small rasps, her heart stuttering. Safe in the pretty guest room, with its view of the sea and its four-poster bed, she put her hands up to cover her ears.

He'd loved her, that boy did. Why did Jenna say nothing? He was willing to take her as his wife, even with her brother's baby growing . . .

His name, love. Give that to me. I swear, he'll bleed for what he did to you. I know this was none of your doing. We'll wed quickly, you and I, and the babe will be thought a seven-month child. You've nothing to fear, once you give me his name.

Becca turned the light out. There was no need for it; her eyes didn't need to see what was there. So long as that voice was moving in her head, loving and imperative, she could close her eyes and listen, feel that warmth and anger and love on Jenna's behalf. She lay across the bed, waiting for his voice.

206

It didn't come. Instead, there was sleep, and there she was, feeling the pull, following a pair of eyes so like her own. For a moment, just a moment, she could see Jenna's face; it was nothing like hers, really, except the eyes. Jenna was round-faced, and she had a high colour, and a snub nose, and a tiny smattering of freckles, weirdly charming.

And there was no more seeing Jenna's face after that; instead she was on the inside looking out, and time was doing cartwheels and handstands, nauseating her, the sky and the sea and her father's garden. Or was it Jenna who felt so ill, the unhappy stomach that came with the early stages of pregnancy? Becca couldn't tell and didn't care. When the world righted itself, she found herself looking up at a boy, a beautiful young man who was looking down at her with love and rage and betrayal and heartbreak in his face. Here he was, then, the lovely shining hope, about to be denied. And he was turning away.

"I can take no more of this, Jenna." His hair was a reddish gold, glinting in the watery sunlight of the new year. "Cann" meant "shining," "bright," "splendour." He was all of that, and he loved her, and wanted to marry her, and now it was all come to ruin, all of it, because of Perran. "For this moment, I can take no more of this."

"Cador—"

He was going, leaving her behind. Around her, the garden was damp, water pooling on the primroses as tears spangled her lashes. Her hands had woven tight across her belly, a hard lump of life growing where none should be.

Becca stirred, coming for a passing moment closer to the surface of waking, closer to herself. What had that priest written? How fear and shame might have driven a girl in Jenna's situation to walk into the sea?

Another twist of the sky, it was where the sea should be, and now the ground shifted again, as well.

He was there, where she'd known he would be: her brother, her ruination, Perran the despoiler and liar, sleeping in his favourite spot in the garden that would someday be his. Even the nurse for their half-brother, Pasco, a woman who had come to their service from Tintagel with the Lady Elyor, knew better than to let the child play here, and none of the servants or the household would dare to tarry here. This corner of the Camborne land, with its old oak trees and its flowering vines, was Perran's own.

He was a handsome boy, dark-haired, his heavy lids over eyes with pouches below them, that somehow reminded Becca of Gowan. On an older man than Perran, those fleshy mounds might have signalled a dissipated life, a taste for the pleasures of the flesh; with his eyes shut, he merely looked young.

She could feel Jenna's jaw, clenched so tight that she might have had a rictus, a death mask of a grimace. She could feel something cold, something hard, something in her hand, in Jenna's hand, nestled there as if it had been made to order.

A stone, smooth at one end, jagged at the other. Her hand, Jenna's hand, she could no longer tell one from the other, holding it, weighing it, looking at the sleeping boy.

The wave of hate that washed through Jenna nearly knocked Becca awake, so potent was it. Jenna was a beam of cold light, nothing but hate and hormones, all of it aimed at the boy sleeping, just within her reach.

Liar, Perran, 'twas naught but lies, you swore to me when you laid me down I'd have no price to pay and none would know, liar, liar, lies, only lies . . .

She brought the stone down, aiming for his face. Just before she struck, the girl's aim shifted—Becca couldn't tell whether it had been deliberate, that downward movement. All she knew was that instead of the disfiguring blow that had clearly been meant, Jenna Camborne had issued a death strike.

Becca, caught and yet detached, felt her gorge rising. She was choking, vomit in her throat, but there was no room to be sick, because Jenna was screaming, raining curses and blame on the boy who had taken her future from her, taken the golden shining boy she would have had, taken her joy and her youth and her innocence, and for what?

Perran's eyes opened and found his sister. Shocked into waking, waking into his own death, he yet managed to speak, a travesty of language, words mangled by the fracture in his hyoid bone: *Na Jenna, mar pleg Jenna, na, hedhi, na, prag, no Jenna, please Jenna, no, stop, why . . . ?*

His eyes, bewildered and disbelieving, were the eyes of another Camborne, not to be born for another five centuries: hazel, with a greenish ring round the pupil. Gowan's eyes.

Everything was moving now, fast and sickening. The stone fell from Jenna's fingers as the last of her brother's words were lost in what was left of his throat. And Jenna was stumbling, backing away from what she'd done, turning to run, to flee, and finding herself caught hard, in the arms of Cador Cann. . . .

Hands on her, but they were on her, no dream, real hands on her shoulder, shoving and pulling.

"Becca! *Becca!* Damn it all to hell, wake up!"

Her eyes opened. Shocked awake, she found herself surrounded: Ringan, fully dressed. Beryen, in what looked to be pyjama trousers and a fisherman's jersey. Lucy, barefoot, but with her shoes in her hand. And Gowan, whose eyes she couldn't bring herself to look at, at the door, looking grim and drawn.

"What—" She sat up, rubbing her eyes. The window caught her eye and showed darkness outside; it was still night.

She knew what had happened now; she ought to tell them. It wasn't fair, keeping it to herself. "What time is it? What's wrong?"

"Get up, will you?" There was something in Ringan's voice she hadn't heard before. "Get up and get dressed. You're needed. And it's ten minutes past two in the morning."

"Why—" She got it, suddenly, and went cold; Lucy, Gowan, Ringan, Beryen. "Where's Aunt Penny?"

"Gone." Ringan was at the door to her room, already heading for the stairs. "She's gone."

Twelve

The knight, he knackd his white fingers,
The lady tore her hair;
He's drawn the mask from off his face,
Says, "Lady, mourn nae mair."

Lying awake next to a lightly snoring Ringan, Penny stared off into the darkness, doing her best to ignore the pounding behind her eyes, and waiting for her pain pills to kick in.

She had reached the stage she thought of as 'busy brain.' Her mind, trying to distract itself from what her body was doing, had gone into an uncomfortably hyperactive mode, forcing her to think about something, anything at all, other than her physical discomfort. As a defence mechanism, it was inherently sound. But it did have the unfortunate result of creating a vicious continual loop. Since her mind was too busy to shut down, the rest of her assumed that wakefulness was what was needed and hurried to catch up.

She felt her legs twitch, bit back a muttered profanity, and shifted her position. The half-pill she'd used was taking its own sweet time being any use; all she wanted was ten hours of sleep, and for this damned headache—which, now she thought about it, seemed to have been with her in one strength or another since that first episode at Gowan's—to go away and give her a bit of peace.

Moonlight moved across the bed, touching her pillow, brushing her cheek. Even the faint brightness hurt, and she closed her eyes against it, her mind wandering down an alleyway she'd only just noticed.

This headache—it really had been here all along. Not a basic migraine, she decided; normally, a migraine and the smell of food were best kept apart. She remembered sitting at lunch the day before, her temples pounding like jungle drums, thinking how wonderful the soup smelled. This was certainly not like any migraine she could remember.

And, thinking about it, the strongest spikes in pain had corresponded with, or been somehow connected to, incidents involving those benighted forbears of Gowan's. Tonight's incident, though, had been something special. What in hell was she seeing and hearing? And why here? Why now?

Her legs jerked again, and she swung them free of the bed. When she'd decided to take only half a pill, she'd been mindful of their strength. She'd wanted to avoid the inevitable fuzziness the next day, but that clearly wasn't going to be enough. Her brain was working on that last question—why here, why now?—and the only way to shut it up looked to be by way of shutting up the headache, as well.

Standing by the window with her water glass, looking out at Beryen's garden, a light went on in Penny's mind. She'd been so knocked over by the strength of that episode that she hadn't stopped to consider whether Becca might have been going through the same thing.

She swallowed the pill, massaging her temples with her free hand. Becca, now—that was a question, certainly. There had been a reaction there. She closed her eyes again, trying to pin it down, and there was the memory, of locking eyes with Becca. It had lasted only a fragment of a second, but those grey eyes had been superimposed on someone else's.

Becca had literally run from them, fled for the shelter of a closed door between her and the adults. And Penny, shaken and sick, had let her go without a question asked.

Dizzy, her legs trembling, Penny climbed back into bed. Her mind was still cycling, but it was lazier now, slowing down. The second dose was kicking in, and bringing the first dose up to speed along with it.

Drowsing, her lids heavy, Penny let the thoughts move, idle and distant. What had she herself seen and heard? She had looked through different eyes tonight, she knew that much. The dead man first, in St. Ives, and now, tonight, the girl Jenna, forsaken by the father who'd doted on her. Tonight, one thing had been quite clear: this had been the first Hywel Camborne had known of his daughter's pregnancy. While nearly everything else about the episode had blurred together, two things remained: the father's shock and outrage, and the daughter's sense of guilt.

She was growing sleepy, at long last. Ringan had turned over on his side, facing away from her. She flexed her ankles, hearing the joints crack and settle, forestalling any more twitches in her legs. The pain in her head was dulling, easing, opening the door to sleep. It was a pity she hadn't thought to close the window, she thought drowsily; the tide must be in, the room smelling of salt and . . .

I've killed him, sweet mother above me, help me, I've slain my brother, oh Perran, father of my child, I've sent him unshriven to his death, there's no mercy for me now, help me Cador, my a'th pys, *I beg you*

Penny, at the edge of sleep, understood, and pulled back. She opened her eyes.

Darkness, everywhere darkness, except for brightness in thumping coloured spots. She could see nothing but vague shapes and her throat, dear God in heaven what was wrong with her throat, she could taste bile and blood and the agony was not to be borne, she must speak, ask Jenna why, how could she do this to one who loved her so dear . . .

Darling girl, stop your trembling. Sav yn-bann, *stand up. You must stop your trembling. That will serve us naught, nor crying neither. Hush now, and let me think awhile.*

Who? Jenna, the faithless little whore, he had loved her more than life. Who dared call his sister their darling?

She knew the voice, she'd heard it before, but she was sinking, the meds were working. She was sliding down, no use fighting the glaze obscuring her vision or the paralysing cold moving through her veins as the blood began a slow settling, preparing for—

Listen to me now, Jenna. Your brother is slain—that cannot be changed except by God Almighty. But no one must know how this came to pass, an they'll take you for it. Trust in me to bring you off safe. Is there some path, some road not often used, where we might go unseen? Show me the way to the shore, so that we may let the sea take him; the world may yet think this a mischance only.

She couldn't see. The world had disappeared behind the hateful cold that was settling in her veins. The meds had never worked this way before; she was going to have words with her doctor next time she saw him.

Dry your tears, Jenna. Your brother is gone; see, you may touch him and all for naught. There's no life left in him, but there is life yet for us, love you and me. Bide here awhile, and compose yourself as best you may, lest your father or a servant chance this way. Into the water I'll put him; the rocks and the tide together should mask what came before. Only do this, an you may yet come off safe.

And now the meds weren't working at all, because she was in pain, serious pain, worse than the headache had been. Her back was in flames, her arms were being pulled hard, her body scraping and bumping, torn by the pebbles and shards of clay beneath her. There was salt in the air, the tang of it strengthening as they came closer to it, a spray as soft as love cooling her skin.

She heard the slap of wave against land, smelled the salt, felt it sting her eyelids. There was little air left in her lungs, and less as the bumping and scraping went on, only the faintest breath, so faint as to be nearly undetectable, slipping in and out of her nostrils.

The burn in her throat was almost gone now, and the pain in her legs was going with it. But this was a miserable dream, dreaming of a dead boy, knowing that he'd been killed by the girl who'd always done his bidding before, knowing that he was going to be thrown in the sea, a genuinely wretched dream—

Na Jenna, mar pleg Jenna, na, hedhi, na, prag . . .

She heard the words in her mind, unspoken, only a thought, nothing more. What small light was left in her eyes was fading; her drowsy limbs were heavy as stone. There was no moving them, hand nor foot nor anything else, and there never would be again.

The water should have been a shock to the system, pushing her awake. Instead, she welcomed it, feeling it soak through her clothing, the finery that had been so badly torn during that dragging down the hillside. No more pain, no headaches, no sense that he must live with the betrayal, that Jenna, sister and lover and mother of his child, had taken away his life. The fabric of his trousers, those fine silk *lavrek,* drank in the water, the heaviest sea water that ever was or had ever been . . .

But you weren't wearing trousers, when you went to bed. You just had on a nightshirt. It was far too hot for pyjamas. Don't you remember? Wake up, Penny, for heaven's sake, wake up. This is danger. This is trouble. This is someone else's death. Wake up. You have to wake up.

"Penny!" Someone was shouting; it was Ringan, trying to get her to wake up. Good. She didn't seem able to do it on her own. "Oh Christ I can't see her—there!"

She opened her eyes. They opened all the way this time, full vision once again at her command; the eyes were hers, and no one else's.

And they were full of salt water.

"What—" Completely disoriented, she opened her mouth. Water rushed in, lungs, stomach, everything, everywhere. She gagged, gurgled, and felt herself sink.

"Gowan! To your left—I saw a hand. Go, you're closer!"

She flailed her arms, feeling her throat close up as it reacted to the unnatural liquid. *What in hell, no way in this world, I am not awake, I refuse to believe this, no way, this simply isn't happening.* Ringan's voice—it was distant, too far away from her. She was wet, and cold, and the nightshirt that she'd gone to bed in, and was still wearing, was plastered against her at the top, and billowed out around her waist and hips. It was pulling her down.

Good, she thought, and forced her body, fully responsive now and wanting to fight against the relentless weight of the water, to relax. In a moment, she would touch bottom, and could push up. And then she was going to wake up out of this dream, because it was scaring the hell out of her.

But there was no bottom, only more water and no way home. It came to her, with a sense of complete disbelief, that she was not in bed, and not dreaming. She was actually in the sea, and if she didn't act, she was going to drown.

She kicked out hard, pushing herself upwards, breaking the surface. There was sky, and moonlight, and where she was looking there was no land, nothing at all.

Then there was an arm around her waist, turning her back toward the land, turning her face from the open water. Breathless and coughing, spitting water, she felt her heart stammering. They were at least seventy feet from the shore. How in hell had she got out here . . . ?

"You're all right." Gowan, panting for breath, wasn't wasting what little he had on unnecessary speech. Someone had got her from the other side; Ringan. "Out you go."

She saw ruins, rock that had once been a castle built to defend the duchy against enemies from the sea, stark and fabulous against the night sky. There was a dark mouth in the base of the cliffs. *I know what that is,* she thought, *that's Merlin's Cave.* She was in the Celtic Sea, and this was Tintagel.

She was limp, and exhausted, and she let the men lead her out of the water. There was sand under her feet now, the weight of the sea becoming small wavelets and then lightly moving foam, as they stumbled onto dry land.

Becca was there, white-faced and wraithlike under the moon. Lucy was there, holding a serviceable torch, with Beryen Cann at her side, holding a blanket. Gowan, shivering and wet, stepped aside and let Ringan cover her with it. She had wakened up.

Her headache was gone. And she was alive.

"Here. You drink this, and don't argue with me."

"What is it? Mead?" Penny took the glass from Ringan, and both eyebrows went up. "You're not expecting me to drink all this, are you? For heaven's sake, there's enough booze in here to knock me out for a week!"

Penny had taken a fast bath, as hot as she could stand it; rather to her own amusement, she'd been accompanied by Ringan, who seemed disinclined to let her out of his sight quite yet, especially, he told her, if she was actually planning to have anything to do with water. She'd responded with a slightly acerbic comment about him handing her a toy boat to play with if he intended to treat her like a toddler, but she'd accepted both his arm and his presence. She was still shaken.

Now, wearing an old dressing gown of Beryen's, she had re-joined the group in Beryen's front room.

"I don't care how much of it you drink, but get some of it down you." Ringan had parked himself at her side. "If it knocks you flat, that'll be fine. You can get some sleep. But really, lamb, I'm think-ing more about warming you up. You were very cold, when we took you out of the sea."

She sipped, relishing the soft burn of the alcohol as it hit her jan-gled nerve endings. The rest of the group were quiet. They seemed to be awaiting her convenience, giving her time to compose her-self, find the words, somehow clarify a situation that none of them could sort out.

It was still night, but the windows of Beryen's front room were showing the first violet reflections that meant sunrise was not far off. When the silence had stretched a few minutes longer, Ringan finally spoke up.

"Penny for them?"

"It'll take more than a penny, darling. You'll need a bank loan for this one, or maybe the bank itself." She set the mead down.

"Lucy—those records you found, about Perran drowning? They were absolutely right. He did drown. That boy was alive when Cador Cann put him in the water."

"Are you sure?" Ringan was fighting down a sense of helpless outrage. It had nothing to do with Perran Camborne, the boy who had seduced and dominated his sister, and everything to do with what Penny had just had to go through on Camborne's behalf. Ringan, not a newcomer to Penny's susceptibility, had already guessed what had happened tonight.

"Yes." She reached for the mead again. "I felt him die."

"You're saying that Cador Cann helped her?" Gowan looked confounded. "He helped her murder her brother?"

"It wasn't murder, Gowan, at least not a premeditated one." From somewhere in Beryen's garden came a small chattering of birdsong. Penny was looking at Becca, waiting for her to say something, anything, but the girl stayed quiet. "She was desperately in love with Cador. She saw him as her rescuer, and she wasn't wrong. She thought he was dumping her—they had a confrontation of some sort in the garden in St. Ives, and either he guessed, or she told him, about the pregnancy. He demanded the father's name, and she wouldn't tell him. He said he couldn't marry her unless he knew, and he turned away from her."

"Ah." Lucy's voice was cool and noncommittal. "Interesting."

"That's one word for it, I suppose." Penny, to her own surprise, found herself not particularly caring about Lucy's disbelief one way or the other. Really, there were very few people out there who'd be willing to accept this situation, and after all, she was entitled to her opinion. She smiled at Lucy, not a warm smile, but a genuine one. "Not the one I would have used. But it doesn't matter."

"I want to know what happened," Gowan broke in. "How in hell did you get from your bed in Beryen's best guest room all the way to the water? Because that's the best part of a mile to the sea, and you in a nightshirt and barefoot. Did you just walk out the front door and away? Or, what?"

"I haven't a clue, Gowan. I'd taken half a pill, trying to get rid of that damned headache. It wasn't working, so I got up and took the other half, and when I got back into bed again I started dozing, and all of a sudden I was back in Perran Camborne, right after Jenna bashed him with a rock. His throat was on fire. So was mine. And he was a rapist and a pervert and you know what? He honestly thought he loved her. That was his way of love. God. That poor girl."

"I'm so sorry." Gowan had caught it, the horror she was leaving unsaid. "Sorry on behalf of my family, even the ones gone five hundred years. That's a sorry thing, indeed."

"I could hear them talking, Jenna and Cador Cann." Voices, the girl at the edge of fragmenting. Had it been pregnancy hormones, adrenaline, realisation of what she'd just done, terror at being found out, a broken heart? "Cador was telling her to calm down—she was in meltdown hysterics. He asked her if there was a nice quiet road down the hill to the water and told her to stay put; he'd take care of it and if they got lucky, everyone would think it was an accident or something. The next thing I knew, I could feel myself being dragged, and then I came all the way out of it, and I was underwater."

Everyone was quiet, watching her. The description had been delivered with a straightforward matter-of-factness worthy of Lucy, but there was no disguising what lay beneath.

"So I must have walked down there." She remembered the bumping, and the tearing of flesh and clothing; Cador Cann, thinking Perran already gone, had had no reason for being careful, and every reason for speed. "Unless I slithered down on my back, or something. Ringan, you washed my back, upstairs. Was there anything—"

"No." He cut her off; his memory of that path, rocky and hard under his feet in the darkness, was fresh and unpleasant; the image of someone dragging Penny made him want to kill something himself. "Just the same pretty back it's always been, thank goodness. You must have walked, and walked into the sea as well." His voice wavered suddenly. "Can I just say, by the way, that if you ever throw a scare like that into me again, I won't be answerable for the consequences?"

"I doubt that upsetting you was her intention." Beryen got up and stretched. She sounded neither sceptical nor convinced, just interested. "All right. What I hear, then, is that these poor dead brother and sister got into Penny's head or her heart or something, somehow. That you tapped into something and had to relive what happened to them. Does that make you some sort of, what? A medium?"

"I don't know what I am. I just know that I'd like it to stop. I could stomach it for myself, if that's the way it has to be, but I don't like it when it affects people around me. This is the first time it's happened where just my being there turned the tap on for someone else who's another of whatever I am."

Penny lifted her head, and for the first time looked directly at Becca. "I'm so sorry, Becca. I didn't know that the song, or whatever it was that did it, would hit you as well. How could I have known? But I hate that this happened. I suppose it's possible that you just were vulnerable to Jenna—same age, all that. I hope that's it. But if you do happen to be a genuine sensitive, you're probably stuck with never knowing when it's going to hit. And I'm sorry, love. I'm so sorry."

Becca had been looking down at her hands, folded quietly in her lap. Now she looked up.

"It's okay." Her voice was calm and very sure. "It really is, Aunt Penny. And anyway, it came in useful tonight, because I knew where you'd gone. But the being stuck? No, I don't think so. I don't think I'm a sensitive—it was just Jenna. And she's gone. I felt her go, down in Merlin's Cove tonight—when they were pulling you out, she just sort of let go of me. I know what happened to her, all of it. I know why she died."

"What?" Ringan was as tense as one of his own guitar strings. "Got something you want to share with us, Becca?"

"Yes, I do." Like Penny, Becca's voice was matter-of-fact. Unlike Penny, however, there was no deliberate effort to keep it that way. Whatever had been riding her since she'd got to Cornwall had been set to rest. "When you woke me up tonight? Well, I was dreaming. I was back in the garden in St. Ives, and she was talking to Cador Cann. Aunt Penny's right about that, they were in love. It was a bit sickening, really. But he was furious. Not at her—he still wanted to marry her, but he wanted to know who gave her the baby. He said . . ." She went pink. "He said that if he had to accept another man's seed as his own, he wanted the man's name as well."

Penny bit her lip. Becca, haunted or shadowed or neither, was still fourteen.

"Well—she wouldn't tell him. He walked away. She thought he was breaking up with her. You know? She was all emotional and flippy over it. She went storming off into the garden, unhappy and scared, and she nearly tripped over Perran. He was asleep in this sort of hammock thing. And, well . . ."

Her voice died away. Penny got up, and sat down beside her.

"He'd cost her everything—or she thought he had." She spoke very gently. "Is that it, love?"

"I think so. I guess." The dark hair swung forward, hiding her face. Her voice was muffled. "She picked up that rock, but she wasn't planning to kill him. I felt it. She wanted to mess up his face, the way he'd messed up her life. But she didn't hit him in the face with it. She hit him in the throat instead."

"All right, love." Ringan came to sit at her other side. "I know it feels fresh right now, but it isn't really. They've been gone five centuries, and you're under no obligation to go on feeling someone else's pain, or fear, or anything else. Let it go, and then you'll be free of it. What happened?"

"She ran." She lifted her face, desolate with remembering, the grey eyes stretched wide. Unnoticed, Gowan's mouth twisted hard and tight. "And she ran right into Cador Cann. He'd seen it. And then I woke up, because you were shaking my shoulder. So I wasn't thinking about it, not just then. But when we went out to look for Aunt Penny, I was at the back, on the path."

She stopped. Ringan, for a moment, saw Penny's ghost-look in his niece's face, that same wide, unseeing stare.

"She was walking to the sea." It was still Becca, after all, a teenaged girl, telling a dramatic story with a minimum of emphasis, trying not to sound like a drama queen, needing to be believed. "Her father guessed about the baby, not who the father was, just that she was pregnant. He'd told her he was calling off the wedding; he said Cador wouldn't marry her. And he disowned her. He told her she was no child of his, and to get out of his sight." The calm shattered suddenly, as Becca's eyes filled with tears. "She thought Cador had stopped loving her, that he didn't want her and couldn't forgive her for making him part of what happened to Perran. She didn't know. How could she? And anyway, she couldn't forgive herself, either, because she really loved her brother, even though he did what he did."

"So she walked into the sea." Penny's throat was tight. Romeo and Juliet, and the whole damned futility of it. Hormones, misunderstandings, and nightmares coming together in a girl unequipped to cope with it. "What were they doing in Tintagel, I wonder? What would have brought them up here in the winter? Because Beryen is right, the roads would have been a mess."

"We may never know that, although I can think of reasons." Beryen had been listening intently. "Sickness, for instance, or anything that impacted the family's revenue—that would have needed seeing to, winter or summer. I can have another look through my things and see if I can piece it together."

"Would you?" Lucy was clearly wrapping the matter in her own mind, tucking the ends neatly in. "I'd be curious."

"I'm more than curious." Gowan's voice was heavy, and his eyes bloodshot with lack of sleep. "The song, Beryen, 'The New-Slain Knight'—you told me, when first you put it in my way, that you'd got it in the north. Not local to Cornwall, you said, and I've looked since. You were in the right of it, it's an old Scots tune. So if it's nothing to do with that poor girl and her pig of a brother—and I'll say he was after getting no less than he deserved—then why did it do to Penny and young Becca, here, what it seemed to do? It makes no sense, none at all."

"Damn. Gowan, you're right." Penny's mouth was half-open. "But it did, didn't it? The song affected both of us."

"I don't know, either. And honestly, I don't care." Ringan was up, holding a hand out to Penny, yanking her to her feet. "Knowing that Penny's alive, that we can hand Becca over safe and sound to my sister in a few days without having to explain all this to her, is good enough for me."

Epilogue
St. Ives,
June 1993

Two o'clock in the afternoon, and Rosevear Camborne was burning five-hundred-year-old family documents in the fireplace of the Cambornes' front room.

It was really too warm a day to be doing any such, she thought. She winced, feeling that hated little pain just behind her left eye. It never went completely away, that headache; the pain was so persistent, it sometimes sounded almost alive, as if it had a voice of its own. At the moment, it seemed to be telling her to burn things, particularly those things she'd always kept in a lockbox in the room she'd shared with Gowan's father until Pedrek had died in his bed, barely forty years old. He'd had headaches, too, had Pedrek.

She was keeping the fire banked low, feeding sheets in one at a time. It wouldn't do to have Gowan come home and ask her things, demand to know what had possessed her to light a fire on a June day. Gowan was going to have enough to cope with when he finally came home from those shows he was doing up in Truro.

Another sheet of parchment went onto the fire. Rosevear was aware of a second voice, her own this time, scolding and hectoring: *Why are you burning the family records, you stupid woman? Your husband's history, your son's heritage, everything you meant to leave behind for him, why are you burning it?*

She giggled. In the quiet room, it sounded loud; it made her jump.

She laid another page on the fire, this one from the diary of one Elyor Camborne. The thin handwriting jumped out at her, a date and some words highlighted by flickers of light, just before the flames took hold:

18 Feb 1481

My husbande goes about his daily busyness in much heavyness of herte, still in gryfe and horror at Jenna's death. No word from me will sway him from his belief that he must bear all blayme for all. Grayte was the shock to mine own system, which shock he considered nowt . . .

Rosevear stopped. Something had moved, made a noise. A damp chilly sweat broke under along her thinning hairline; had that been a footstep from above? No, impossible; there was none alive up there to make a noise. It was just a creaking board, or the house settling, or a conniving little tart from America, swinging slowly from a heavy beam as her naked body stiffened into rigor in the warmth of the June day . . .

Rosevear giggled again, her hand clutching another page of Elyor's journal, free of the pile that had been so well-kept, passed down to the next generation. Five centuries, but that was over now, and there would be no future Cambornes in this house, with its beams and its fireplace and its headaches.

Rosevear knew the truth, understood it. Gowan would never wed; she had read every word of Elyor's diaries over the years. She knew the entire story. Gowan, her boy, had the flaw of all the Camborne men; he could never be true to one woman, never in this life. It had been Pedrek's failing, as well.

. . . visit to Sennen, to the weddynge of Cador Cann to the Lady Merryn Roache. I think this marriage will bear little fruit, for I bore witnesse to his silence and grimnesse of demeanyr. Cador has in no wise revived from Jenna's death, the mannyr of which was so dredfyl as to cast her out of propr burying in hallowed earth . . .

The room was extremely warm, and Gowan's piano, silent, seemed too large for the space it occupied. Rosevear, suddenly claustrophobic, emptied the rest of Elyor Camborne's papers into the fire in a single pile. The flames jumped, licking the walls of the fireplace, taking hold and sending a jet of ash halfway up the chimney.

Pandra hwer genev?

"Stop that, now." She heard her voice, perfectly ladylike, echoing around the superheated room. There was no one there, no one in her head asking what was happening to them, nothing at all, no one. There was certainly no one alive to talk to her. She really must be quiet, now, and get on with it, before Gowan came back.

She stirred the remains of the Camborne family history with a poker, watching the black sooty remnants dissolve into ash. The American girl, that scheming conniving Jenny—she'd been a bit disturbed, really. Off balance. Rosevear remembered her showing up here all too well that first day, looking too young to be let out alone, reaching out a hand to Gowan, suddenly a woman, adult. Give a girl like that her head, she'd be the ruin of the boy. And really, there had been enough of that in this family, over the years.

Then I kissd her with my lips, and stroked her with my hand

A voice, ghostly as a distant echo, singing. Rosevear whimpered.

Had it come from upstairs? From that infernal nuisance inside her skull? Had it been mocking? Would she never get those words, that melody, out of her head? All those hours spent locked away in her room, two solid years of it, the better to not have to listen to the pair of them, her boy and his whore.

Win up, win up, ye well-fair'd maid, this day ye sleep oer lang.

"Shut your noise!"

She heard herself say it, and bit the words back. This house was too confining for her taste just now; the gloves she'd pulled on so that she might handle the heavy ropes with no trace left had gone first into the fire. There had been no need for them using the poker itself—after all, what was a poker's handle for? And the heavy iron handle had done what she'd wanted; the lightest possible tap, and down the girl had gone. It hadn't left so much as a bruise. Served her right, sneaking into the house, stripping herself like a corner whore, offering herself up to the boy as some sort of gift. Indecent, that's what it was.

Besides, she'd been unbalanced. Not for Gowan. It was better this way.

Rosevear set the poker back in its proper place on the hearth. There was a bit of ash on the lid of the Brinsmead, and she pursed her lips. It wouldn't do, to let Gowan's precious piano gather fireplace ash. She wiped it off delicately, with the tip of her finger.

It was time to go, to let herself out, to walk into town as she always did. She would stop and chat with Mrs. Tregarren at the produce shop and perhaps steady her nerves with a cream tea. And while she was out, she really must remember to ask the pharmacist if he might recommend something for these wretched headaches.